"I've got a mental picture of the roof, lover, and it's red."

"What's she talking about, Cawdor?" the sec leader demanded angrily.

"Krysty can 'see' things, Rollins. I'd say it's about to hit the fan."

"Shut her up. We don't have time for crazy mutie talk."

The small radio on Rollins's gun belt squawked, the shrill tone adding to the mounting tension between the two men. He snatched up the comm unit and thumbed the send button. "What?"

"This is Jameson, sir, from the west wing."

"I've got problems of my own, Jameson. Make it quick."

"The stickies, sir. The bastards are coming at us from all sides. One dropped a load of napalm onto the roof. We're boxed in. What are we going to do?"

All eyes turned toward the red flames, shooting into the sky.

**Other titles in the
Deathlands saga:**

Pilgrimage to Hell

Red Holocaust

Neutron Solstice

Crater Lake

Homeward Bound

Pony Soldiers

Dectra Chain

Ice and Fire

Red Equinox

Northstar Rising

Time Nomads

Latitude Zero

Seedling

Dark Carnival

Chill Factor

Moon Fate

Fury's Pilgrims

Shockscape

Deep Empire

Cold Asylum

Twilight Children

Rider, Reaper

Road Wars

Trader Redux

Genesis Echo

Shadowfall

Ground Zero

Emerald Fire

Bloodlines

Crossways

Keepers of the Sun

Circle Thrice

Eclipse at Noon

Stoneface

Bitter Fruit

Skydark

Demons of Eden

The Mars Arena

Watersleep

Nightmare Passage

JAMES AXLER

DEATH LANDS®

Freedom Lost

A GOLD EAGLE BOOK FROM
WORLDWIDE®

TORONTO • NEW YORK • LONDON
AMSTERDAM • PARIS • SYDNEY • HAMBURG
STOCKHOLM • ATHENS • TOKYO • MILAN
MADRID • WARSAW • BUDAPEST • AUCKLAND

Back before predark, during the even darker days of my stint at North Surry High School, Lowanda Shaw Badgett taught me a few things about writing and about being a professional. This one's for her, and for her father, James Irving Shaw, a man I recently was delighted to discover has been a fan of the Deathlands series since the beginning. I hope these novels keep entertaining him for a long time to come.

First edition April 1998

ISBN 0-373-62541-3

FREEDOM LOST

Copyright © 1998 by Worldwide Library.

Printed in U.S.A.

Now that the Atomic Age has apparently passed, future historians may well coin this the Shopping Center Age, the United States of the Mall, the New Mall-en-nium. Love them or loathe them, malls are a major economic force and a modern fact of life, a powerfully pervasive—and privately controlled—cultural phenomenon. These placeless, misplaced Main Streets are no longer part of the community, someone once said, they *are* the community.

—Excerpt from *The Mall-aise of America*
by Jeff Huebner, 1992

THE DEATHLANDS SAGA

This world is their legacy, a world born in the violent nuclear spasm of 2001 that was the bitter outcome of a struggle for global dominance.

There is no real escape from this shockscape where life always hangs in the balance, vulnerable to newly demonic nature, barbarism, lawlessness.

But they are the warrior survivalists, and they endure—in the way of the lion, the hawk and the tiger, true to nature's heart despite its ruination.

Ryan Cawdor: The privileged son of an East Coast baron. Acquainted with betrayal from a tender age, he is a master of the hard realities.

Krysty Wroth: Harmony ville's own Titian-haired beauty, a woman with the strength of tempered steel. Her premonitions and Gaia powers have been fostered by her Mother Sonja.

J. B. Dix, the Armorer: Weapons master and Ryan's close ally, he, too, honed his skills traversing the Deathlands with the legendary Trader.

Doctor Theophilus Tanner: Torn from his family and a gentler life in 1896, Doc has been thrown into a future he couldn't have imagined.

Dr. Mildred Wyeth: Her father was killed by the Ku Klux Klan, but her fate is not much lighter. Restored from predark cryogenic suspension, she brings twentieth-century healing skills to a nightmare.

Jak Lauren: A true child of the wastelands, reared on adversity, loss and danger, the albino teenager is a fierce fighter and loyal friend.

Dean Cawdor: Ryan's young son by Sharona accepts the only world he knows, and yet he is the seedling bearing the promise of tomorrow.

In a world where all was lost, they are humanity's last hope....

Prologue

The Past

The figures were locked in a two-step, supporting each other as they weaved across the arid landscape. Their feet stumbled, uncertain of the next step as they walked clumsily over the uneven terrain. Above their heads, the wild sky was a deep, striking blue, without a single cloud hanging in place to battle back the hot sunlight.

There was an absence of any kind of hill, or mountain or cover—just flat, broken highway—six lanes of highway—as far ahead as the eye could see.

Pieces of broken pavement and scraps of long-dead automobiles littering the roadway kept tripping up the two men—that, and the state of near exhaustion they barely endured as they picked their way northward along the abandoned stretch of road.

Once, the highway had been known as Interstate 77. Now it was just another road, one of thousands that still crisscrossed the former United States of America, unmaintained and forgotten.

Far behind them, long hot miles back down the interstate and directly off an exit ramp near the remains of a single ruined overpass, were the burned and crumbling remains of the play palace and amuse-

ment park that had been known to many as Willie
ville. But it had an earlier incarnation meaningful to
good Christian soldiers, as Freedom City, U.S.A.

Before the darkness fell across the world, the site
had been a queer mix of Bible-thumping religion and
overblown Vegas-style entertainment. The crown
jewel of the attraction was a sparkling, modern,
twenty-four-story hotel with all of the amenities, including a private, hidden casino in the basement for
those "very special" guests of the Lord.

Freedom City U.S.A. was also equipped with an
amusement park for children, a fully functioning television studio with satellite hookup and live feed, a
radio station broadcasting on both AM and FM wave-
bands, private quarters for the staff and employees,
and an eighteen hole golf course with special tee off
spots for senior citizens.

All of these diversions were offered for free to select members of the church group who sponsored the
dream of the compound's owner and president. The
master of Freedom City was a "born-again" show-
man, promoting his land of fun through publishing
and radio, but primarily via cable TV with regular
appeals for money to help do the Lord's work.

He had taken the title of televangelist, one of those
new words that sprung into being when meshing the
old and the new.

He claimed to be able to produce miracles, healing
the sick on a daily basis. The lame threw down their
crutches. The ones committed for life to wheelchairs
stood up and danced. The blind were made to see.
The men, women and children who held their diseases

close, hidden in their bodies as cancer tumors, were made whole and well again.

These acts were performed live with a very special handpicked studio audience who got to enjoy the pleasures of Freedom City after their television debuts. And for the poor souls unable to travel, they too were offered salvation by pressing their hands up against their TV screens at home, and told to channel their energies through the very lines of fiber optic cable carrying the broadcast signal into their neighborhoods.

The Lord had chosen to respond to all of these good works done in his name by allowing the miracle producing head of the church and complex of Freedom City to be exposed as a lecherous and greedy little troll, who wept like a baby once his sins became public. Once the word was out that their leader—the good married reverend himself—had been discovered in a bedroom of one of the hundreds of hotel rooms housed in the twenty-four story crown jewel of his empire with two women half his age, the holding corporation for the entire kingdom had been plunged into a non-ending series of investigations and exposés. All of the media attention culminated in the leader's imprisonment, bankruptcy and ruin.

The dream was over.

The park was closed. The golf course was padlocked shut. The hotel was turned over to private enterprise, rented a few times a year for business conventions.

Then, less than a decade or so later, the literal end of the world the former Baptist millionaire had promised for so long finally did happen. When it did, concepts such as religion, and inventions such as television, and businesses with corporations and strong men of leadership involved in tawdry affairs with young girls were utterly, totally, completely moot.

Over a hundred years later, Freedom City, U.S.A. had become a ville run by a man with an iron fist and a handpicked team of security men. At first, the area was under the command of one Baron George Frederic Sokolow. Sokolow was a brutal man, but trusting and fair. His successor, by way of betrayal, had been one Baron William Elijah.

Unfortunately for Freedom City, U.S.A., the good and proper Biblical name of Elijah was not chosen as the site's new appellation. The name of the place became Willie ville.

Now, all gone, Freedom City had died thrice. The first time had left the structures intact with the soul removed. The second had seen all around it fall into waste and ruin.

The third found it blown into bits and burned to the ground, overrun and destroyed by legions of muties.

The two figures fleeing from Willie ville kept moving. To their right, skeletal skyscrapers of the city known as Charlotte towered high, but the city and its artificial canyons lined with sidewalks and parking meters wasn't their destination.

"We there yet?" the taller of the two asked in a drugged, slow voice, a voice like a sleepy playback on an elderly tape recorder with dying batteries.

"What do you think?" the other retorted, his voice

a wet, phlegmy sound. "Look around, stupe. We're not even past Charlotte yet, and I sure as hell don't want to go in there. I hear there's patches of hot rad spots."

The shorter of the pair, the man with the fast quip, was hairless, and his scalp was a mix of bright red new skin intermingled with blackened scabs and old scar tissue. His companion had enough shaggy brown hair running down from above a lean, hairless forehead to the nape of a narrow back to provide ample tresses for each of them.

Both of them were wearing sunglasses. The bald one with the ugly head had a pair of black knockoff Ray·Ban eyewear, in the classic boxy style of the 1950s. The long-haired figure wore a pair of amber aviator's glasses, with thin metal frames of gold. The glasses were a size too small, but still better than braving the sun without any eye protection.

The first man with the injured head and face had been trapped when things had gone to hell weeks earlier in Willie ville. A semicompetent sec man and hired mercie by trade, he'd been unlucky enough to rouse the ire of the now-deceased Baron Willie Elijah, and on the day the ville was blasted into ruin, he'd been strapped with other unfortunates to a great wheel used to raise and lower the elevator car that traveled between floors of the twenty-four-story hotel jutting from the center of the baron's ville.

Unfortunately for those who manned the elevator wheel, the baron had chosen the penthouse as the roost of his domain, where he could look out on all that was his and rest assured it was good.

This aerie was also home to his family and followers, and where many of his sec men who hadn't in-
curred his wrath and been banished to the wheel
stayed, as well. All of them, and more, had been up
there on top of the world the day Willie ville began
to die.

There had been an explosion within the upper
floors of the former pleasure palace, and the elevator
car—full to overflowing with panicked men and
women—had come crashing down at a terrific rate.
The wheel that the slaves had been strapped to spun
faster and faster, whipping them around like insects
struggling to keep their footing on a traveling vehicle.

Under the sounds of the explosions and screams
came the sickening snaps of breaking bones and the
haunting noise of naked flesh being ripped open and
torn apart. Then there were more blasts of horrific
intensity, followed by fire as the entire twenty-four
floors of the hotel came tumbling down into the basement.

The two men now leaning woozily on each other
for support had been among the few survivors from
the devastation in Baron Willie's headquarters.

In the instance of the man wearing the Ray·Ban
sunglasses, the end result created by the flames was
a scarred visage that suggested the aftereffect of a
novelty wax head placed within a microwave oven.
Flesh had bubbled and melted. The forehead was
slashed with still healing wounds and bits of black
shrapnel that had yet to work themselves out of the
skin. No eyebrows were above the currently hidden

eyes, but one eyeball was wide-open, glaring and minus an eyelid.

The other eye was half-closed in a mess of scarring.

The nose was missing, gone as if it had never existed, and when he breathed, air was sucked in through the remaining narrow holes above the ruined mouth. There were no lips to be seen, only a wet orifice cluttered with scraps of white teeth and a bright red tongue between cheeks stubbled with clumped patches of beard and blotches of crimson.

His injuries made it impossible for him to fully close his mouth. Like his nasal cavity, his mouth hung open, panting as air went in and out of his lungs like an overworked bellows. Smoke inhalation from the fire had created a permanent rasp when he breathed. The fire had also claimed the man's ears.

He fell to his knees, his chest rising and falling as he struggled to regain his breath. The second figure placed a hand on his fallen friend's shoulder and waited silently.

The placed hand was strange, inhuman, dirty and...wrong. The fingers looked as though they had an extra joint between the midbend and the knuckle, and indeed they were so equipped. The fingers also came with two additional bonuses—a multitude of tiny suckers, each little mouth capable of sticking to almost any chosen surface, and a thin secretion of bioproduced adhesive.

The hand was the first clue in separating the pair, for the man on the ground, despite his horrific injuries, was a human. A "norm" by birth, now a freak by accident and lucky to be alive.

The standing figure behind him was a mutant, and there would be no changing that birthright. The mutie was commonly called a "stickie" due to the suctioning fingers, which could tear flesh off bone.

Stickies had the same suckers on their long tongues, as well.

There were also other ways of identifying a stickie. Their speech patterns were usually slow and monosyllabic. Many times their teeth were sharp, both by nature and because stickies enjoyed filing their teeth down into needles for shock value. And many had the unusual trait of being born without any ears, so their hearing was limited, making them seem even slower and dumber to a human foe. The lack of ears also forced most stickies to be loud talkers, making them seem even more annoying to all except for their own kind.

No one knew why most stickies were missing ears.

There were two kinds of stickies. The one in the aviator's glasses was the more intelligent kind. A second breed of stickie came with very little in the upstairs attic, no body hair and suckers on their feet. Also on the hands and feet of these murderous unfortunates were highly developed sucker pads instead of fingers and toes, the digits exuding a gelatinous ooze even more adhering than the secretion characteristic of their brighter kin.

"How much longer?" the stickie asked slowly.

"I don't know," the scarred man replied as he gulped oxygen. "We're heading north, so I know by the sun we're going in the right direction. I couldn't begin to tell you what kind of time we're making.

We're killing ourselves now, and we haven't gone near far enough. Trip is going to take weeks on foot in the condition we're both in. Mebbe even months, unless we find some kind of wag or horse."

The listening stickie used its other hand to adjust the cap it was wearing. The letters "PTL" were stitched in yellow on the blue hat, a souvenir of time spent in servitude in Wille ville. The creature had no idea what the initials stood for, nor did it care, since it couldn't read anyway. The hat had three things in its favor: it fit snugly over long hair, it wasn't filthy like the rest of the stickie's clothing and the wide brim kept the sun off its pale face.

"No wags here, norm," the mutie said, its shaded eyes surveying the surrounding landscape. The closest thing to a means of vehicular transportation were the stripped frames of abandoned automobiles.

"Don't call me that," the man snapped. "I'm not a norm. I'm no longer a man. I'm one of you now. A filthy, stinking mutie."

The stickie pondered this for a long moment. "You want me to call you Lester?"

A wet rasping sound came forth as he inhaled, then exhaled. "Hell, no."

"That was your name."

"Not anymore. Forget you ever heard it."

The stickie pondered this before answering. "Have to call you something."

"Just shut up, okay? Shut up and keep walking. Let's see if we can make that tractor-trailer rig up there. Can use it to camp in tonight."

"Whatever you say, Norm, whatever you say." The stickie reached down and offered a helping hand.

The newly christened Norm knocked the assistance away and awkwardly got to his feet on his own.

"Fuck you, mutie," he said proudly.

The stickie looked at him, its expression unreadable behind the aviator's glasses. "Saved you, Norm. Saved your life."

"I can't say I'm grateful, you ugly prick." Spittle and drool flowed freely from the slash of the man's ruined mouth, splashing out in drips and drabs and hitting the mutie in the face. The mutant didn't appear to mind. "Did I ever say thank-you? Can't remember that I did. Wish you'd let me finish burning like a candle in that shithole."

"Need me," the stickie said, pointing a long bony finger to itself. The finger turned and pointed at Norm. "Need you."

"Yeah, yeah, you've told me. Word got out before everything back at the ville went to hell, didn't it? About the western part of Carolina crawling with muties? Fucking Lord Kaa-kaa and his plans to unite all the mutants."

"Lord Kaa," the mutie said in tones of reverence. "Lord Kaa."

"Yeah, whatever. Lord Kaa sent word out—how, I have no fucking idea—to all of you freaks in the baron's mutie zoo about this place."

"Budd wasn't in the zoo," the stickie said firmly, identifying itself by name.

"Excuse me, all the freaks in the zoo combined with all the mutie turds working the grunt detail on the elevator wheel with us dumb-ass norms who were stupe enough to get Willie-boy all pissed off. I was a good sec man for a long damn time for my baron, the dried-up old skank. I make one mistake, and he drops me. Just because I missed that old bastard's blade hidden in his walking stick.''

Norm muttered all of these details in a singsong voice. Reciting the same account over and over had committed the rant to memory. Budd didn't protest, but merely listened.

"Bet ol' One-eye put his pal up to hiding the shiv. Yeah, I miss one old fart's blade, and my boss fucks me up the ass in front of everybody and next thing I know I'm stuck in the basement turning the elevator wheel with guys like you.''

The mutie pondered the words. "Budd had been at the wheel for many days. Weeks.''

"And what did you do to earn your stint?''

"Nothing. Budd did nothing.''

The scarred man stopped walking and turned to face his associate. "Wrong. Budd was born with oozing hands and a strong back. Face it, *all* you stickies were fucked from birth. But you'd learned to accept it, right? Until you mutie bastards got the word Kaa was coming to save your sorry asses, freeing you from the fields and the wheels and the baron's mutie zoo. Kaa might have pulled it off, too, except the cannies and the scabies and all you stickies got a serious murder lust and started killing one another off.''

"Lord Kaa couldn't contain us all," Budd said simply. "The blood fever came. We were unable to stop ourselves.''

"Good thing, or we wouldn't be going north. Kaa had the right idea, but he was too weird to pull it off. Muties always have needed a strong hand."

"Like yours, Norm."

"Yeah, like mine. We'll go to Winston, Budd. We'll start over there, me and you both. Hell, guys like us, we're heading for the promised land!"

The stickie didn't answer as it continued concentrating on putting one foot in front of the other. Norm was allowed to straggle along under his own steam now. Despite what some said, muties did possess rudimentary emotions, and Budd was both hurt and angered by his companion's caustic comments about Lord Kaa. The mutant could have broken the smaller human into pieces, if it had chosen to. Instead, Budd had accepted the responsibility of companionship.

"What happened to Lord Kaa, anyway?" Norm asked after a few moments, growing bored with the sound of his own labored breathing.

"Budd doesn't know. Lord Kaa was there, then he wasn't. He disappeared."

"Chilled, most likely. Yeah, he's probably back there in Wille ville under a ton of burned brick and dead muties."

"Budd doesn't agree. Kaa lives."

"Budd can kiss my ass. I don't give a shit what you think."

"Then, leave me."

"You wish. Of course, we both know that's the problem here," Norm said, his voice trailing off. "The fact is this—you stickies couldn't find your dicks with both hands in a stiff wind."

"Norm helping Budd."

The man took off the sunglasses for a moment and rubbed his injured eyes. "I guess so. Somebody has to. Navigation isn't your strong suit, and I've heard about this stickie hive where we're going. Some of the other sec men I worked with back at Willie's before the ville got toasted had pulled duty time at the human outpost near our new home. Muties have the entire city to themselves, and the norms live farther out from it, safe and snug in their own pocket of protection."

Norm took another breath. "Yeah, I guess we're in this together, mutie, like it or not."

"Why?"

"Like I told you…I'm mutie now. I'm Norm the half-melted mutie. Way I look, your kind is the only ones left in the Deathlands that can accept me without gagging."

"You are a strange norm, Lester," Budd said.

The shorter figure's one good eye flashed with anger. "For the last time don't call me that. Call me Norm. Lester's dead. Buried back in Willie ville. If we make it to where I'm planning, I've got some plans, Budd. Big plans. Your Lord Kaa? He was a friggin' piker compared to what I'm planning to take over and rebuild. All you stickies need to take over your lives is some guidance…and me and you, we're going to give them all the lessons they need."

Silence. More steps.

"Norm?"

"What?"

"Are we there yet?"

Chapter One

The third planet from the sun seemed to explode in the old calendar year of 2001. In some parts of the now-hemorrhaging world, the continual explosions were of such terrible force, they could be seen by orbiting spacecraft. Whole pieces of continents ceased to exist as they were obliterated in expanding mushroom clouds of radioactive dust and debris.

Satellite cameras on high recorded the horrific images for the unbelieving observers below, and for their eventual descendants to view one day via decaying videotape.

The exact date of destruction has been recorded as occurring precisely at noon on the twentieth day of January, early in the new year. In Washington, D.C., where the power elite chose to live and work and plan and play, the first blast of the countless more to follow fell on a bitter cold day—perfect weather to welcome in the end of the world.

All within a five-mile radius were instantly vaporized.

The actual battle was over in minutes. However, the ramifications of what had happened took longer. In mere hours, chaos reigned in the rapidly shrinking pockets of survival in every country of the world...and as the verbal accusations and the barrages of hellfire and destruction flew back and forth, the doomsayers with their predictions in tabloids and the self-appointed prophets with their posterboards of admonitions were proven right at last.

The world was ending—welcome to the new millennium.

That one black day when the fighting began and ended in less than twenty-four hours was forever known by those who lived through it as skydark—the time when the very sun appeared to have fallen from the sky to be reborn in a conflagration that enveloped the Earth. The firestorm that burned the green away, and replaced it with the blackness.

Yet, there were survivors. A small percentile who were in the right place at the right time, or who were in locales where the rad blasting did not occur and the nuclear rains did not fall. Slowly, hesitantly, in packs and pairs over the long years following the conflict, men and women painstakingly crawled out of the wreckage. They looked with weary eyes upon the new world their leaders and their hidden agendas had wrought.

Overhead, the sky had changed from a bright blue to a smoky purple—purple being one of the dozens of colors the sky took depending on which section of the former United States one lived in. Everything was lost—even the color of the sky; an eternal reminder that things would never be the same again.

These survivors bravely decided that, yes, while most everything of value had *indeed* been turned to shit, there was still life to carry on.

Staying alive at all costs was such a frank, unadorned methodology that it revolted some. Still, it was better to wake up tired and paranoid than not to wake up at all. The world wasn't a very nice place to live in anymore—in fact, it was worse than ever before.

The current incarnation of what some called "Old California" would have been unrecognizable by using the old maps. From the air, this stretch had been transformed into the multitude of floating hot spots called "The West Coast Islands." Any sane man stayed as far away from them as possible. The former California coastline had been hit hard at the beginning of the war by a planted barrage of earthshaker bombs, seeded from Soviet submarines. These seeds of death had been left behind to decimate their intended targets—the many winding fault and fracture-lines of the lands underneath the waves of the Pacific Ocean.

At the same time these hidden devices had been activated in conjunction with the sneak attack in the Soviet embassy in Washington; the Cascades, from Mount Garibaldi in British Columbia down to Lassen Peak in California were showered with ICBMs and sub-launched missiles. The combination pulverized the entire stretch from the lower regions of Washington State past Los Angeles. The volcanoes from Mount Rainier and Mount Saint Helens and Mount Shasta literally blew their stacks, blasting rock and magma into the arid sky.

The San Andreas Fault opened like a cheap zipper on the back of a jolt-addicted whore.

Today, if one came inland from the West Coast

Islands, all that was left in the resculpted southwestern United States was desert.

One section was notorious. The Barrens. A place of heat and sweat.

There was nothing here in this festering hellhole to greet a visitor but a few valiant, brittle attempts at flora and fauna...and, in this particular area, an innocuous gray halfdome rising from the sand. The one-story building had no windows or doors. The only apparent way into the place was via a rectangular shaped portal. The portal was smooth, without any kind of handle or other sort of push/pull opening system. A single numeric keypad with a red liquid crystal readout display was recessed into the wall next to the entry way.

These types of code protected portals were familiar to the group of seven people who had disappeared inside the nondescript bunker-like installation.

The people who had just arrived weren't in the Barrens for the view, nor did they give a damn about the single dwelling jutting against the orange mustard color the sky had chosen for today. They knew what was inside the dome, and what was below the placid, boring surface. From the crumbling to dust protective body suits in the labs down under, to the red and white strident warning signs, to the emergency decontamination chambers—all of this and even more evidence was housed within...pointing to this lonely lair as being the nest of a plague sower.

A happy home for the most deadly of biological weapons.

Chemicals were used in the conflagration that

sparked the end of the civilized world, but used far less than might have been intended once the nuclear fire began to burn relentlessly across the globe. More intelligent denizens of the appalling new world that followed suspected that mere radiation couldn't account for the perverse genetics that had been spawned after skydark. A released biological agent—a single mutagen or perhaps an infinite number of dozens from unknown origins—approached the truth more about the many humanoid mutations that had come about following the holocaust.

All of the new mutations striving for survival alongside the ''norms.''

However, no truces were forthcoming. Along with the rewritten genetics that created the mutants came what one long forgotten wag termed as "brain rot."

The Barrens

THE TRAVELERS had arrived at the redoubt after an arduous journey across barren wasteland. Their mode of transport had been a fantastic mix of ancient chariot and powerful motorized carriage, but the vehicle's engines were nearly drained. An electrical recharge would have been needed if they intended to carry on farther, but fate had intervened. They had reached an intended destination safely and had gone inside to initiate their locational remove from the gateway. Then something had occurred to Ryan, and he cursed at himself. He should have thought of it before. Now they were all outside the vanadium doors again.

"I don't think we were followed," J. B. Dix said,

taking what he hoped was a final look at that stretch of California. He reached up and pulled down the brim of his battered fedora to shield his eyes against the sun. "If anyone was on our trail, they're too far back to try anything now. Flat as it is around here, we would've seen them if they got too close."

"Let's keep it that way," Ryan Cawdor muttered by way of a reply. By his very carriage and attitude, it was obvious the lean man with the scarred visage and eye patch was the leader of the group. Ryan had taken the controls of the vehicle and kept them on their course for the duration of the journey back to the redoubt, trusting his comrades to keep a watch on their potential pursuers.

Miles away, back along the path they had come, was the city of Aten, a construct of ancient Egypt standing hale and hearty on North American soil. Aten was where the Pharaoh Akhnaton had once reigned, until a final, fatal run-in with Krysty Wroth, one of the two women of the group. A hypnotic mix of man and mutation, the pharaoh had been named Hell Eyes by complacent followers, a title bestowed upon him in a mixture of awe and fear.

Ryan Cawdor was in a triple bad mood. He could still taste the grit between his lips from his desert flight. The air was hot, like breathing vapors from the back of a overheated war wag. When they had first arrived here, guesses as to their location had included the Sahara and the Gobi. Logistics aside, that's still what it looked and felt like.

Ryan sighed. They needed to keep moving.

"We can't leave this contraption here," he told

them. "Jak and Dean, you will take the chariot out back of the dome. If anybody does come looking, no need to advertise this is where we stopped."

"Right, Dad," Dean replied, as he and Jak, a whipcord lean, ruby-eyed albino teenager stepped up. Ryan passed over a fleeting desire to burn the sturdy little vehicle—the smoke plume would be visible for miles.

"We could always bury the damn thing," J.B suggested, echoing Ryan's own unvoiced worries.

"You feel like trying to dig in this bastard heat?"

J.B. grinned tightly, his teeth hidden behind thin lips. "Hell no."

"What are you two talking about?" Mildred Wyeth asked as Dean and Jak returned from the rear of the building.

"Way the wind tends to kick up out here, our tracks won't be around for long—I hope," Ryan stated, pointing at the obvious trail left by the tires of the chariot. "But leaving this thing here out front is a red flag in a bull's pasture."

"Pardon me, my dear Ryan, but might I make a suggestion?" The request came from the skeletal man in the faded frock coat who had been hovering around the edges of the conversation, listening intently, one hand stroking his narrow chin and the other working a black sword stick through his fingers like a baton.

"Not now, Doc," Ryan replied.

"No need to be so abrupt, lover," Krysty Wroth interjected, her long prehensile red hair resting gently on her shoulders. "Let Doc speak his piece."

Krysty's green eyes caught Ryan's single blue orb.

He glared back—annoyed at the interference when their safety was uppermost in his mind. Then he let himself relax. The fight or flight adrenaline was raging inside him, the survival instinct keeping him on edge. As far as Ryan's weary body was concerned, until they were far away from the Barrens, they weren't safe.

"What's on your mind, Doc?" he allowed himself to ask.

"Might I suggest we take yon chariot into the redoubt with us?" the oldish-appearing man said. "While this installation is much smaller than the usual military installations we're used to taking refuge in, I think we can spare the room this once."

Ryan and J.B. exchanged embarrassed glances—their combined years of training in tactics had been dulled enough by near exhaustion so that they completely overlooked the obvious. The dome's portal was plenty wide enough to pull the vehicle inside once the door was fully open.

"Damn straight, Doc," Ryan replied. "Good thinking."

"Naturally," Doc Tanner replied modestly. "I am a college graduate."

DOCTOR Theophilus Algernon Tanner was more than a mere college graduate, much, much more. In fact, despite his elderly appearance, he was beyond mere age—having lived within the constraints of three lifetimes—a reluctant time traveler plucked from the year 1896 and drawn forward to 1998 as part of a secret government project known as Operation Chronos.

"Hell of a lot of candles to stick on a birthday cake," Ryan had once said.

"I never cared for birthdays," Tanner had replied.

The concept behind Operation Chronos was simple to describe and impossible to truly understand in terms of what passed for so-called current day physics. Whitecoat scientists might toss jargon around about "using a quantum interface in conjunction with a matter-transference booth to pierce the space-time continuum to pluck random subjects from the past or future and bring them safely, intact, whole and breathing, to the current day," but when the veneer of scientific babble was stripped away, they really had no idea of how the setup worked since the builders of this magical device were compartmentalized. Technicians might never even see the engineers.

The military leaders of the operation referred to the time travel process as "trawling," since there was no visual or physical confirmation available on what they picked up during the experiments. The work was dangerous and crude. The Chronos scientists had no idea who—or what—they might latch on to and bring back into their midst, and all involved had heard stories and rumors of the fates of previous teams who had locked upon the whirlwind.

Doc was one of the few living "trawling" success stories. At first, his captors were elated—if they were able to pluck a man from one hundred years in the past, surely they could go back even further.

However, as months passed, they discovered their transport of Doc had been a fluke. Virtually all of their other trawling expeditions had failed horribly, bringing back nothing but hunks of wet meat mixed with shredded flesh and splintered bone into the hexagonal mat-trans chambers. The temporal storms of time weren't forgiving to their crude attempts to shuttle living tissue from one era to another, and even the rare living creature brought back physically intact was always a fragmented mess mentally.

Doc, who had been isolated for study in a cell in the sprawling Chronos laboratory, found his jailers to be more insistent than ever. No longer was he allowed to lie idle, watching television and reading books as he struggled to acclimate himself with his new world. Now he was constantly questioned, prodded, hypnotized and drugged.

What was different about this one man? What made him appear intact and sane, while other humans and animals were brought into the present as unrecognizable masses of gore, or with their bodies relatively intact but their minds forever twisted into knots of insanity? Even non-living tissue was disrupted by the time jumps, although there was a higher rate of success in beaming back simple objects and hunks of rock and metal.

Perhaps what none of the Chronos scientists could bring themselves to admit aloud was that Doc Tanner possessed an unstoppable desire to live. Even then, they knew that physically, Doc's body had accelerated due to the forces he endured during the journey. But there was a bright fire burning within his weakened frame. His life, his world, all had been stolen, and Tanner had rolled with the punches and still asked for more.

He retained his antiquated speech patterns, and clung to his out-of-date attire and identity, defying the scientists who questioned him to figure out how he still lived. He clung with a parent's possessiveness to his memories of his long-dead wife, Emily and his two young children, Rachel and Jolyon, and their faces and names kept him sane. Tanner wasn't an old man when they had first latched upon his body and ripped him away screaming into the void, but the shock of transport had altered him somewhat. His very skin seemed to tighten on his skeletal frame, his entire gaunt physique always sunken down inside his faded academic frock coat.

By December 2000, the whitecoats had had enough of Doc's uncooperative attitude and his attempts to escape, and had thrust the defiant Doc Tanner one hundred years into the future, into a world that had become bitterly known as the Deathlands.

However, even in the Deathlands, some areas were safer than others, and the Barrens where Tanner and his friends were now standing were definitely not on anyone's top ten places to stay.

WITH THE CHARIOT now inside the redoubt, they again went along the passageway leading down. Nothing had changed. The passageway leading down appeared the same as they had left it—the concrete floor sprinkled with a light smattering of sand from outside.

"Looks clear," Ryan said, still following his safety procedure even if they'd been there a very short while ago. "Let's do it. Triple red until I give the word."

Ryan brought up the rear, lingering behind the others. Krysty Wroth hung back too, waiting for him. Her keen eyes searched his face, looking for some sort of outward manifestation to reflect the feelings she knew were churning inside his guts about what happened to them in Aten.

Perhaps J.B. had summed up the experience best when he remarked—''Like being trapped in one long wet dream without a climax, and even if you could come, you'd still feel like you'd done something wrong.''

The only one of the group to escape the sexual sadism of the place had been Dean. Perhaps sensing some of the debauchery to come in their destination, Ryan had taken up a man named Danielson on his offer of sanctuary for the boy in the bosom of Fort Fubar—a safe haven en route to the walls of the Egyptian-styled city.

All the way back to the dome-shaped redoubt, Dean had been chattering away with questions. Where did they get the awesome chariot? What had taken them so long in getting back? Why couldn't he go to Aten and see the pyramid for himself?

For once, Ryan hadn't even possessed the strength to summon the anger to shut the boy up, but since all of them shared Ryan's exhaustion, no one had bothered to answer Dean's queries, and the boy had soon given up out of boredom.

''Lover...?'' Krysty began, wincing at the hesitation and embarrassment she felt. Feeling ill at ease with Ryan was a new sensation for her, and she didn't like the unfamiliar emotion.

"Uh-uh," Ryan cautioned, knowing from her tone she was getting ready to walk down a road he wasn't interested in traveling just yet. "Let's get to the gateway first. Sooner we find out which way the stick floats, the sooner we can plan for the future."

Krysty knew Ryan's words were law when he was in this sort of mood, but she didn't care. This was the first instant they'd been alone since escaping the city, and the air had to be cleared before she could allow herself to go forward.

She blocked his path, and, choosing her words carefully, said, "That's what I want to talk about. Our future and how the recent past may affect it."

"What?" Ryan asked dumbly, his eye questioning her.

Krysty's hair undulated, reflecting her own confusion and turmoil. "I know what's troubling you, lover."

"You do." His tone was flat, cold. Krysty knew she was inching out onto dangerous ground.

"Yes," she said firmly.

"Your mutie senses tell you that or are you coasting on feminine intuition?" Ryan asked softly, the tone of his voice easing back the sarcasm of the words.

Krysty held his gaze. "Tension's been thick enough to reach out and hold. Not just affecting us. Affecting everybody."

Ryan looked away. "It'll pass. Until we know whether or not this bastard mat-trans unit is going to work this time, we're all going to be in a pissy mood."

"I'm not talking about the mat-trans unit, and you know it."

Ryan shrugged, making a move to step around her. "You weren't responsible for what happened back there."

Krysty caught his arm, her strong fingers biting into it. "You say that, but you don't know how sure you are of it," she laughed bitterly. "I was under Akhnaton's will, I can't deny it."

"So don't," Ryan replied. "He makes a dandy one-stop scapegoat."

"Dammit, Ryan, I love you!" Krysty cried. "I will always love you! My love warred with Akhnaton's mental power even as he tried to make me his own."

Ryan's head throbbed, along with his injured shoulder, the blood pulsing through his veins. He wished Krysty could have waited for this discussion. He wished they were all inside the gateway now, their ticket out of Aten punched. He wished he could make her understand he wasn't upset with her, nor had what she'd endured made him love her any less.

Krysty reached out and stroked both sides of the beard stubble on his face. "You aren't physically hurt too badly, but your spirit is wounded," she said softly. "Your pride bleeds because you think you were unable to protect me."

"I don't 'think,' I *know* I was unable to protect you."

"But, don't you see?" Krysty asked desperately. "You did protect me. It was your love for me and my love for you that broke his power, broke Nefron's power. It was your strength and courage that gave me the resolve to battle him. Every time he reached for me, touched me, spoke to me I was fighting back. We defeated him together.''

Ryan closed his eye, releasing his breath slowly, letting her words wash over him. Comforting, soothing words. He pulled her to him, holding her tightly. He nuzzled her hair, pulling her scent back into his lungs and being.

"Living is struggling," Krysty whispered to him. "The unavoidable thing. But love makes it worthwhile.''

"Yes," he replied very quietly. "You taught me that.''

Ryan relaxed his arms around her and she stepped back to face him, her eyes shining with tears, like wet emeralds. Her mouth was smiling as she reached out and took his hand.

"What's the holdup?" J.B. said suddenly, his voice coming at them from around the bend in the passage. Apparently the Armorer and the others had continued ahead, but had grown tired of waiting for the pair.

"Just restating the obvious, J.B.," Ryan called out, squeezing Krysty's hand. "We're right behind you."

Chapter Two

A military redoubt was a boring place. There was little in the way of decoration or personality, only a cold professionalism. These hidden installations varied in size, from the massive maze of passages and rooms located behind the stone-faced facade of Mount Rushmore, known as the Anthill, to this tiny little hive of less than a dozen or so labs, dormitories and control rooms.

No matter the size or the complexity, there was a predictable uniformity that cried to the rafters of calm, plodding, rubber-stamped government bureaucracy.

Checking each of the rooms was quick and effortless, and no time was wasted in search of food or supplies since they had examined all the redoubt had to offer during their earlier stay.

"Gunmetal gray." Mildred Wyeth sighed. "There's no place like home."

"Familiar is good," J. B. Dix replied. "I like familiar."

"You would, John," she retorted.

"What? You want change?" the Armorer asked in disbelief. "Hell, Millie, every time we walk into one of these redoubts, we end up jumping to another part of Deathlands. Only good thing about this mode of transportation is that it's quicker than riding in a wag, and a hell of a lot safer than walking or trying to ride a motor bike.''

''All I'm saying is, would it have killed whoever came up with the design of these lairs to consult a decorator?'' Mildred asked. ''Some different colors of paint? A pair of frilly curtains? Hell, I'd even take throw pillows and doilies just to break up the monotony.''

Mildred's comments were directed at the sameness of the redoubt's walls. For all of its many uses in security, vanadium wasn't a reflective or attractive metal. The genetic installation's underground level was constructed of smooth alloy wall plates, which absorbed the faint light given off by the fluorescent light strips overhead.

J.B. looked exasperated. ''I'm going to check on Ryan and Krysty. After all we've been through, Ryan's probably forgotten the combination to close the sec door.'' He was referring to the treatment the friends had received from Pharaoh Akhnaton in the city of Aten, and the arduous journey across the Barrens to this redoubt. At the back of their minds was the possibility that the gateway wouldn't work—as it hadn't days earlier when they had attempted to jump out of there.

J.B. stomped off, only to quickly return with the missing pair. No words were spoken as Ryan made his way past, the others falling in behind him. The low-wattage lighting conspired with the vanadium walls to create a multitude of faint shadows, skittering pieces of dark against the light as the group made its way down the hallway.

Now that all had been reunited, the order of their descent back into the lair was a traditional, predetermined one, a secure wedge of seven friends who had grown to rely on one another despite the brief internal squabbles that might occasionally erupt. Tempers sometimes flared, but when the time arrived, they stuck together firmly as a family to survive the harshness of the world they were forced to call home.

Ryan turned to face the group after they had determined the redoubt was secure.

"Fill up the canteens," the dark-haired man said. "Might be a while before we get another chance. Every one take a good long drink, but not too much. Our trip isn't over yet, and I don't want to have anybody puking up water if it can be avoided."

His young son, Dean, collected the canteens and left to start filling them in the tiny kitchen.

After their thirsts had been quenched, there was nothing left to be said.

Taking up the triple-red-alert positions again, all gathered and waited, standing before the only door they hadn't yet entered. They knew what was inside from the last time, and none of them relished going back through for a return visit. The door was different from the others in the redoubt in both shape and design, its surface bearing a disk sheathed in silvery metal surrounded by three concentric collars of thick steel.

Another keypad was on the wall, and next to it was a laminated sign bearing red letters: Biohazard Beyond This Point! Entry Forbidden To Personnel Not Wearing Anticontaminant Clothing!

"Oops," Ryan said mildly. "Any of you remember to pack a pair of anticontaminant coveralls?"

The mock query went unacknowledged. Their fears of a rogue biological agent having been loosed inside the room they were about to enter had been debated last time. Mildred had felt sure the combination of the passage of time and the lack of obvious damage in the redoubt would indicate their safety against being infected with any killer microorganisms.

"Guess not," Ryan murmured, answering his own rhetorical query. "Looks like we're going in dressed as we are."

He reached out and pressed in the familiar sequence to open the door. Ryan was standing to one side, his blaster held at the ready, braced against his lean right hip. The other companions were arrayed behind him, their own weapons held tight in readiness to pour a vicious drumming of full-metal-jacketed death into anyone—anything—hostile that might be waiting inside.

Following the hiss of pneumatics and internal machinery, the metal door rolled slowly to the left, disappearing into a open slot to allow entrance.

The room that was now revealed was dim. Ryan could make out dark blocks of shapes inside the immediate threshold. He exhaled a deep breath and stepped into the chamber. This motion caused an automatic lighting system to kick in the moment his presence was noted. A sickly greenish fluorescent bank of overhead lights illuminated the complete contents of the cluttered twenty-yard-long room.

Ryan strode quickly through, his eye noting the tables loaded with pristine glass tubes and beakers, silent gauges and softly humming comp terminals. His blaster stayed in his right hand, cocked and ready, as he headed for the door on the other side of the biolaboratory.

"Hope no bugs have gotten out since last time," J.B. muttered as he followed Ryan inside.

"Now, that's a cheery thought," Krysty Wroth retorted.

"Doubtful," Mildred said, her own dark eyes scanning the hidden genetics laboratory. "If so, there's not a damn thing we can do about it now."

"I feel a most distinct tickle in my nostrils," Doc Tanner began. "Do you think perhaps—?"

"No. Like I told you the last time, any virus that might be loose in here was most likely designed to attack through the skin. Your nose is itching from desert sand or your own weak nerves," Mildred snapped, her voice slightly hollow in the chamber. "And if you're going to sneeze, use your handkerchief! You're probably carrying around a more dangerous disease than we'd ever find creeping around in here."

"Don't get your germs on me," Dean said, scooting past Doc with Jak Lauren close behind.

"Me, either," Jak added.

Doc made a brief show of taking out his stained swallow's-eye kerchief and putting the rag to his face in time to catch the spray as he unleashed a terrific sneeze. Everyone turned back to glare as he gave a weak smile, folded the now damp kerchief into a square packet of cloth and placed it in a rear pocket of his trousers.

"Apologies, friends. But there is no stopping a sneeze once it begins," Doc said. "One might as well hold back a howling tornado or stop a crushing tidal wave."

"Or stifle the verbosity blowing out of an overeducated windbag," Mildred added.

Ryan stood waiting at the door on the other side of the lab. This silver door was a twin for the first one, with the same configuration and security keypad. Ryan waited for Doc to compose himself and keyed in the entry code, commanding the door to roll aside and allow access to the last stop on their tour.

They stepped into a foyer that led to a small anteroom containing nothing but a utilitarian metal table and two steel-and-cloth office chairs. Several fluorescent light strips gave off a feeble glow. Another vanadium-alloy-plated corridor led to a large modern room, filled with an array of more-elaborate comp consoles and readout monitor screens than seen in the lab.

Some of the comp screens were dark, but others glowed in tones of amber and blue, with lines of strange symbols mixed together with letters and numbers in incomprehensible codes. Oversize comp banks as tall as a man lined one wall, and on the other was a sharply cut series of brown panels of armaglass.

None of the group seemed surprised or impressed by the control room they were now standing in. All of them had seen this kind of setup before.

"There's the mat-trans chamber," Mildred said,

pointing at the armaglass and stating the obvious. The walls of the gateway chamber she was pointing to were a rusty brown shade.

"The color of runny crap," J.B. muttered. "From a frightened man…"

"What is *that* supposed to mean?" Ryan snapped back. "Want to go back and visit in Aten again? Play some Blood Stomper with the Pharaoh? Maybe dig him out from under that ruin of a pyramid so we can continue our friendly chat?"

"Hell, no," the taciturn Armorer grunted. "Making an observation, that's all."

"I don't give a shit what color this thing is. It's our ticket out of this mess, unless Nefron's still got the controls frozen. If that's the case, we're all going to have to figure out how to survive a trek clear across the Barrens. I guess we can all take turns pushing the chariot!" Ryan said, continuing to mine the vein of sarcasm J.B. had inadvertently opened up.

"Didn't say anything about that. You did," J.B. replied.

"Drop it, lover. Please," Krysty said, lightly touching his arm. "We're all on edge. Don't need to start carving one another up."

Still, the notion of being a coward rankled Ryan. J.B. was right—what were the gateways really, but the ultimate escape route? Maybe it was the easy way out if the damn thing worked this time…but after all they'd been through, Ryan really didn't care.

One by one, each of the party stepped into the chamber and sat on the floor. Ryan waited patiently until everyone was inside and accounted for before stepping into the room himself. He turned back and stared at the door of the low-ceilinged chamber. Once closed, the advanced matter-transfer unit should automatically begin to power up and then they would be free, their very atoms reduced to mere components and shot out screaming into the void to be reassembled in another place.

Hopefully a better place than this.

"Close it," Jak said bitterly. "Close door on fucking place."

"Amen," Doc echoed. "I would rather be anywhere besides here, even if I must endure this hellish mode of transit."

"You could always walk, Doc," Ryan said. "The offer's still open."

"No, I do not relish a rematch with those most unusual followers of our friend the pharaoh. Even though the good Miss Wroth has eliminated Akhnaton from this mortal coil, I shall take my chances with the matter-transfer process, thank you very much— though we all know how well it sits on my aged bones."

"Aged bones, my ass," Mildred said. "You'll outlive us all, Doc."

"A fate I do not relish, Dr. Wyeth...although in your case, I must make an exception."

"All right, then. Let's do it," Ryan said, and pulled the chamber door closed, feeling the heavy steel panel click shut, an action that would result in the activation of the mat-trans unit.

A second passed, then two.

Ryan felt sweat begin to bead under his armpits.

And then, as it always did, the unit's security lock caught true, and the metallic clunk of magnetic bolts being thrown into the place was followed in turn by the spectral tendrils of the sinister pale mist that signaled the beginning of a jump.

"Hot pipe!" Dean said excitedly.

Despite his tension, Ryan grinned at his son's sense of adventure. "They don't make 'em any hotter," he acknowledged.

The white fog continued to gather, thickening around the unearthly shimmering disks in the floor and ceiling, and an almost inaudible hum from within the bowels of the chamber began to make itself heard deep inside the very core of their individual beings, a hum that increased slowly in pitch, making their skulls vibrate. For a few fleeting seconds of sheer agony and discomfort, it always felt as though the flesh were being flayed back from the bone.

"I could use a bottle of extrastrength headache pills," Mildred mused. "I used to eat them like candy back when I was in med school. Pulled many an all-nighter with them and the radio as company, and got to where I'd bite down and chew them up one by one without water. I actually developed a taste for the flavor. And I thought I had bad headaches then!" She paused, then went on. "Now I also feel as if a whole hive of electricity generating ants were running all over my body…and I want to talk and talk so I won't notice as much."

"Any of the stuff we grabbed out of here good for headaches?" J.B. asked. "I got a pocketful of drugs and syringes."

Mildred shook her head. "What you're carrying are just broad-spectrum antibiotics. Good for infection, but they're not painkillers in the sense I'm needing."

"Too bad. Bad enough taking a mat-trans jump when you're feeling good. Triple bad when your head's already hurting."

"I know," Mildred replied, snuggling in closer to J.B.'s lean body. "I'd have to wait and take them after the jump anyway. Otherwise, I'd probably just vomit them up once we got to where we're going— wherever in the hell that might be."

John Barrymore Dix—better known as J.B.—was Ryan Cawdor's longtime companion, best friend and his own personal walking and talking cache of knowledge of all forms of weaponry and how they could most effectively be used. J.B. wore the title of Armorer with quiet pride, a title given to him by the legendary Trader in the days when J.B. and Ryan rode with the grizzled old master of survival before fate stepped in and set them on their own path.

Trader had respected Dix and made him his head weapons master and booby-trap expert. J.B.'s encyclopedic mastery of blasters and their specs was invaluable to anyone attempting to traverse the Deathlands. From simple black-powder muskets to rumbling war wags equipped with high-tech lasers, J. B. Dix had obsessively spent his childhood and young adult life studying and memorizing how to use and repair any kind of offensive weapon.

He was still learning, but it was the rare weapon indeed he hadn't read about or seen.

With J.B. was his companion and lover, Dr. Mildred Wyeth, a "survivor" from the period before the nukecaust that ended the civilized world. Like J.B., Mildred was also a rare find for the Deathlands, since she was a trained physician and pioneer in the field of cryonics and cryogenics, a talented woman whose abilities had saved more than one member of the group.

Ironically, due to an illness near the end of the year 2000, she had been frozen by the very same cryonic process she had helped to develop, and had remained that way until Ryan and the others had found and managed to restore her to life, not knowing she was a physician.

Of even more practical use in her new surroundings, Mildred was a crack shot, having participated in the Olympics of 1996 as a free-shooter and taking home a silver medal for the United States. She carried a ZKR 551 Czech-built .38 target revolver, and while she took her oath as a healer seriously, she had seen enough and experienced even more since her reawakening to know the old saying "he who hesitates is lost" was written with the Deathlands in mind.

But for now the Armorer and the doctor were both at rest. Although they kept their relationship restrained and private, Ryan couldn't help but notice the comforting arm J.B. had placed around Mildred's shoulders. She leaned back into the side of the Armorer gratefully. Out of all the band of friends, Mildred came closest to actually understanding the hellish process they were about to endure, but that didn't mean she particularly enjoyed it.

J.B. was ready. Ryan saw the lean man had already

removed his steel-rimmed eyeglasses and tucked them safely away inside the front pocket of his worn leather jacket. J.B.'s other hand gripped his Smith & Wesson M-4000 scattergun tightly, reminding Ryan to check his own weaponry. Ryan caught J.B.'s eye, and the Armorer nodded an affirmative, tilting his battered fedora down over his eyes as if readying himself for a late-afternoon nap.

Ryan smiled at the gesture. J. B. Dix didn't like to use words when a gesture or a nod would do the job. Saved time. But he spoke up when things needed saying, or at times, when Mildred needed something a little extra from him.

"Planning on standing up for this trip, lover?" Krysty asked.

Staying upright during the matter-transfer process was never a good idea, since they usually ended up after a jump flat on the floor and unconscious anyway.

Ryan sat down in the graveyard mist next to Krysty, and she gave him a brief wink. As always, he couldn't help but marvel at her striking beauty—the flawless pale alabaster skin that managed to keep its purity even under the adverse conditions they sometimes traveled in, the radiant green of her eyes and the passionate fire of her long red hair. It was odd considering the amount of time they spent outdoors that there wasn't even a hint of a freckle on her nose or cheeks. Such a lack of freckling was very unusual for a redhead.

"You're staring," she whispered, taking his hand in her own and squeezing.

"Just thinking about how lucky I am to have you," Ryan replied.

"Nice to be appreciated."

"I'm just glad to be moving again," Dean Cawdor remarked to his father. The boy was seated next to Krysty, his knees drawn up tight to his chest. Ryan could almost swear the lad had grown an inch during their brief separation. If the growth spurts continued, the boy would soon be as tall as Ryan himself. They already shared the same dark complexion and curly black hair.

Like many young people of the Deathlands, Dean was chronologically poised to enter his teens with the life experiences of a much older person.

Across from Ryan was a young albino he considered his second son. Unlike Dean, there was no sharing of bloodlines, nor any resemblance—but the mutual feelings of love and respect ran deep. The teen's features were distinctive enough to bring more than a glancing notice, even among the more unusual appearances in Deathlands. Jak Lauren's pallid complexion was paler than usual, throwing the crisscrossed scars on his face into sharp relief. His ruby eyes were half-closed, and his mouth was drawn tight in anticipation of the jump to come.

A heavy, well-used but well-maintained Colt Python blaster was safely fastened down in a holster on one of Jak's legs. As a rule, Ryan didn't want his party to have weapons combat ready before a jump, so there was no need to have the handblaster cocked and ready. The mental and physical condition of everyone after a jump prevented the use of any weapons. Even if they were to beam into the midst of a firefight or a band of scalies, the group wouldn't be able to lift a finger to fight back until recovering from the physical toll the mat-trans experience took as payment for the instantaneous method of travel.

Besides, hidden on his person, Jak had several leaf-bladed throwing knives, their hilts taped for perfect balance. The young albino didn't need to worry about using a blaster when he had access to his knives, and he never went anywhere without one or more within instant access.

As usual before a mat-trans jump, Jak had nothing much to say, unlike the thin man beside him, who kept up an ongoing discussion with anyone who would listen or, when that option was out, keep a dialogue going with himself.

Next to Jak's eerie whiteness was the weathered face of Doc Tanner, a man trawled from the 1800s and thrust into present-day Deathlands. A lifetime of sights was etched into his skin—and his eyes. Doc gripped his ebony walking stick tight, the silver lion's-head handle keeping the secret of the hidden and honed blade of Toledo steel housed inside the body of the cane.

A most unusual handblaster was holstered at the man's thin hip. It was an ornate Le Mat, a weapon dating back to the early days of the Civil War. The weapon was almost as much an antique as Doc himself, but probably in much better condition. Engraved and decorated with twenty-four-carat gold as a commemorative tribute to the great Confederate soldier James Ewell Brown Stuart—or Jeb Stuart, as his friends and folks in Virginia referred to him—the massive hand cannon weighed in at over three and half pounds.

The blaster had two barrels and an adjustable hammer, firing a single .63-caliber round like a shotgun, and nine .36-caliber rounds in revolver mode. Finding ammo was difficult, but the old man refused to give up the sometimes clumsy blaster for a more modern weapon.

"Once you are set in your ways, there is no reason to change unless absolutely, positively necessary," Doc intoned.

Ryan did a quick inventory of his own personal arsenal. The 9 mm SIG-Sauer P-226 blaster was at his side like a loyal dog, the weapon's bulky baffle silencer digging reassuringly into his hip. The twenty-five-and-one-half-ounce weapon served as his third hand.

He had looped his bolt-action walnut-stocked Steyr SSG-70 rifle over one shoulder. Also on hand were two bladed weapons, a large eighteen-inch panga strapped to his left hip and a flensing knife, hidden away at the small of his back. Various bits of ammunition and a talent for the lost art of hand-to-hand combat made for a dangerous two-legged killing machine.

"Dad don't take shit off nobody," Dean had once said in awed wonder to Krysty as they both watched Ryan take out twin attackers in less than thirty seconds.

"I know. He doesn't have to. And what have I told

you about watching your language?'' the redhead replied.

This same incident had caused a third foe to cry out in exasperation at the firepower Ryan was using and the skill in how it was deployed, ''It's a wonder the one-eyed son of a bitch doesn't clank when he walks!''

''That's mister one-eyed son of a bitch to you, stupe,'' Ryan spat back, before unleashing a single shot from the SIG-Sauer pistol and turning the upper part of the attacker's head into a messy mix of brain, blood and bone.

The memory comforted Dean. More often than not, he viewed his father as more than human. Oh, not in the way one might view a mutie or doomie, but instead in how a man might step back and look at a force of nature. Ryan shared one trait with the unpredictable weather patterns that circled the globe—once you unleashed the whirlwind, there was no stopping him until the course was completed.

The mist of the chamber began to creep into everyone's being, tendrils of pale smoke sparking with miniature bursts of lightning, working its magic as the group prepared to be taken to an unknown site at an undisclosed location. No one could know for sure where they might end up. The band of travelers had traversed most of what remained of the United States and even visited other continents during their time of hopping around via the gateways.

How the mat-trans units really worked was anybody's guess. Mildred's theory—based on the quick study of the precious little documentation she'd been able to scan, the discussions she'd had with the rare few in the Deathlands who appeared to know something about the devices and late-night talks with Doc in the man's more lucid stages—was that both organic and inorganic matter were reduced to digital information and instantaneously transmitted on a form of carrier wave to another gateway, where it was then reconstructed, molecule by molecule.

None of the group had ever taken the time to try to dismantle any of the gateways; after all, once you'd taken one apart, there was no guarantee of being able to put it back together again. Ryan didn't want to find himself in a situation where they'd broken down their only avenue of escape because they'd gotten creative.

Nor had they been able to completely figure out exactly how a destination was chosen for them. The process was unpredictable—some jumps seemed to take only seconds, others hours or days. The time spent in transit always varied, surprisingly enough, even from person to person, depending on how their own perceptions colored the excursion.

"I'm really not looking forward to this," Krysty said softly.

Ryan moved closer to her in silent reply, acknowledging the journey to come.

Chapter Three

Exposing body and psyche to the forces of the mat-trans gateway was never a pleasant experience. At best, one might hope to walk away with a nosebleed and a feeling of nausea. Vomiting was a frequent companion to those who dared partake of the unforgettable mat-trans experience. At worst, a traveler arrived on the other end in a near coma, vital signs at a low ebb. There was also the haunting possibility of coming out of a jump in a state of dementia, thrashing around and causing injury to oneself and comrades.

Days before, when the group had first arrived at the gateway chamber inside the biological and genetics laboratory, Ryan and Krysty both were unconscious and dreaming, their sleeping minds locked in a simultaneous dream vision of erotic horror.

Later, all had determined that this shared dream—pieces of which Doc had also been privy to, minus the erotic element—had been brought to the forefront by the pharaoh and his formidable mutant gifts. But it was ultimately connected by their own psi abilities. Ryan was latent sensitive, which in many ways accounted for his own finely honed survival instincts. With the damage Doc had suffered by being time trawled, it was hard to determine how strong his own "psychic" abilities might be—or had once been.

Of the three, only Krysty possessed any outward manifestations of true extrasensory abilities. Her gifts were strong, skirting doomie status when in full bloom and serving as an advance-warning system for the group in times of uncertainty and danger.

Still, any example of a shared dream was most unusual. As a rule, everyone enveloped within the gateway process dreamed, and usually the experience wasn't pleasant. More often than not, what Ryan and the others were forced to endure while in the midst of molecular meltdown and reassembly was forgotten once they were awake and safe, the only vestiges being fleeting images of evil and feelings of unease.

Some of the dreams triggered by the mat-trans jumps they underwent were amazingly banal when exposed to the cold light of unforgiving reason and logic: vicious gunfights in the Old West along muddy streets and wooden sidewalks; card games with elegantly dressed gentlemen scalie gamblers on riverboats made of thick plastic and spun glass; a fistfight with a walking, talking plant that spouted platitudes from Plato; wild, unbridled sex with a multitude of partners.

Anything and everything burbled up from the subconscious and intruded when it came to the insanity of a mat-trans dream.

Ryan had asked Mildred what she thought caused the dreams to be so vividly violent, and she'd told him that the mind was only able to absorb and comprehend so much. When they took their places in a mat-trans chamber to go spiraling off into the infinite, perhaps the dreams were a defense mechanism to deal with sights and sounds that could otherwise drive them to insanity.

Not a bad theory, but Ryan had later placed his own spin on why the dreaming was induced. Depending on the level of just how psi sensitive you might be, tapping into the place where time and space met might also allow one a subtle, cloaked and symbolic glimpse into the future, such as the recent precognitive visit in the Egyptian-styled halls of Hell Eyes.

"There is truth in dreams, my dear Ryan," Doc had intoned more than once after recovering from a jump. "Ignore them at your peril."

"Dreams, hell—nightmares is more like it," was how Ryan defined them, both at that time for Doc and even now, at the present, when he was caught up in such a jump state.

Nightmares.

RYAN LOOKED DOWN at his hands. His scarred fists were stubs of raw, red meat from where he'd continued the pounding on the thick armored glass of the room's lone doorway. His bones ached, and his back was one long knot of pain. The shoulder he'd injured and Mildred had reset was a glistening mass of aches. His mouth was desert dry, and his breath was a long rasp as the oxygen-rich air went in and came out through lips that were cracked and bleeding.

He needed a drink. He needed a long cool drink of water, or even better, a bottle of vintage predark Scotch whiskey, a large heaping tankard filled with nothing but the finest whiskey and pure spring water and cracked ice.

Hell, at that very moment in life, Ryan felt as if he could drink a five-gallon bucket of the liquor, especially if it was the good stuff. Scotch like he was dreaming of could only be found in the secured wine cellars of the most powerful land barons—fat, swaggering, evil men who reeked of corruption and decay. Most barons were a silly, idiotic lot, content to feast on the downtrodden and keep all in their so-called kingdoms for their own private use and gain—but they always had the best booze.

A lot of baronies were nothing but cesspools of slave labor and sexual cruelty, sadism for sadism's sake: a child pulling the wings from a fly, or the torturing of an injured animal caught in a bear trap; the crushing of a man's self-respect and honor; the joy of watching the light of life slowly die in the eyes of anyone who dared get in their way. That's all many barons stood for...and Ryan had no use for them. However, barons could also be dangerous when provoked, and the one-eyed man and his ragtag band of friends seemed to have a knack for pissing off all the right people at all the wrong times.

Ryan wasn't the most patient of men, nor was he the most compassionate. He worked hard at holding back the red curtain of anger that would start to descend at the slightest provocation, knowing that to give in would leave him vulnerable, at risk.

But at that very moment, Ryan was prepared to endure the most debilitating bout of red-eyed rage if he could gain a bottle of Scotch whiskey in the bargain. Even the kiss of a baron was preferable to sitting in the near darkness, alone and in pain, for Ryan knew there would be no drink coming, neither of Scotch nor of water.

Not here. In this room there was nothing but madness and the dead.

Ryan studied the walls of the chamber, which seemed to flicker with hidden fires. The air was filled with shadows, physical and mental, but all were black.

The shadows were his protection against seeing his oldest friend with his arms wrapped in a death's grip around the body of the black woman in his embrace. Ryan felt his eye involuntarily tear up as he tried not to see the lifeless, pale, scarred man-child or the lean, weathered face of the elderly dead man tangled together on the floor. He tried not to notice how the flames flickered and created after-patterns in his retina when his gaze passed over the long, flowing, sunburst flame of hair of the woman he loved.

The woman he *had* loved. Ryan's tenses kept scrambling up—past, present and future. He made a valiant attempt to cut his lone eye away from the broken sight of his only son, the heir to the Cawdor name and bloodline.

Madness.

Ryan remembered now the reason why all of the walls in the chamber were spiderwebbed with cracks. Krysty had called on the terrible power of Gaia, the Earth Mother, closing her emerald eyes to slits as she sat in the lotus position on the floor and began to whisper in a half voice a mantra of assistance, "Help me, Mother, help me and give me the strength."

She had been trained since childhood to hone this empathy by being in tune with the electromagnetic energies of the very Earth itself. By tapping into these deep pools of energy, Krysty was forced to sacrifice her humanity in order to become a creature with untold strength.

The transformation lasted only a limited time, and took a terrific toll on her physical and mental being. Still, she'd tried her best to free them from the armaglass trap, but her efforts had ultimately proved useless. Her human frame could only trap and house the near molten force for so long before her bodily functions began to shut down, and she had pushed way beyond her limits this time.

She was dead twenty minutes after the attempt. Mildred noted the last of the woman's vital signs as they faded away.

A second bitter tear welled inside the duct of Ryan's blue eye.

"I know you, Ryan," a voice said. "I remember your face."

The rangy, muscular man whirled at the words, peering into the gloom of the room, trying not to look down at the limp, unmoving bodies.

"I remember what a cold-eyed, bitching bastard you were. Even as a young kid."

The voice came from none of the people at his feet. Ryan tried to focus and came up with the face from his own brain to go with the easy, mocking tone.

"Harry?" Ryan asked, startling himself with how

flat and dry his own normal baritone came out. "Harry, is that you?"

"If you say I am, I guess I am," Harry Stanton replied. The King of the Underworld of Newyork was sitting across from Ryan in a far corner of the hexagonal-shaped room. His eyes twinkled and he smiled broadly. He was dressed in the same outfit as Ryan had last seen him wearing many months ago amid the ruins of old Manhattan Island. Harry favored red and crimson apparel, and with his long beard and ample girth, he looked like a Deathlands version of jolly old Saint Nick.

Only Santa Claus had never looked so maniacal when smiling.

Ryan actually knew a bit about Christmas. He'd read an illustrated children's book—a poem really— over and over as a kid during his privileged childhood as the son of Baron Titus Cawdor in the ville of Front Royal. There was time for reading then. All the time in the world for anything he might have wished, until his mad brother and equally insane stepmother had taken all of that away from him.

"'Merry Christmas to all,'" Ryan said weakly.

"'And to all a good night,'" Harry finished. "Never took you for a poet, Ryan."

"I'm just full of surprises," he said after considering the concept.

"Oh, now, that I can certainly attest to, yes. Ryan Cawdor? A one-eyed chill-crazy bastard, filled to the apex of his pointy head with jolly surprises."

"What brings you out here?" Ryan asked, bored already with the rambling chatter that Harry adored.

"Out here, you say? Oh, we're outside?" Harry asked with a smirk, staring at the oppressive armaglass walls surrounding them.

"I mean, in here, I guess," Ryan added lamely. Fireblast, but he felt...broken. Drugged. Weary. All fought out.

"You'll do, Ryan! You'll do fine—you always have, damn your luck," Harry boomed. "Last time I saw you, you left me and my men asshole deep in a blizzard back among the skyscrapers of my beloved Newyork, Newyork."

"It wasn't personal, Harry. Otherwise I never would have left you stuck there alive. You saved my ass. J.B.'s, too."

"Glad to know you remember. Hell, I had to, Ryan. We had a history. I was there, you know, only a few weeks after you first joined up with the Trader. Damn, you were a sight back then," Harry mused, his ruddy face glowing with the memory. "You were too busy keeping the cheeks of your ass pressed together and walking tough to notice me, except as a potential enemy."

"My instincts weren't that far off."

"Yeah, me and the Trader, we go way back," Harry continued. "And since you were there in training pants running along behind, you and I, we go back, as well."

"Trader used to say a man with a long history was a walking corpse," Ryan said.

"Trader used to say a lot of things, most of it useless, but damn, it was entertaining. Life with the Trader was many things, but it was never boring."

Harry crooked a finger, and Ryan slid over closer. "I have something to tell you. Six degrees of separation is all that exists between any of us."

"Huh?" Ryan asked dully.

Harry sighed. "In between launching your salvos of bullets, you should think about reading a book every now and then."

"I have. I must've read *The Night before Christmas* fifty times," Ryan protested in a voice that sounded remarkably childlike. The timbre of his words frightened him enough to make him fear taking a look down upon himself, fearing he might see the fleshy body of an eight-year-old kid with proper depth perception.

"Let me put it this way—it's a small world after all, but we're all connected in some form or fashion," Harry said. "Not like spokes on a wheel, either. More like a patchwork quilt."

"Okay." Ryan coughed, suddenly impatient. He wasn't sure where Harry was going with this latest crock of shit about wheels and quilts, and he didn't care. Time to change the topic of discussion before he was forced to get to his feet, stagger over and strangle the talky bastard with his bare hands.

"How's the vid collection coming along, Harry?" Ryan asked, recalling the stacks and stacks of old videotapes Harry had shown him during his time in the man's lair beneath the streets of Newyork. Some of the vids were in protective plastic cases or tight cardboard boxes, but most were open—piles and piles of black plastic shells filled with spools of endless miles of recording tape.

"Coming along quad-triple fine!" the overweight man replied, excited to talk of his hobby. "I guess every man, woman and child must've owned a vid machine in the old days. More tapes floating around than a man would ever have time to watch. I can't figure out the logic behind some of the shit people recorded and saved, but any tape is usually a gem. You want to know what I find the most?"

"Not really, Harry. I was just trying to make conversation," Ryan retorted. "And you picked a lousy time for a visit."

"All depends on the interpretation."

"Yeah, right. Why *did* you pop up here anyway?"

Harry rapped a gloved fist on the top of his own head. "Why, I'm a cheesy fragment from your subconscious mind, Ryan, here to tell you to keep your possessions close...and your loved ones closer."

Ryan exhaled noisily. "Fuck, Harry. I already do that."

"Or so you think."

"No thinking necessary. I don't think. I do."

Harry fell silent, looking around the fiery walls of the hexagonal chamber. "Looks like you're in a bastard fix, Ryan my boy. Yeah, One-eye Cawdor's not going to fight or trick his way out of this one. Hell, I don't know why you're acting so surprised. We both know you were expecting this to happen sooner or later."

"What are you talking about, Santa?" Ryan had decided to give up on trying to maintain a semblance of a true conversation—he was saying whatever came into his mind now, flowing with the fever-dream logic being presented to him.

Harry beamed at Ryan, running his fingers through the snowy white beard the fat man was now sporting. "Come, now. In the darkest part of your heart you anticipated this happening. Now, there's no more dread, ho-ho-ho."

Ryan digested this latest piece of information. Harry had seemed to tap into a private dread, and from the looks of things, the evidence was clear. Was Santa Harry right? Did Ryan's fear of ending up trapped in a gateway cause this? Ryan pondered the concept, his own hidden fears peeled away and put on display in such a destructive fashion before his own remaining eye.

Then he rejected such analysis. No way. Every reassembled atom of his being rejected such a notion.

"No way, Harry Claus. I'm not dead yet."

"No, you're not. Not yet. Soon, mebbe. Sooner than you think. But jolly jumping Jesus, boy, take off the patch and look around you, because everybody else is stone-cold dead in the marketplace, one hundred and ten percent chilled!"

With that, Harry Santa Stanton Claus, the once and future King of the Underworld of Newyork, laid a finger up the side of his nose, and with a nod and a wink, up the brick-and-mortar chimney he rose.

Ryan gaped. He managed to crawl over to the mantel, his knees uncertain as he crossed J.B.'s lifeless leg, for a better look at the flickering fireplace, the source of the strange light and shadows that had been bothering him since he arrived here, in this place, in this state of mind. His gaze delivered more details about the fireplace.

There were photographs on the mantel, framed pictures of himself as an older man, with a hint of silver in his hair; of himself and Krysty together, smiling, at ease, with a tiny red-haired child held proudly between them; and of Dean, only Dean at the age of thirty, with the lines of maturity and age set in his cheeks and forehead.

Photographs. Memories. Visions of things to come?

Ryan took all of this in and was moved to speak a final time.

"I didn't know there was a fireplace in here," he whispered, half-hypnotized by the flickering of the flames, and then he woke up.

Chapter Four

Even through his closed eyelid, Ryan could still see the light.

A second ago, he had opened his right eye and immediately snapped it shut. In the instant Ryan had looked up into the blinding light, he'd been struck down hard by the coruscating illumination surrounding him. His lone orb ached, like someone with a massive fist had smashed a hairy knuckle into his lone good eye socket.

That wasn't a light caused by smoldering embers glowing inside a jump-dream-inspired fireplace. The light seemed to come from all sides, washing down from above and splashing up from below, bathing him from all angles in white brilliance.

Flat on his back, Ryan willed himself to reach down blindly for the weapon holstered at his hip and was rewarded with the comforting feel of the butt of the SIG-Sauer in his palm. He pulled the weapon free of its holster and scooted backward until the base of his spine hit the solid surface of what he figured to be the mat-trans armaglass wall.

The nova-hot light had begun to slowly fade to a more reasonable wattage. Through the spots dancing in front of his vision, Ryan was able to make out the forms of his companions, all of them scattered like discarded shell casings across the floor around him, their positioning identical to how he'd seen them in his mat-trans induced nightmare.

Krysty was to his right, facedown and unmoving. Her flowing red hair was shining bright in the brilliant illumination. Near her was Dean's tense body. Ryan gathered that the boy had also come to consciousness and been exposed to the sheer ferocity of the light—he was on his side, his eyes clenched shut like a fist. A dark streamer of blood covered his lips and chin, the standard nosebleed the mat-trans jumps so frequently induced. Ryan had come to consciousness many a time to find a smear of red across his face.

"Dean, you all right?" Ryan barked.

"Yeah, Dad. Got a triple-bad hammer going at my head," the boy replied. "Eyes feel awful. Like somebody rubbed ashes in them."

"Open them," Ryan ordered. "You've got blood on your face."

Dean carefully opened one eye, then the other. He touched the sticky blood on his chin and sighed. "Gets old. Wish I could figure out a way to stop this from happening."

"Don't we all. Anybody else awake yet?" Ryan asked the room, regaining his usual composure as the light continued to fade to a normal level.

"Yeah, but I wish I wasn't," Mildred Wyeth replied. "I think I scarred my retinas."

"Light was pretty damn bright. Never seen it go so high," Ryan said. "Guess it doesn't matter much as long as we're all here in one piece."

"Speak for yourself, Ryan. I haven't tried sitting up yet," the black woman replied.

The last thing the physician remembered was feeling all of the fillings in her teeth starting to vibrate and a metallic hum rising within her mouth to match the pitch and frequency of the teleportation disks overhead and underfoot in the small redoubt in the desert.

Then came the smoke, and the blue haze, and the long, lazy tendrils of fog. Unlike most of her companions, all of whom subconsciously held their breath as the eldritch process of the jump began, Mildred always breathed deeply, taking the ion-charged atmosphere deep into her lungs. She believed it helped with the dispersal and recalibration of her individual molecules when they where broken down and reassembled at their eventual destination.

So far, she had managed to avoid any references to *Star Trek*, Dr. Leonard "Bones" McCoy, having her "atoms scrambled" and the Starship *Enterprise*—not because she didn't think it would be funny, but because it was tiring to be the only person in the room laughing at a joke—though Doc might get it—and by the time she'd explained everything it wouldn't be funny anymore.

"Like looking into sun," Jak said softly, speaking for the first time since their arrival. His own ruby orbs were infinitely more suited for low levels of light and shadow instead of the bright lighting in the new mat-trans chamber.

"It's not that bad, Jak. Wasn't that bad, I mean," Ryan replied, getting slowly to his feet and keeping his blaster leveled at the door. "I took a good look when I came to, and I seem to be all right. The spots'll fade."

"Thank Gaia. You don't have the sight to lose," Krysty replied, revealing she, too, was awake.

"Hell of a ride," J.B. announced, sitting up and stretching. He took out his glasses and placed them on his lean nose before standing.

The mat-trans chamber they occupied was the traditional hexagonal shape, but everything else was different. A lower than usual ceiling tapered to a central point. Ryan had to duck when crossing the center of the room. An array of open silver mat-trans disks were overhead, close enough for Ryan to reach up and touch. A smooth, flat floor that appeared to be made of a thick clear substance with the lower mat-trans disks sealed within like insects in amber rested beneath the group's bodies. The disks were softly creaking as they contracted from their expansion, cooling down from the incredible heat unleashed during the jumping process.

The usual metallic smell was in the air, a flat, bitter scent of pressurized oxygen from the gases released during the jump.

There was nothing pleasant about a matter transfer jump. However, everyone was relieved to know that the odds were in their favor of being a long, long way from the Barrens, and that knowledge alone was enough to help relieve some of the feelings of illness that came with gateway transport.

However, this mat-trans chamber came with yet another new twist.

What could only be interpreted as a clear ob window was embedded in one wall, next to the doorway. At least the familiar thick armaglass that served as the walls of the chamber was in evidence here, although colorless in a dingy opaque gray sort of way. Trying to see through it was impossible, like trying to peer through a window covered in grime.

"What gives?" Ryan asked. "This place is a mat-trans chamber, but the feel is all wrong."

"I agree," Krysty answered. "And I don't think we're the only ones here."

"Think we're being watched?"

"Hope not."

Mildred was standing in front of the ob window with J.B, who had unlimbered his Uzi and was standing combat ready.

"One thing's for sure. This isn't just another redoubt," the Armorer murmured. "If you think the chamber's different, get a gander at the control room."

Everyone but the still unconscious Doc clambered over for a look, keeping their heads low as they peeked outside. The window revealed a wide, low-ceilinged—like the chamber—room that was antiseptically white. A series of black lines gave the floor a checkerboard pattern. A single white desk with a comp and monitor rested directly across from the window.

"Simple, stripped down. Where's all of the hardware?" Mildred wondered aloud.

"Another room, perhaps?" J.B. replied. "There's

a small anteroom off from the gateway between us and main control anyway.''

"Mebbe. Mebbe not," Ryan said. "Still, I do see a door, off to the far left."

Everyone looked in the direction where the one-eyed man was gesturing. There was a door, which appeared to be painted eggshell white with a simple silver doorknob. No high-tech locking systems or security key pads were visible. The frame had the look of being reinforced, and a thin rubber seal could be spied for an extraclose fit, but that was all in the way of modification.

"From the lack of security, I'd guess this place is commercial. Not military," Mildred mused. "I wonder what part of Deathlands we're in this time?"

Ryan tried the handle on the heavy armaglass door. It lifted up easily, and the door opened a crack.

"Never seen a mat-trans unit like this, and the colors of the walls are new. We're in unexplored territory here," he replied. "May want to take another jump out of here triple fast. Might be safer."

Doc remained oblivious, still unconscious and coiled in a fetal position on the floor. "Don't think these jumps are getting less stressful for Doc," Krysty said as she knelt next to him and pushed back a few wisps of long white hair from his face and forehead.

"My dear, you have a singular talent for stating the obvious even as you soothe my troubled brow," Doc retorted, smiling at her while keeping his eyes closed. "I do wish, however, the fates would choose the easier path and set me down gently upon it."

"You're not dead yet," Ryan said. "Get your skinny ass up, you old faker."

"I believe a predark expression was, 'My eyes feel like poached eggs,'" Doc volunteered, then curled his long, hawkish nose and sniffed. "Burned poached eggs, at that, if the scent my nose has detected is true."

Ryan smelled the odor, as well, which was now wafting into the mat-trans chamber through the door he'd opened.

"J.B., you smell it?" Ryan asked urgently.

"Dark night," the Armorer replied as an affirmative, "smoke."

"And where there's smoke..." Doc said, his voice trailing off.

"There's fire," Dean finished. "We've got to go. Now."

"Can you move yet?" Ryan asked, striding over to where Doc sat.

The old man shook his head slowly. "No," he whispered. "Not yet. Not at any kind of speed."

"I'm not asking for a sprint. I just want you to walk fast."

"Alas, my dear Ryan, I fear even elementary locomotion is beyond my reach. A few moments more, and I might rouse myself—"

"We don't have a few minutes," Ryan snapped. "Guess you get to improvise, Doc."

"My good man," Doc said indignantly, "my life thus far has been nothing but one long improvisation."

"We'll have to carry him," Ryan said simply.

"Krysty, you take his feet. I've got his upper body. J.B., take the point. Mildred, Dean, fall in behind him. Jak, you're on the rear. Let's see what's burning. If there's a fire in the control room, we might not be jumping back after all. Triple red, people. Let's move!"

"Didn't count on fighting any fires today," Mildred said, glancing through the ob window at a bright red extinguisher hanging against one of the white walls outside the gateway. "And I imagine the charge in that old extinguisher wouldn't even put out a match."

"That's what we get for jumping into something besides a good old-fashioned military redoubt," Ryan retorted. "At least in those, we know what's coming, most of the time."

J.B. gripped the heavy handle of the chamber's door and jerked it open farther. The door responded easily enough, then the Armorer was outside.

Unencumbered, Mildred and Dean were close behind J.B. as he took extralong steps and flattened himself alongside the single door to the small control room.

"Go ahead," Ryan said after the seven friends were safely out of the mat-trans unit. "Open it."

THE UNDERGROUND SECTION of the Wayne Feldman Baptist Hospital and Medical Center was burning, and Alton Adrian knew it was only a matter of time before his pursuers discovered him. Once he was found in his hiding place, he'd be a dead man, his freshly chilled corpse nothing more than new kindling to toss on the bonfire of the world. He'd been warned to tread softly into this maze of hospital corridors and hidden stairwells by the old-timers, the scavengers who eked out a living by picking through the remains of the past and bringing back items that were still of value.

By the very nature of their business, scavengers liked to talk. Information was just as valuable as something solid you could hold and touch, some times even more so. There were always rumors of lost caches of ammunition, secret stockpiles of gasoline or mother lodes of precious metals.

Some of these tales were close to home.

Such as a hidden lair below the medical center.

Adrian had been told time and time again the hospital was essentially clean of any valuables, but if a man wanted to go down deep, he might find comps or medicines or other high-ticket items worth their weight in jack as barter to a better life. Only problems with that course of action were the stickies—the Baptist hospital was dangerously close to the part of the downtown area of the city they called home.

He had two choices, three, if he included the logical decision of never going near the abandoned hospital complex. The scavie could go in alone and quiet and try to avoid alerting any muties of his presence, or he could take in a team of mercies and openly engage any hostiles who might have set up squatter's rights within the hundreds of rooms.

With a team on his side, any loot would have to be shared. Adrian wasn't greedy, but he was practical. Not to mention the element of trust. He could round up a few good men, but it would take time, and the smell of possible big jack had a way of driving even the best of allies apart. So far, he was the only man with an investment in this scheme, and he'd paid in jack and favors to find out the secret of the med center's hidden basement.

Days before, Adrian had been across the old state line to visit a tiny ville in Virginia known as Cana. A friend of his father's was rumored to live there, a colorful coot named Willard Boyles. Boyles was a semilegend in the scavenging business, with rumors and stories passed from ville to ville about his prowess and sense of fair play. The wily practitioner had been at it for thirty years before making his big score and hanging up his walking shoes.

The only reason he'd admitted Alton Adrian into his home was due to the younger man's bloodline. Scavengers were sentimental like that. A few cheap self-brewed beers later, and the usual protective mask Willard wore had been discarded and he was speaking as bluntly and honestly as if he'd known Adrian all of his life.

"Experiments, boy! No telling what went on down there. Never been in those black labs myself, and I have no intention of going, either. Who knows what you might find…or what you might let loose in the process!" Willard had said.

"Don't think I'll find anything to add much worse than the shit already running around Deathlands, Will," the younger man replied. "And if I do, it'll probably chill me first."

"I'm not saying you'd go marching in and unlock Pandora's box intentionally. Hell, some doors were never meant to be opened. Excuse the pun, but that old hospital is bad medicine.''

Adrian grinned. ''Sure, you can say that. You're set until the last train goes West. Me, I'm still trying to make the big score.''

Willard paused, remembering his past and his own endless days of traveling around the Eastern Seaboard of Deathlands while mining out a living from finding, repairing and selling pieces of the past. Perhaps it was the home brew or the sense of obligation to his old friend, Lee Adrian, the boy's father. Either way, Willard Boyles was indeed set for life, and as such, he had taken pity and offered up a secret he'd never had the courage to fully explore himself.

''There's a hidden basement level in the medcenter tower in that hospital, you know,'' he said casually, confirming what the young scavie had previously heard. ''Not on any map or chart.''

''So, the legends are true?''

''In this case, yeah. Tale I got was that there were freezies down there. Hundreds of them. All with jewels and jack to start a new life once they woke up.''

Adrian listened to the older man speak, spellbound. A treasure trove had been kept in stasis along with the near dead. It was the ultimate score—*his* ultimate score.

''Why so hush-hush?'' he asked.

''Had to keep it a secret. Didn't want grave robbers going in.''

''How'd they keep it hidden?''

''Money, of course. Jack. To be put in with the other freezies, you had to pay dear. The freezies' lair was private. Getting down there involved some trick with the elevators, back when they were functioning. I don't know the details. Don't matter anyway. They had to have a backup plan in case the elevators fucked up, and that's where you'd go in.''

"Will I have to rappel down the elevator shaft?'' Adrian asked nervously, already feeling his arms ache. "I'll have to lose some weight and get in better shape.''

"Shit,'' his new benefactor replied, taking another long swig of his beer, "you think I'd want to go diving down an elevator shaft? No way. No, what you'll need to do first is to find the stairs.''

"All right. That I can handle.''

"When you enter the main floor of the med-center tower, there's an admitting desk. You'll have two choices. Right or left. Go left. Take the stairs down all the way to the bottom.''

"Okay.'' The scavie started to take out a scrap of paper to make notes, but Willard's stern glare made him tuck the paper back in a pocket.

"What you doing, boy? First law of scavenging is to never write anything down.''

"I know. Sorry. Nerves.''

"This isn't that complicated. You'll remember it.

"Now, you'll have to go by feel, since the walls in the bottom look blank. There are no doors or windows. If a man was to have walked down there long ago, he'd never have suspected anything, and gone back up a level to the last floor listed on the guide maps. Keep running your fingers along the wall. I think it's the wall on your left. Feel around until you notice a small indention. That's the spot. Rig a series of explosive charges to take out the wall, and you should be in.''

Adrian could scarcely contain his mounting excitement. "This is fantastic! What's inside once I bring the wall down?''

Will paused with an expression of guilt. "I don't know. I never was brave enough to go see for myself. Like I said, I've been told freezies, but who can say? I went down once, had a bit of plas ex in my backpack and a time-delay fuse, and I was ready to go, oh yeah. But hell, I'll admit to you, Alton. I got scared. The stairwell was pitch-black, and I was alone and afraid of what I might find. So, I went back up and on my way, fully intending to go back down there with a partner, but I never did.''

"And you think I should.''

"Isn't my knowledge and advice what you came all the way to Cana for?''

"Yeah, but—''

"It's an easy score for a smart man.''

"Hah. Easy for you to say, Willard. You've made your bank. You'll live here in this cabin with your woman and your guns and your sec systems until you dry up and wither away.''

"It's all up to you, boy. You're still young. How hungry are you?''

A FEW DAYS AFTER LEAVING Cana and returning home, Alton Adrian decided he wasn't just hungry—he was a starving man.

So he had taken the long walk down into the dark

and, once at the bottom of the stairs, he'd worked the claylike plas ex in his hands, molding and shaping it into four clumps of equal size. He pressed two of the clumps at eye level separated roughly by eight feet. The other two he placed low. Then he took out the wiring and used it to attach the four clumps of explosive to a single fuse. Extending the fuse as long as he dared, Adrian crept back up the stairs, knowing he'd need to be a floor away when the fireworks began.

He had no idea how thick the door or walls might be, so he overcompensated.

The wall went up in a sound of thunder.

The scavie crept back down to admire his handiwork, and artificial light spilled out into the darkness. The room he had opened had electric lighting from within. He'd been inside for only five short minutes when he heard noises and smelled burning oilcloth.

Adrian realized with mounting panic that he'd been followed into the dark...and now into the light. The sound of the overheated explosion had been catnip to his visitors. Stickies. Six of them.

He ducked, hiding. If the underground chamber was filled with freezies, the crazy muties would probably burn them, too.

Adrian laughed bitterly. At least he could console himself with the sad realization that no matter how bad it got before the end, at least he wouldn't die alone.

"Wonder if you poor bastards start to drip and melt?" he asked aloud.

No answer was forthcoming.

THE EGGSHELL WHITE control-room door had opened into a much larger room filled with the missing comp banks and other hardware normally associated with a working mat-trans unit. Ryan's keen eye raked over the room, looking for any signs of fire. The room appeared to be intact and unoccupied. All of the screens were flickering. No flashing red lights or warning systems had erupted…yet.

J.B. glanced down at the button radiation counter he wore on his lapel. "No indications of rad leakage in the area," he reported.

Another door at the end of the room waited. Next to the door was a sec keypad to keep out the unwanted and unauthorized.

"Look alive, people," Ryan said. "Appears the gateway has been uncompromised. We can still jump out of here, or we can take this door and see what's causing the smoke."

Doc was now on his feet. "I regret the lack of choices, my dear friend. I prefer two options—the lady or the tiger."

J.B. laid an open palm against the door. "Doesn't feel hot," he said. "Whatever's burning on the other side hasn't gotten out of hand yet."

"Guess it wouldn't hurt to take a look, would it?" Krysty said.

"Guess not," Ryan replied, before reaching down and pressing the short sequence of numbers. However, instead of the door sliding up into the ceiling or into one of the walls, it merely gave a loud clicking sound.

"What was that?" Dean asked.

"Door unlocked," Mildred said. "I'd been wondering if the redoubt codes would work here."

Ryan pushed the door carefully, allowing it to swing open into the next room. Smoke billowed in from the burning walls and furniture inside the new room, which appeared to be a kind of waiting area or lounge. The haze in the air limited his visibility. Ryan brought up his blaster and readied it to fire, then took a single step inside.

A stickie, dressed in a dirty black pullover turtleneck and jeans, staggered out of the smoke with both arms outstretched, in a mockery of a vaunted embrace.

They looked at each other, man and mutie, brothers through a distorted looking glass.

"You...you're a norm," the stickie said slowly as the information began to sink into the wrinkled morass the mutant called a brain.

"And you're chilled, asshole," Ryan retorted before pulling the trigger of the SIG-Sauer.

Chapter Five

The single shot of the SIG-Sauer was explosively loud within the confines of the underground network of labs, so loud that Alton Adrian easily heard the shot from where he was hiding inside a silver steel entryway outside of the main cryogenics laboratory.

"Skrag! One of the muties must be packing heat," he whispered to himself as a chill went down his spine and settled in the small of his back. A stickie with a blaster was triple-bad news. Weapons were hard enough to find in that part of Deathlands.

Blasters were hard to obtain and costly to maintain. Even with a blaster, finding ammunition was even harder unless you had the extra jack to pay top price. Most of the stickies Adrian had ever heard of or seen went for a more basic approach to offense—they used their own substantial strength and incredible mutant abilities to attack their foes bare-handed or with clubs.

Taking a deep breath, he warily slid out of the cool entryway and crawled on his hands and knees down the corridor. The smoke was thick there, and by staying low he could breathe easier and have better visibility.

He paused, wondering if he was indeed heading in the right direction, when more sounds of violence came crashing around the corner less than fifteen feet away from where he was crouched. Already he missed the cool of the room near the freezie chambers.

He had two choices: go back the way he came or investigate what was causing all of the stickie ruckus.

"Follow the ruckus," he decided. Perhaps he could gain the upper hand somehow. He hadn't spent all this time hoping for a big score to see it pissed away by a bunch of idiot muties who liked to set fires.

ONCE RYAN HAD FIRED the first shot, the battle was on. He flattened against the wall, firing a few more rounds blindly into the smoke.

"Come on," he barked, and the rest of the group filed in past the burning parts of the room. The fires didn't seem to have opened into full flower yet, blossoming out in red-and-yellow petals. The walls, while scorched, weren't ablaze.

"Want to seal off the gateway, Dad?" Dean was standing at the door, where a twin for the sec keypad was recessed in the door frame.

"Do it," Ryan replied. "We might need a back door if things get bad in here."

The boy reversed the order of the locking code, and the door gave off the same queer clicking noise that indicated the magnetic lock had thrown true.

"The fire may burn itself out," Krysty said. "Not much here to flame on, really."

"Mebbe," Ryan agreed, coughing from an unintended lungful of smoke. He strained to see as they stepped farther into the burning room and near a doorway that led into a wide corridor. He could see more humanoid figures at the far end of the wall, slowly moving closer.

"More stickies heading this way," he reported to his friends.

Then, before any sort of battle could begin, the ceiling fell in, the smoky air above them transformed into a mass of cool white clouds, jetting down violently and without warning.

"What is this bastard stuff?" Ryan bellowed.

"Stay calm," Mildred yelled back over the rattling of the released emissions. "It's halon gas! I've seen it before. They used it in predark times to fight fires instead of water in sensitive areas with computers."

Looking up, they all saw that the gas had been released from a series of shiny sprinkler heads mounted into the ceiling tiles.

"Can it hurt us?" Krysty asked in a concerned voice. "Should we hold our breath or something?"

"No. It's a chem dump, a deluge. Expensive as hell, but it won't harm anything, including people. It's inert. Can't damage equipment or paper and disappears like a vapor. Leaves everything behind except for fire untouched," Mildred replied.

"Sounds more like the neutron bomb of the firebug set," J.B. observed sourly.

Already, the chemical was doing its magic, beating back the flames and clearing the air, revealing the damaged lounge area and the remaining three stickies who now could see the humans quite clearly, and vice versa.

"Feel wet," Jak said, running the palm of a hand down his pant leg.

"Halon gas dries quickly, Jak," Mildred told him. "You'll never know it was there in a few minutes."

"This fire was big enough to trigger any safeguards. I wonder what took the gas so long to launch?" Ryan said, watching the stickies regain their equilibrium from the sudden appearance of the artificial cloudburst.

"No telling," Mildred replied, sharing Ryan's attentive gaze on their foes. "Since this isn't a standard redoubt, I'm wondering what's keeping this place powered up enough to operate a gateway anyway."

"Must be a nuke gen somewhere around here," J.B. said bluntly.

Mildred chuckled. "If this is more of a private setup, I'll bet the locals never dreamed there was a small nuclear power plant right under their feet."

Like others of their kind, the muties were clumsy as they entered chaotically into what passed for a stickie attack stance. The freakish deformity of their bodies was painfully obvious as each of them turned to face Ryan and the rest of the group of friends.

The only weapons they carried were torches, and a few blades and other sharpened hand-to-hand weapons. No blasters were in evidence.

Normally the muties didn't need them. However, in such close quarters, their attack against human rifles wouldn't last for more than a few seconds. Chilling the stickies would be a simple task.

But then the ceiling fell in for a second time, the lightweight tiles buckling on top of the group of friends as two more of the murderous muties came crashing down into their midst.

One of the stickies bounded forward with a wordless cry, slamming into J.B. before he could raise his scattergun. The mutant's hand adhered instantly to the side of J.B.'s face, the suckered touch driving a scream even from the stoic Armorer's throat as he tried to twist away. His wire-rimmed spectacles were slung from his face as he struggled.

Afraid he'd hit one of his comrades in the now tightly fought battle, J.B. took out his Tekna knife and used it against the stickie who was intent on ripping away his face. He slashed out with his blade again and again at the stickie's arm, hitting a vein that carried what passed for blood in the mutie. A thin film of tacky ichor sprayed out, coating the stickie's face and upper body.

"Fireblast!" the Armorer cursed, throwing himself back in disgust even as the upper epidermis of his face tore away from the stickie's finger-pad attachments. With the pain came relief, the pain of freedom much preferable to the horror of being drawn closer to the subhuman mutation.

The moment direct contact with J.B.'s skin was broken, Mildred squeezed off a shot from her pistol, finishing the job J.B.'s blade had started when he cut a hunk out of the stickie's arm. However, Mildred wasn't going for the extremities. She went for the head shot, the chunk of lead escaping her blaster with a loud crack as it almost instantaneously entered the stickie's nasal cavity, entering in a clean, deadly motion and crashing through the lower part of what passed for the mutie's brain.

The bullet exited the back of the stickie's skull,

punching out in a spray of gray matter and blood and bone. As the grue flew out, it splattered against the back wall of the hallway with a wet slap, narrowly missing Doc, whose swordstick's blade tip just slid into the eye socket of the second attacking stickie. Doc slid the stick out and back a second time with all of his strength, shuddering when he felt the blade scraping bone in the pulped socket.

J.B. stumbled forward, his normally weak vision seriously compromised by the loss of his glasses and the blood pouring down from the torn flesh of his forehead into his naked eyes. He kept moving, to provide less of a target while keeping his immediate area clear of attackers.

"Son of a bitch!" J.B. cried out, incensed by his handicap, swinging his knife in a searching circle. "I'll gut all of you bastards!"

In the heat of the battle and confusion, no one even noticed when J.B.'s booted foot came down hard on his dropped spectacles, shattering the already cracked right lens and cracking the left lens.

Across the room, Ryan was involved in his own struggle. The distraction of the pair of muties falling into the band's midst had given the other three stickies time to advance. Having lost one eye, Ryan was well aware of the fear men possessed when it came to preserving their vision. Taking his cue from Doc's fancy work with the ebony swordstick, Ryan also went for his opponent's eyes. Muties, at least stickies, shared this phobia, and the lead one screeched out in terror as Ryan dug both of his thumbs into the freak's ghastly pale eye sockets and pushed with as much force as he could muster.

Thin blood, sticky and pink, came squirting forth like tiny fountains from the twin thumb gouge. It ran down the stickie's cheeks like tears and covered Ryan's hands and upper arms.

The mutie's tongue came slithering out, long and lank, adorned with dozens of tiny suckers mirroring the ones on the creature's hands. Ryan bit down hard on the impulse to gag. His adversary's creature's breath was unbearable, and the odor coming from the stickie's burst eyeballs was even worse.

The tip of the tongue brushed against Ryan's wrist, slithering like a snake over the band of his wrist chron before touching flesh.

The thought of an oral caress from a stickie was too much, even for a hardened warrior like Ryan Cawdor. He pulled his thumbs back and locked his hands and fingers together, swinging them down, then up in a rapid, fluid motion. As he brought the double handful up, he smashed a twin fist into the unfortunate mutie's chin, slamming the already maimed creature's mouth shut with terrific force, causing the dumb, blinded bastard to bite off its own tongue.

The abnormally long tongue fell to the floor, and the dying stickie soon joined it.

The remaining two were summarily dispatched with equal and deadly force. Shots rang out from Krysty's .38-caliber Smith & Wesson and Dean Browning Hi-Power. Unlike Mildred, Krysty was no former Olympic champion when it came to target shooting, but she was a fine shot at such close range.

The volley from Dean's pistol also struck true, but the boy had gone for a shot to the heart instead of the head, forgetting that stickies had internal organs that were sometimes positioned differently than those belonging to an ordinary man.

The shot was a killing wound, with an assist. On the fringes of the action, peering in for where his talents might best be needed, was Jak. Spying Dean's quandary, Jak calmly whipped out a throwing knife and sent it spiraling into the neck of the stickie that Dean's bullet had previously entered. The combination of critical injuries finished off the mutie.

And then all of the attackers had fallen, and the conflict was over.

"Everybody okay?" Ryan asked from behind clenched teeth, his injured shoulder singing a lusty song of agony now that the adrenaline surge was fading away.

A chorus of replies came back affirmative.

"You don't look all right, J.B.," Ryan noted. "Mildred, see if you can get his face to stop bleeding."

"On it," she replied, striding over with a clean cloth and a small bottle of disinfectant she kept packed away in case of injuries such as these. "Need to find a few bandages or some med tape. That should take care of you, John."

"You're the doctor, Millie," J.B. replied. "Don't think the bastard had a chance to get too much of a grip. Feels like he just took off a top layer or two."

"Well, I'll be the judge of that. Ugly as you are, a few more scars won't hurt," the woman teased.

"Thanks," he replied glumly. "Nice to be loved."

"Where are your glasses, John?" Mildred asked, noting their absence for the first time since the struggle had ended.

"Damn stickie knocked them clean off. Must've landed on the floor somewhere."

"Shit," Jak said. His tone made them all look at him.

"There a problem?" Ryan asked.

"Found specs. What's left," Jak replied from a squatting position near a bloody corpse. The albino held up the twisted frames. One of the lenses was shattered, with bits of glass hanging in the frame and scattered like fine grains of salt on the floor. The other lens was in better shape, but not by much. A crack the size of a bolt of lightning stretched down the center.

"Aw, hell," the Armorer said as Jak walked over and handed him the remains of his eyewear. "Don't think duct tape is going to help hold these together."

"How's your vision minus the specs, J.B.?" Ryan asked, concerned that his friend might be crippled without the glasses.

"I can get around, if that's what you're getting at. Just don't expect any precision shooting from me and I'll be okay."

"Soon as we get out of here, we'll try to find you a replacement pair. I can't have my best shot stumbling around blind."

"I'm your best shot," Mildred protested. "And don't worry about John, I'll be there to help keep him from stumbling."

"Not ready for a damn white cane yet," J.B. said.

"Glad to hear it," Ryan replied.

"You think we're underground, lover?" Krysty asked Ryan as he turned to let Mildred finish ministering to J.B.'s facial wounds.

He considered the question for a moment. "Probably. Least ways, I'm guessing we're underground. Fits the usual pattern, even if this is the most fucked-up redoubt I've ever encountered."

"Still say this isn't a redoubt," J.B. protested as Mildred dabbed some of the antiseptic on his chin. "Son of a gun," J.B. hissed. "What's that, Millie? Acid?"

"It's germ-free John. It's supposed to hurt. Kills the infection."

"Ever hear of the cure being worse than the disease?"

"If this isn't a redoubt, let's start exploring and see what it really is," Dean suggested, hopping down from an abandoned gurney and stepping over the dead stickies to check out the end of the corridor.

"Wait, Dean. Don't go running off on your own," Ryan growled, but the impetuous boy had already gone around the blind corner.

And come face-to-face with the haunted eyes of a new threat.

Chapter Six

Dean Cawdor was sometimes headstrong and impulsive and all of the other things a boy his age could be called, but certainly he wasn't a coward. That much of his makeup came from his gene pool.

Still, he could be startled and react accordingly.

So when his choked cry of surprise reached his father and friends, they knew something unexpected had happened.

After Dean yelled, he almost fell backward as he tried to put distance between himself and the unexpected figure he'd nearly run over. The boy pulled out his blaster as he retreated and leveled it at the intruder.

Already heading toward his son, Ryan had unholstered his own weapon and readied it. "Back off, Dean," he yelled, lining up the sights of the pistol to fire a killing shot as he waited for whatever it was to advance carefully around the blind spot of the corner.

"D-don't shoot, for Christ's sake!" the offstage figure said.

"Doesn't sound like a stickie," Krysty remarked.

"Come on around, then, nice and slow," Ryan ordered, the barrel of the blaster unwavering.

Dean was still in the vantage point. "He's got his hands up, Dad."

A man stepped carefully around the corner, his hands held high over his head, smooth palms out and open to show his nonmutie status. His mouth was hanging open in complete and utter shock. The entire force of stickies had been cleared in less than thirty seconds, their lifeless bodies littering the floor.

"You got them all?" he asked.

"No. There's still you," Ryan growled.

"Don't shoot," he cried. "I'm a norm!"

"Good way to get chilled, norm or not. Toss your blaster over here, nice and easy. Take it out with two fingers, and try not to drop it and shoot yourself in the foot."

"How do I know you won't chill me?"

"What's stopping me from chilling you now, stupe?" Dean retorted, his courage flowing back into his veins.

"Got a point, I guess."

"Been enough chilling in here. Until you do or say otherwise, I'll take you as a norm. Keep your blaster on him, son," Ryan said as he holstered his own drawn pistol and handed over the captured piece to J.B.

"Colt .45 auto," the Armorer said. "And even without my specs, I can tell it needs a good cleaning. What do you want to do with this dumb shit, Ryan?"

"Ryan?" the scavenger repeated, a light of recognition in his brown eyes. "You're Ryan Cawdor! And that must be J. B. Dix! I'll be dunked in honey and oven-roasted—you guys rode the wags with Trader!"

"That was a while back. And you seem to know a hell of a lot about us for a stranger."

"I get around, Mr. Cawdor. Heard some things. Talked late into the night with a guy named Abe who was trying to track down Trader after he'd heard the old salt wasn't as dead as had been previously reported. Abe told me some stories and described you two. Not that many people walking around Deathlands with features as distinctive as yours—at least, traveling together with other people like the redhead and the albino. Uh, no disrespect intended," the man babbled nervously.

"What's your game?" Ryan asked.

"I'm a scavie—a scavenger. I find and I sell."

"You're a damn bone-picker, is what you mean," J.B. muttered.

"We all got to make a living, Dix. But I don't pick no bones or truck with dead men."

"Speaking of dead men," Mildred said. "I'd just as soon get the hell away from all these stickies. Find another place to quiz our new buddy."

"Okay. You keep quiet, and you might get out of here alive. Got it?"

The scavie nodded eagerly.

"You're a fast learner," Ryan noted approvingly. "Most people screw up and say 'Yeah.' Can't seem to keep their mouths shut."

The travelers split into two teams, with J.B. and Dean staying in the corridor to keep an eye on the scavie. Doc and Jak took one end, Ryan, Mildred and Krysty the other. The rooms and corridors were laid out in a simple rectangle shape. They passed a cryo lab, a suite of empty hospital beds, a single nonfunctioning elevator, a front reception area with long dead phones and other such hardware and a sizable hole that Adrian had blown into the wall for admittance. No armory, no food and no supplies, except for a small first-aid kit Mildred found in a bedside drawer.

"Got J.B. some adhesive bandages at least," she announced. "There's a brand-new box in the kit."

"It's not a redoubt," Ryan said. "Just like J.B. predicted back in the gateway."

"Feels and smells more like a hospital," Mildred observed.

"Perhaps we need to question our new friend. I wonder how long he's been down here anyway?" Krysty said.

"Blast in the wall looks fresh," Ryan replied, picking up a chunk of concrete. "New grit on the ground from the explosion. Our timing might have been better or we might just be unlucky. I'd say the guy with the beard hasn't been stumbling around in here for very long."

"Could've done without him and those stickies. He probably brought them in here in the first place," Mildred said.

When the two groups had converged, the scavie suggested adjourning to the cryo room, away from the smell of the fire the muties had set and the stench of death where the dead stickies had fouled themselves as they died. Ryan agreed, wanting to get the man away from the still intact and working gateway as quickly as possible.

They talked as they walked to the labs. The newcomer seemed to take particular delight in discovering Ryan had a son. His own boy was down south in Georgia with his mother and her kin.

"Guess you can say she left me. Her loss, as well as my own. Glad to meet all of you. I'm Alton, Alton Adrian. I guess you heard the explosion. That's what brought you down here."

"Uh, right," Ryan improvised. "The explosion. Made my eardrums pop."

Adrian shrugged. "I overdid it. Not a demo man. Better too much than too little."

"Not always," J.B. replied. "Can bring the roof in on your head."

"I'll remember that. Well, I owe you, I guess. I'd be chilled for sure if those stickies had got their hands on me. I've got squatter's rights, so I'm claiming half, you all can divvy up the other part between yourselves. Fair?"

Ryan frowned. "What are you talking about?"

"Scavenge the cryo spots. Try and thaw a few of the freezies, see what valuables they decided to hang on to during their stay in the cooler."

"Yeah. We were looking like anyone else," Ryan said gamely. If the man wanted to think they were fellow ghouls, so much the better. Such beliefs saved questions, including the big one of how they'd gotten into this area in the first place.

"I didn't think anyone else knew about this hidden level but me. I got sloppy and used too much plas ex. Muties must've heard just like your group did and followed me down here. Good thing you came along."

"Timing is everything," Krysty said with a smile.

"Don't I know it," he replied, reluctantly pulling his eyes away from Krysty's beauty to peer back at Ryan and J.B.

"Listen, Cawdor, don't take this wrong, but you and your pal there are two of the most curious-looking fellows I ever seen around here. The stories Abe told me didn't say you had such weird coloration."

Doc cackled. "I take it you are in awe of their dusky pigmentation."

"Say what?" Alton asked.

"Their skin, man! You are talking about their skin!" Doc replied.

"Yeah. Take the lady doctor here," Alton said, gesturing to Mildred, who was busy applying the bandages she'd found to the coin-sized flesh wounds on J.B.'s face. "She's beautiful. Don't get me wrong. Skin color don't mean shit to me. Attractive is attractive. And the rest of you look like any other poor white bucks running around Deathlands, even the albino."

Jak glared in way of response. The teen wasn't sure if he trusted Alton yet or not, and as a newcomer the man invited and deserved extra scrutiny.

"But I never seen men with skin color like Ryan's and J.B.'s," Alton continued. "It looks, well, it don't look natural. Looks kind of funny."

"Well, it isn't. We got into a scrape a while back and had to dye our faces and J.B.'s hair. Long story, but we got out alive," Ryan replied. "You should have seen us right after the deed was done."

"Man does anything to stay alive," Alton agreed, not pushing further. Curiosity could get a man chilled triple fast, and the bearded man had escaped death already for the day. He believed in playing the odds and not causing problems. Whatever had forced Ryan Cawdor to dye himself a new skin tone was the one-eyed man's business, and since there was no offer of volunteering to explain what had happened, it would remain a mystery.

"Good thing most of the dye has worn off, lover," Krysty said. "I was starting to get used to your new look until our new acquaintance pointed it out."

"Here we are," Alton said, gesturing toward the door of the cryo laboratory. He'd been very close to entering the actual lab. His chosen hiding place was outside the main doorway in the air lock, with the contents behind him kept sealed by a single steel door. He'd peeked inside through a small round window, but had gone no farther. Again, as in most of the lab complex except for the gateway, there were no codes or secrets for full access and entry, just a simple Admit button to cycle the air lock.

"Ready?" Mildred asked, an anxious tone in her voice as she stood in front of the doorway, clenching and unclenching her hands.

Ryan waved her on, and the woman stuck out a stocky finger and pushed the button. The air lock hummed, then opened with a sigh, and the pressure quickly equalized, allowing easy entry to a pair of double swing doors hanging on the far wall inside.

Mildred stepped through, followed closely by the others.

Ryan held out an arm, stopping the newest addition to the group. "Why don't you and Jak stay out here," he said, nodding toward the waiting albino. "A pair of jacks to back up our hand once we're in."

Blocked by Ryan's arm, the scavenger's eyes narrowed and his face took on a suspicious look. "I've played straight with you and your group. You're not looking to cheat me, are you, Cawdor?" he asked.

"Not much you could do about it if I was, is there?" Ryan asked.

"No, but—"

"I was just thinking we needed some men outside in case another band of stickies came calling. Don't worry, we'll protect your interest."

The scavie looked dubious and glanced at Jak.

"Okay, Cawdor. I owe you anyway. I guess you know best."

"Be here," Jak added. "Come running if hear shots."

"Like the wind," Ryan said, stepping into the cryo facility and sealing the door to the air lock behind him.

"OUR FRIEND'S OUTSIDE with Jak. Told them to watch out for muties."

"Good idea," Mildred said. "We can talk more freely."

As in other cryo centers, the layout was elementary: a control room filled with comp panels dominated by a mammoth central unit in the center and a long side wall of clear glass. However, the difference came from behind the glass. There, angled on a raised platform, were a dozen silver capsules, and recessed farther into the wall on metal shelving behind the capsules were an additional twelve smaller cylinders.

"I confess, I have seen the larger cryo beds, but what are the little containers for?" Doc asked, his face reflecting his confusion.

"I don't know. Midgets?" Dean guessed.

"Little people," Mildred retorted. "And no, there are no little people in those casks."

"What do you think?" Ryan asked, looking at Krysty. "Anybody in there still alive?"

"No, I don't think so. Feels wrong," the crimson-haired woman replied, her voice whispery as she struggled to concentrate and expand her consciousness outward. "Feels empty."

"How so?" Mildred asked as she continued to inspect the room's equipment.

"Not like when we found you," the green-eyed beauty said in response as she blinked and tried to focus a second time. "Or Rick."

"Rick" was Richard Neal Ginsberg, born March 22, 1970. Ryan and his band—before Mildred and Dean had joined them—had discovered the man housed within one of the cryo chambers inside a military redoubt in California. An expert in the operation of the mat-trans units and the gateways, Rick had been frozen to halt the spread of the disease that was slowly killing him, waiting in the hopes of being revived when a cure was available.

Suffering from an advanced case of Lou Gehrig's disease, he'd been a companion for only a short time before determining that the disease was still relentlessly killing him. When the opportunity arose for a valiant sacrifice to save his new friends, Ginsberg had made the gesture.

Like Ginsberg, Mildred had also been placed in cryo sleep, but her problem was different from a life-threatening disease. Instead, the doctor had been hospitalized to undergo abdominal surgery for a possible ovarian cyst when an unexpected and completely idiosyncratic reaction to the anesthetic plunged her into a coma.

As Mildred's life signs plummeted, her personal physician—as well as her best professional colleague—had chosen to take the step of placing the then dying Dr. Wyeth in cryo suspension in order to save the woman's life. In an ironic twist, some of the tech used to preserve her fading vital signs had been invented by Mildred herself, but the sleeping physician was in no condition to appreciate the irony.

When Ryan and company had reawakened the woman from her deep sleep, her life-threatening symptoms and coma had miraculously vanished during the long years she'd been under. "Must've been like a healing trance," she'd later decided.

"I'm not getting any sort of vibe, lover," Krysty finally said, putting her hands to her forehead and massaging her temples. "Usually with freezies, I get a strange, creepy-crawly feeling. Alive, but not alive. Dead, but not dead. A suspended-in-limbo, hovering sensation."

"Trapped between two worlds," Doc whispered. "Sleeping, but not breathing."

"I don't have the poetry you do, but yeah, exactly," she agreed.

"And this time?" Ryan asked, already knowing the answer.

Krysty shook her head to the left and right. "Nothing."

"Then they're chilled," J.B. said. "Literally and figuratively," he added laconically.

"Not necessarily," Mildred mused, who had been examining the cylinders with a careful eye from her vantage point behind the glass wall. She was now sitting at a comp station and rapidly typing in commands. She was amazed—usually these systems were encrypted and required a series of passwords to enter, but for some unknown reason, she was being provided full access to the information stored within.

"There's a dozen freeze tubes in there, Mildred. I can tell from here none of them are operational," Ryan said firmly. "The liquid displays are all off-line and blank. And all of them have red malfunction signs glowing across the tops of the pods."

"Just give me a minute," Mildred said softly. She slid across the polished floor in the wheeled desk chair, checking a panel marked Coolants Input. The readouts were all blank, matching those on the canisters and coffinlike tubes. She flicked a switch, once, twice, before pounding a fist against the inert panel in protest.

"Dammit," she said in a tight voice.

J.B. had been carefully squinting down over her shoulder and peering at the cryo controls.

"Don't see an emergency-mass-release box," he

said. "Course, I still can't see much of anything without my specs. Point it out to me and I'll blow the sec locks. See about doing a quick meltdown in here."

"There isn't a mass release for this setup, J.B." Mildred replied tiredly. "This isn't a redoubt, remember? Some military technology is here, but not enough. This has the smell of a bought-and-paid-for kind of deal. There are no secrets hidden here to require locks. In case of an emergency, you just hit that red button and there's a quick coolant drain and shutdown. Or if you're at a computer like I'm sitting at, you just enter the correct computer command and it also engages the primary release."

"So, go ahead and do it," J.B. urged.

Mildred looked sadly at the controls. "There's no need. Krysty's right, as far as I can tell."

"Sorry, Mildred," the redhead said.

"I'm being irrational, I know, but I feel a kinship to many of these freezies," the physician continued. "Would've been nice to find another batch alive, safe. But if there are no vitals, I'd be wasting a lot of time we don't really have. Takes hours to do a cryochamber drain and hours more to resuscitate, and there's no rushing the process. Those stickies could have friends, and we don't want to get caught down here a second time."

J.B. took one of Mildred's hands and squeezed it tight. "Millie, those people in those chambers died over a hundred years ago. Not a damn thing could be done for them then, or now."

"Any idea who they were?" Ryan asked.

Mildred went back and starting tapping keys on the

keyboard. "From what I can tell, this place was designed with one purpose in mind. Preserve some of the finest leadership and military minds until the conflict was over. It's not the worst plan I ever heard, but as usual the x-factor came stomping in and trod all over the best-laid plans of mice and men."

Mildred stood, gesturing toward the units housed inside the glassed-in area.

"At some point in time, the power here must've gone off-line. I'd say it happened within days after the bombs fell. Could've been a fluke, but my guess is a techie took particular offense at being left behind to die in the brave new world once the bombs actually started falling, and he or she sabotaged the chambers. Once the damage was done, he turned the systems back on to cover his actions, or perhaps a fail-safe device came on-line and reactivated. Either way, the end result was the same. I suppose, in retrospect, I should be grateful the same thing didn't happen to me."

"Hell of a way to die," Ryan said, peering inside the sterile room. "You think you're going to take a long nap and pull a cheat and, boom, you die a second time in your sleep."

"Well, no matter how you look at it, half of them were dead the minute the war broke out," Mildred replied enigmatically.

Ryan turned to look at her. "How so?"

"Doc, you were asking about those smaller containers, the barrel-shaped ones?"

"Yes. What is the concept behind those?" he replied.

"In those casks are twelve more cryo subjects."

"I don't get you," Ryan said, perplexed.

"The twelve smaller tanks held human heads, Ryan, awaiting possible future transplant onto new bodies."

Chapter Seven

Mildred sat in the swivel chair behind the main comp bank and began to type at the keyboard once more, pausing only to move the mouse to click onto new screens of information.

"You know what they used to call freezies back in my day?" she mused aloud. "The 'frozen chosen.' Like you were saying, Ryan, we were the ones lucky enough to cheat death and waggle our fingers bye-bye at man's final frontier. We were being put on ice to await the coming of the new technologies, capable of saving our dying asses."

A screen blinked and a set of tiny speakers beeped, indicating the search of the data bank Mildred has asked for was finished.

"No wonder health care was so expensive in my day," she said. "Most of the people in that room who underwent the cryo process weren't even sick. I'm talking about the ones with bodies, not the headless horsemen. I see three senators, a governor, four millionaires and some other names and rankings I don't recognize here listed as being put into the program within hours after skydark."

Doc slowly shook his head. "More madness."

"Not true," Mildred replied. "You forget, Doc. I was one of the whitecoats involved in cryo research.

Cryonics was a complex, controversial medical procedure that stored either the whole body or just the head of a clinically dead person in liquid nitrogen, at a temperature of minus 196 degrees Celsius. After the big chill, a suspension team prepared the body for its icy descent into a large Dewar flask, where it was stored until time for revival. Doing so took some effort to mount."

Mildred turned from the screen and ran her fingers through her long beaded hair. She looked very sad as she started to remember, and to speak.

"We were all mavericks in cryo research back then, driven by an insatiable urge to stop time and restart it on a schedule we dictated, not the predetermined one set by fate or nature. Looking back, I guess I was considered one of the tamer practitioners. Others, like Saul Kent, one of the founders of the Cryonics Society of New York, had his own mother decapitated and frozen in the hope that she could be reanimated sometime in the future."

"Geez, he chopped off his own mom's head?" Dean asked. "Gross."

"Who better? I mean, let's face it. The prospect of immortality inspires the unusual. He loved his mother, she loved her son, ergo, she willed her body to science and upon her death, he decided to test his theories. If it had worked out, he could have saved her life. Brought her back from death as we understood it."

"I cannot help but comment that all of this sounds most grotesque, Dr. Wyeth," Doc said with an exaggerated shudder. "The removal of the head and brains and dropping them into cold storage puts me in the mind of the most outlandish of Lovecraftian horror.''

"Why not? Lovecraft was predicting this sort of thing in many of his short stories. Course, I didn't read them until when I was in college," she replied. "No, my interest in this branch of science came early. I was in an accelerated program in school and had an adult's library card with full access to all of the closed stacks. I guess that's where I first found Professor Robert Ettinger's book called *The Prospect of Immortality*. That book came to be considered the flashpoint of the concept of life-extension technology. He believed in it so strongly, he froze *his* mother, as well—in fact I guess he was the first.''

"Entire generations suspended in time. Barbaric," Doc declared.

"I thought it was marvelous, although some of my more religious kin didn't find the suggestion of avoiding the hereafter by sticking your body in a freezer a proper way of following the plans of the Lord.''

"Your father was a preacher," Krysty said. "I'd say he had trouble accepting some of the more fantastic theories you were spouting off.''

"Actually my father wasn't the problem. He didn't care for the idea, but he let me be. Most of my grief came from two meddling aunts, the old biddies. They were always coming to him as his concerned sisters, worrying about my welfare. My brother, Josh, after he became a minister like our father, also showed more compassion and understanding of my chosen career.''

"Yeah, relatives can make your life a living hell, bastard quick," Ryan observed, thinking of his own corrupted family ties.

"Professor Ettinger's book suggested that people could be frozen in 'suspended death' until medical technology was able to cure what killed them and breathe new life into their bodies. No big deal to us now, but at the time, it was considered all-out voodoo," Mildred mused. "See, his problem was, his attempt to achieve immortality conflicted with some of the most conventional truths modern science had been built upon up to that point, including the premise that death is final in a world of mortals."

"Nothing is absolute," Ryan said reflectively. "Trader used to say that."

"Correction, my dear Ryan. One thing is absolute, and that is if there is a cliché for the occasion, the good Trader was wont to have uttered it," Doc muttered as he slumped down like a weary scarecrow into one of the free chairs near Mildred.

"You're just jealous, Doc," Krysty said.

"Pray explain," Doc said with mock severity.

"Trader's the only man in the Deathlands with more arcane sayings than you."

Doc sniffed. "The mantle of Trader is not a title I envy."

"In Ettinger's book, I remember his saying that mankind had been conditioned to accept death for thousands of years. However, he grew up in a new world expecting that one day old age would be preventable and reversible. And the man practiced what he preached. Ettinger was a pioneer and helped in the formation of cryonics.''

"Pardon me, but I thought the term was 'cryogenics.''" Doc said, unable to pass up the opportunity to correct Mildred in her own branch of science.

Mildred shook her head and smiled wistfully. "No, Doc. Common mistake. Cryonics was, and is, a more radical branch of cryogenics—cryogenics being really nothing more than the recognized field of cold-temperature medicine. You know, research contributing to the aging process, the best way to preserve human organs for transplant, bloodless surgery. Nothing half-baked or hidden about it.''

"Cryogenics. Like the swapping of organs for the tech Lars Hellstrom was so fond of back at Helskel.''

"Exactly, but with more humane intent. But cryonics went further in design. Cryonics were designed to slow and eventually halt the process of death. In my case, putting me under saved my life until I was found and awakened by all of you.''

"Sounds good to me,'' Dean remarked, entranced by the story Mildred was telling. "Who wouldn't want to live forever?''

"Out of the mouths of babes,'' Krysty said, winking at Ryan.

"Indeed,'' Doc added. "Trust me, young Cawdor. As a man who has spent over two hundred years bouncing around this mortal coil, I can say that immortality always comes with a price.''

"Yeah, but you're *old*,'' Dean protested.

"Not as old as you think, young man.''

Mildred grinned at Dean. "In a discussion like

we're having, the idea of beating death does sound promising. It's when you start putting such ideas into motion that people get nervous. The world was different in my time. In the mid-1960s, cryonics advocates were a small fringe group. The structure of some organizations was rocked by scandal, sometimes at the hands of incompetent people and equipment, and other times because of sensational media coverage.''

''Media?'' the boy asked.

''Newspapers. Video. Tabloids. The media. They broke all of the news stories that made people nervous...stories such as how in the early days of the programs, scientists were having to make do with storing bodies in the surplus wingtip fuel tanks of Air Force jets. No big deal, until it got out that the tanks weren't 'one size fits all,' and when they had people too obese to fit, they'd chainsaw their arms off and stick them in that way.''

Mildred paused, looking lost and far away for a moment. ''After my father's murder by immolation at the hands of those Klansmen, I wondered—could cryonics have preserved him until such a time as miraculous regenerative processes would be the norm? I'm sure he might have seen it as an abomination, but I've always wondered. I suppose that curiosity is what continued to carry me into the field. I wanted to go beyond theories and tests. I wanted to be one of the new, innovative thinkers blazing onto new ground....''

''So, what happened?'' J.B. asked. ''Why did the cryo program go the way of mat-trans units and Operation Chronos and Overproject Whisper and all of the other subtly named covert government projects?''

Mildred chuckled bitterly. ''Believe it or not, what really, truly, undeniably saved the program was government interest and involvement. If the average hardworking American believed cryonic suspension to be the stuff of bad science-fiction novels, so much the better. Grants and equipment were available to the right doctors, and my own profile was high for a number of reasons.''

''How so?''

Mildred counted down the list on her fingers: ''I was a woman, I was black, my theories made sense and I was a former Olympic medalist. You couldn't ask for a more suitable candidate. Once I was in the door, I soon discovered that organizations such as the American Cryonics Society and the Alcor Life Extension Foundation were all smoke screens. Only a few dozen people were listed officially as ''being frozen'' at the end of the year 2000, with a waiting list of hundreds wanting to join the program.''

''We all know that's a crock,'' Dean interjected.

''Of course. In actuality the number stretched into the thousands, with chambers and preparations being made for thousands more in case of war. Cryonic suspension was expensive, too. Only the rich and the powerful—or the very important—got a seat in the freeze chambers. I made it because of my research and because of the woman who operated on me pulling some strings. She was my friend, and she didn't want me to die on an operating table.''

"So there could be an untold number of freezies waiting to be discovered?" Krysty asked.

"Yeah. I imagine some high-muck-a-muck couldn't resist the idea of a cryo version of Noah's Ark, which means any and all living creatures up to skydark may be safely tucked away somewhere sleeping."

"How much jack are we talking to freeze somebody?" Ryan asked, his own fascination coming into play. Some of what she was telling the others wasn't unfamiliar to him after what he'd seen going on the Black Hills laboratories of the Anthill. In those frigid chambers, he'd held conversations with men dressed in business suits with wag coolant for blood.

The woman thought for a moment. "Seems like I recall the official public price as being something along the lines of one hundred twenty-five thousand dollars for a whole-body suspension or, in the case of just wanting to preserve the head in a procedure called neuropreservation, that was around fifty thousand dollars. Pricey, and beyond most people's means."

Mildred stopped talking and stood. There was nothing much else to say.

The group left the cryo labs quietly.

Outside, the scavie became most distraught, begging Mildred to "Unchill the bastards so we can divvy up the loot."

"There's no 'loot' to be had, Alton," she replied tiredly. "Cryo patients aren't placed inside their capsules wearing rings on their fingers and bells on their toes. This process isn't like preparing the dead for a burial in a coffin with jewelry and their favorite things to take along on their journey into a new life. You go into a freeze tube as naked as the day you were born, with only a sheet to cover your soon-to-be-lifeless body."

"Aw, shit," he said sadly. "Are you sure?"

"Yeah."

"Hell, much as it cost to do this, no wonder there's no valuables with these freezies," J.B. told the man. "Spent all their loot getting put them in this condition."

"Lighten up, Adrian," Ryan said, handing back the glum scavie's captured Colt .45. "Let's blow this joint before another party of stickies decides to come looking for the batch we chilled."

Chapter Eight

The stairwell was pitch-black and cold. Even with the hidden nuke generator that still possessed enough juice to keep the freezies on ice and bring the oddly configured mat-trans room safely on-line, apparently there was nothing left over for illumination except for the essentials needed back in the subbasement.

Alton took out a small pocket flashlight and started rapidly squeezing a trigger over and over. A whirring sound came from the tiny device as a beam of light shot out of the clear plastic end. "Self-generating. Long as my finger doesn't give out, we got some light," he said proudly. "You want me to take the lead?"

"You've got the light. Don't worry, I'll back you up." Ryan turned back to his own group. "We go up until we're out. Take it nice and slow, and we should be all right. I don't like traveling practically by feel, but we don't have any other options."

The steady climb upwards was uneventful, except for a brief moment of chaos when Dean inadvertently stepped on something small and alive, losing his footing and falling backward into an unprepared Doc Tanner. Other than a boomed "By the Three Kennedys!" exclamation from the surprised Doc, there were no injuries.

No one knew what Dean's foot had found, and none of the assemblage wanted to find out, either.

Onward the group traveled, past levels of different colors—blue, orange, and red. Alton tried one stairwell door, and it opened into a wide corridor that led into a ruined chapel, the stained glass shattered, the pews ripped up from the flooring and removed. The light beam coming from the hand-powered flashlight picked out brief images of the desecration before Alton closed the door.

"Wrong floor," he said.

The next level proved to be correct, depositing them first in a once-glassed-in corridor that was now nothing more than some empty framework that led out to a parking deck.

Rusting frames of automobiles lined the sides of the deck. Some of the designated slots were empty, but most still housed the remains of their former tenants of rubber, chrome and steel. A Cadillac Seville over here, a Chevrolet Lumina over there. Any part of value had been long since scavenged, leaving gaping holes beneath the hoods and inside the interiors. Engine blocks were MIA, along with head- and taillights and any other instruments that could be used elsewhere in the mass of retrofitting that kept automobiles and wags moving along in what passed for the society of Deathlands. All that was left of the cars and trucks housed in the deck were the frames and the metal wheels.

"Triple cold in here," Dean said with a shiver, hugging his jacket close to his body.

"Nothing around us but concrete. Walls. Floor. Ceiling. Feels damp," Krysty said.

"Not like," Jak said quietly. "Get hell out. Like open."

"I prefer open spaces myself, Jak," Ryan agreed. "At least you can always see what's coming."

"Where are we?" J.B. growled, already annoyed he couldn't deduce their location for himself without his glasses and proper vision.

"Carolina. The northern part, near the Blue Ridge Mountains. Go up about fifty miles or so, and you'll be in the lower part of Virginia," Alton replied.

"The South rises yet again," Doc murmured.

At least with having the scavie along, there was no need for J.B. to take out his small but sturdy mini-sextant and take a reading to determine their location. At one time, the Armorer had access to one of the finest collections of predark maps and atlases in the country, thanks to the supply the Trader had collected and kept aboard his own vehicle over the years.

Now, without the storage space provided by the fleet of war wags the Trader had maintained, J.B. had to rely on his memory. There was no room in his pack for heavy books and maps. A man on the move had to travel as light as possible, with the weight he carried devoted to ammunition and essential supplies.

Luckily J.B. possessed a near photographic memory, and he had managed the feat of retaining thousands upon thousands of roads, borders, star charts and anything else of use in the fine art of navigation. When his own internal library of information was combined with the reading he could retrieve from the minisextant, J.B. could almost always tell his friends with a fair degree of accuracy what part of Deathlands they ended up in.

"This area doesn't look all that rural," Krysty observed, leaning out over the railing of the deck and into the afternoon sunshine, which cascaded beautifully off her red hair. "Looks more like a city."

"It is. It was. This is Winston-Salem, one of the bigger metro areas of old Carolina. Made cigarettes here. You can see what's left of the downtown over there," Alton said, pointing out a cluster of skyscrapers beyond the tall redhead. "I don't recommend going there for a sight-seeing tour."

"Why's that?" Krysty asked.

"Stickies," the bearded man replied. "Downtown belongs to them. For a long stretch of time, there's been an unspoken truce between the Carolina norms who live in this region and the muties—stay away from the claimed grounds and there'll be no fighting or retribution."

Doc had a sinking feeling in the pit of his stomach. "And do tell, where does this hospital fall?"

The scavenger smiled. "No-man's-land. Stickies are technically closer, but since anything of conceivable practical use had been long taken out, I was gambling there would be no reason for them to be in here."

"Only a fool gambles with a retarded deck of cards, and any group of stickies is full of jokers and deuces," Ryan said. "There is no rhyme or reason as to what they do and when they do it. Crazy bastards."

"Amen, brother," Alton agreed. "Still, we could

be in worse shape. We're in the middle of what used to be called Medical Row. Go along Hawthorne for about two miles until you hit what's left of Silas Creek Parkway and Highway 40. Nothing in between but a few residential sections and rows upon rows of doctors' offices. Had a doc for any ailment that plagued you back then.''

"Not anymore," Mildred said quietly to Ryan. "I knew this place—spent some time at this very hospital, in fact. By the 1990s, North Carolina had some of the finest physicians and medical equipment in the entire country.''

"The old road's still intact more or less. We'll follow it toward Freedom. I've got some business there, and it'll give us a safe place to spend the night.... What's wrong?" Alton allowed his voice to trail off as he tried to comprehend the sudden dark expressions that crossed the faces of Ryan's group upon the mention of the word "Freedom."

"This Freedom—that the name of some kind of ville?" Ryan asked, his mind involuntarily crawling back to another Freedom, the Freedom City Motor Hotel and Casino, located in the southeastern part of the Carolinas. It was the lair of the former Baron Willie Elijah and his mutie-hating mercies, the site of a vicious battle with Lord Kaa, a self-styled "lord of the mutants" who had confronted Elijah and his humans in a brutal fight ending in the baron's ultimate demise.

"Yeah, sort of," the scavie replied with a grin. "But better. You got to see it to believe it.''

"Already have," J.B. said firmly. "Don't want to go back, either."

"No, this is a different Freedom," Ryan replied. "Has to be."

"What's the Southern fascination with the word *freedom* anyway? Seems half the places we've ended up in the Carolinas has been named 'Freedom' this or 'Freedom' that," Dean groused.

"White guilt," Mildred guessed.

That got J.B.'s attention. "Huh? I don't get you, Millie."

Doc was quick to offer his interpretation, delighted at the opportunity in fact, J.B. thought glumly. "The War Between the States was triggered by many pivotal events, John Barrymore, one of which was the thorny subject of slavery. The white overlord and his darker-hued property. Those in power in the South said they needed the slave labor to maintain their fields, and when President Lincoln signed his fateful proclamation, mounting tensions went beyond discussion and boiled over into full-scale conflict. The South seceded from the North, and there was holy hell to pay."

"Everyone pays the freight in a war, Doc," the Armorer replied.

"Indeed. After the war, many of the more forward thinkers in the Carolinas, Georgia, Virginia and so on entered into a spell of overkill, and in response to the new freedom of the black man, a freedom that did not fully come until decades later during the famed civil-rights movement, the name Freedom worked its way into many a new Southern building or street. The traditions continued well into the late 1900s, and up to skydark.''

''Well, that's one interesting thing about the end of the world…it tends to be a great equalizer,'' Mildred quipped with little amusement.

HOURS LATER, after making their way down from the parking deck to the road below, Mildred was feeling much better. She whistled a slightly off-key fragment of a bouncy tune, snapping her fingers in accompaniment. The beaded strands of her plaited hair clacked softly as she moved her head in time to the music.

''What's that you're whistling, Millie?'' J.B. asked, trying vainly to identify the music. ''Sounds familiar, somehow.''

''Before your time, John,'' she replied, pausing to breathe deeply of the mountain air. ''Way before your time. Came from an old television show. So old, it was in black and white—not color. The show always started the same. The opening credits would show a father and his barefoot son walk down an old back road to a lake, fishing poles over their shoulders.''

''Kind of like you and me, Dad,'' Dean interjected. ''Except we haven't gone fishing in a triple-long time.''

''Don't interrupt,'' Ryan replied to his son. ''Mildred's talking.''

''Show took place in North Carolina, and that's what I always think of when I think about this area. Back roads and fishing,'' Mildred continued. ''Damned if this place doesn't look just like what I

remember from the series, even if it is part of Deathlands.''

"Television," Doc snorted disdainfully. "Mind
rot. I regret the loss of the films of the world, but I
cannot say the same about what wags dubbed 'the
idiot box.' Too many hours of potential achievement
were wasted staring at the daily parade of misfits and
dysfunctional families on a never ending barrage of
so-called talk shows, programs where the talking con-
sisted of nothing but screaming and accusations over
intentional betrayals between men and women of ill
repute and worse behavior."

"I'll take a little mind rot over senility any day,
you old fool," Mildred said with a chuckle. "Besides,
from the sounds of it, you wasted more than a few
hours of your own life watching the daily parade of
the misfits."

"At times, dear Doctor, that was all I was allowed
to do to pass the time during my incarceration. And
I can assure you, my jailers gave no choice of channels."

Mildred fell silent after that.

THE PARTY OF EIGHT continued to follow the broken
pavement of the old Hawthorne Road. Extra care had
to be given to watching where they stepped, as the
road was pitted with small holes that could easily
twist an ankle or cause a fall. At times, the blacktop
disappeared entirely to be replaced with a mix of lush,
ankle-high green grass and the hardy, small white dai-
sies that seemed to bloom throughout Deathlands.

After Mildred had stopped reminiscing, a slight pall

seemed to hang over the group. About a mile into their trip, the silence had become almost tangible.

Ryan took notice of the lack of sounds in the air. Before there had been faint reminders that life was still here among the ruins—the hum of insects, the discussions between the arguing friends, the sound of footsteps rising and falling on the road. Now it was almost as if each of them had subconsciously started trying to move more silently, a hidden command to breathe easy and keep noise to a minimum.

The absence of birdcalls was especially noticeable. Once, Krysty had wordlessly tugged at Ryan's long coat. When he glanced back, he couldn't help but see she was troubled, as well. Her sentient red hair was coiling and uncoiling in a manner that indicated that she, too, subconsciously knew something was wrong.

Still, the tree-lined roadway gave all indications of being safe, and their guide had no problems with striding ahead without fear. Alton apparently knew where he was going, and the closer they got, the more at ease he acted.

"Been a while since I got out this way," he said. "Like you, I been traveling myself. Back and forth with no permanent place to hang my hat."

Dean, bored out of his young mind and looking up at the blue sky, noticed the movement in the trees first. His keen eyes detected a slight movement in the leafy covering of a particular large tree directly next to the scavie's head. The mighty oak's branches were hanging out like spread wooden fingers over the asphalt path they were traveling.

He thought about mentioning it, but he didn't want

to look like a stupe over a squirrel or other arbor-dwelling creature. Besides, his father didn't seem to be worried, and the boy knew Ryan's survival senses were honed by experience to a much finer edge than his own. As Alton and then Ryan both passed under the long branches, Dean held his breath until they were on the other side.

The boy exhaled with relief.

Until the leaves parted with a sudden, frantic rustling, and the hidden men leaped out and were upon them.

Chapter Nine

"Ambush!" Dean cried out in a voice pitched high and tight with shock, but his warning arrived a second too late as the men in the tree revealed themselves with a sudden, murderous intensity.

Alton Adrian fell like a dropped doll, taken totally by surprise as the weight of his attacker came down hard and swift upon his head and upper body.

The second man wasn't as lucky.

He had chosen Ryan as his target.

The one-eyed man reacted much more swiftly than the bearded guide, his reflexes inhumanly quick as he brought up the muzzle of the SIG-Sauer in a swift, practiced motion and fired off a trio of shots, each slug catching his assailant in the chest. The force of the bullets at such close range flipped the attacker backward, causing him to hurl his weapon away.

He landed hard on his lower back and rear once his feet clumsily hit heel first on the broken road. Between the force of the bullets and the impact of the fall, the man was wheezing, gasping for air as he writhed helplessly in pain.

J.B. was in motion the instant the ambush begun, swinging the butt of his own weapon in a forward arc across the back of the man who had focused his energies on the unsuspecting scavie. The sound of hard blaster on softer skull was loud and unforgiving. Even with the disadvantage of poor vision, the Armorer was a deadly foe in close-quarters fighting.

The others—Jak, Mildred, Doc and Krysty—all came to instant readiness, their own individual weapons springing up from their holsters and other places of concealment to find safe haven in their hands.

No other ambushers revealed themselves.

"That it?" Jak asked in disbelief, still peering hard into the foliage above.

"Looks like it." Krysty said.

"Stupes," Jak muttered, shaking his head in amusement.

Mildred was kneeling and checking the broken cranium of the man J.B. had taken down. She felt the bloody skull and winced.

"This one's alive, but he won't be answering any questions for a while. Some lump he is growing on his skull."

"Could improve his dumb-ass looks," J.B. muttered angrily.

The sec man Ryan had drilled staggered to his feet, holding his chest and ribs with both hands. His face was a twisted mask of agony as he tried awkwardly to stand. Ryan reached over and shoved him back down hard on the ground.

"Ow, goddammit!" the man roared.

"Wearing armor under those work clothes, aren't you?" Ryan remarked calmly.

"Best purchase I ever made. Saved my ass twice before," he managed to gasp in a voice tight with pain and fear.

"Too bad they don't make it for the head."

"You weren't aiming for my head."

"I am now," Ryan said, making a point of aiming the SIG-Sauer right between the man's eyes.

"Shit!" the man cried out, bringing his hands up to his face.

"Hold still. No, don't keep trying to get up or I'll drop you coldcocked like your pal over there."

The man looked over at his comrade lying unconscious at the edge of the road.

"He chilled?"

"No, just sleepy. What I want you to do is roll over flat on your stomach with your hands above your head. Cross your legs like a bashful gaudy slut and keep them that way until I tell you to move," Ryan ordered.

The man complied, groaning with the effort of contorting his already aching body.

"Now, I'm going to ask you some questions," Ryan said. "I want answers and I want them fast, or I'm going to start blowing you apart piece by piece, and no body armor is going to stop it. You get me?"

"Wait a second. We're sec men out of Freedom. You're getting awfully damn close to the area we're supposed to protect."

Ryan looked to Alton for confirmation. Alton shrugged and pointed to the identical green denim jackets the two men wore. On the right arm of each was a white patch with an ornate cursive *F* in a circle.

"They're wearing Freedom colors and patches like sec men. Could be telling the truth."

"Don't mean much. They could've stolen the

clothes from Freedom or even chilled the real guards for the threads and hardware,'' J.B. said.

"What are your names?" Ryan asked.

"I'm Michaelson. The guy you knocked cold is Isaac."

"Mike and Ike. That's real cute," Ryan said mockingly.

Dean had collected the dropped handblasters the men were carrying in the attack and gave one of them to J.B. for identification.

"Twin Colts, the 2000 model," the Armorer said. "This was the first gun from Colt that broke away from the old John Browning original design of the locking breech that drops and swings. The top lug locks into a recess in the slide, and the bottom lug rides in a cam path cut into a cam block—see? The block rests in the frame. The firing mechanisms on these pistols were also innovative. The mag release is ambidextrous, and there's no form of applied safety. The self-cocking mechanism is set up so you can't accidentally shoot yourself in the foot."

"Thanks, J.B. That's probably more than I needed to know," Dean replied.

"One more thing—these blasters use 9 mm ammo."

"Good, we can use the bullets," Ryan answered, turning his full attention back to the prone captured man. "Ready to talk, Mike? Why were you and your buddy out here?"

"Looking for stickies. They been giving us holy hell at Freedom. Every night they slink around, starting fires, chilling travelers, blowing things up. Not only is it a major pain in the collective ass, but the sons of bitches are getting dangerous. We've started widening the perimeter of our patrols to see if we can catch them out in the daylight.''

Ryan nodded. ''And what happens if you do?''

''Then we chill the stickie bastards.''

''All two of you?'' Mildred asked sarcastically. Jak snorted in derisive agreement.

The fallen sec man looked insulted. ''We're the advance team, the lookouts. Looking down, we got carried away and thought you were stickies.''

Ryan lashed out with the steel-reinforced toe of his scuffed boot, catching the man in the hipbone, making him cry out. ''Wrong answer, friend. Want to try again?''

''Damn, mister, you don't have to kick me!''

''I'll kick your teeth in if I take a notion, and stomp your balls for an encore if you don't stop jerking me around.''

''It's the truth, it's the truth!''

''Do we look like any stickies you ever saw before?''

''No, not now. Up in the trees you did. Sun's going down. Getting harder to see. I guess we acted without thinking things through.''

''That's the first honest thing you said to me yet.''

J.B stepped forward and added his opinion. ''What kind of strategic genius thought it was a good idea for two men to jump a party of eight? Your odds aren't worth a damn.''

''Thought if we took out you two, we'd have hostages.''

"Stickies don't give a rat's ass about hostages."

Mike's partner, Ike, gave a groan as he started to come around. "Perhaps your partner over there can tell me the truth before we decide whether to waste two bullets on your sorry asses."

Alton Adrian's voice broke into the interrogation. "Wait, I think I know who these two are now—or rather, why they're slinking around and jumping people. They're highway robbers. Thieves. Hiding out here to steal the jack off any visitors before they can get to Freedom safely."

"You lie!" Mike roared.

"No, I think he's made a good point," Ryan replied, pulling out his panga with a flourish. "Now, I'm not one for torture, but let's see if cutting off some fingers and toes loosens your memory."

"Someone come," Jak said, pointing down the stretch of road.

Off in the distance, a group of men was riding toward them on horseback. They paused a good distance away, and the leader took out a small handheld bullhorn device to amplify his voice.

"Hoy to you, friends. We're sending out a representative to talk with you. Hell, I'm coming myself. Don't chill my ass until you hear what I've got to say," the man called

"Getting interesting," Jak said softly, readying his blaster.

"Tell me about it," Mildred agreed.

The man who'd spoken through the bullhorn handed it to one of his men and rode slowly toward the waiting group. On his approach, the beautifully marked reddish-brown-and-white paint horse became identifiable.

So did the black man's attire, which matched the suits worn by Mike and Ike.

"Good evening," the man said, keeping both hands on the horse's reins.

"Whatever," Ryan replied, alertly insolent.

"I'm Rollins, out of Freedom Mall. I head up the sec operation there."

"Mall?"

"Mall. Freedom is completely enclosed," he replied. "Didn't you know that?"

"No. We just thought it was a fancy ville."

" 'Fancy' isn't the right word. Who are you?"

"Ryan Cawdor. Mebbe you can answer a few questions about the men on the ground there."

Rollins took a look. "Seems to me like you found Mike and Ike."

"Wrong. They found us. Tried to get the drop on us for our blasters and jack. Some kind of shitty welcoming committee. You came along just in time. We were debating whether to waste a bullet on them."

"Rather you not do that—waste a bullet, I mean. We've had them hiding out, looking for stickies," Rollins said.

"That's the tale they shared with me. Thought it was bullshit," Ryan retorted.

"Some of us still think it's bullshit," J.B. added.

"No, it's true. They were up there looking," Rollins insisted. "Not the spot I would have chosen, but I'm not them. We got worried when they hadn't radioed in with a report."

"Comm units were off when they came falling out of the tree," Ryan observed.

"Standard operating procedure. A live radio unit could give them away."

"Is it standard operating procedure to go jumping down on stickies when you're outnumbered four to one?" Krysty demanded.

"Not hardly. They sure as hell weren't supposed to try and take them on alone," the leader replied. "If you give the two men to me, I'll see to their punishment."

"What is this? Grade school?" Mildred said with a sneer. "Take away their blasters and armor and make them stand in a corner in a pointy hat with no chocolate milk at recess?"

Rollins looked at Mildred blankly. "Don't know rightly where you're coming from, ma'am, but these two are my men. My responsibility. I'll take care of them."

"We're keeping their ammo," Ryan said matter-of-factly.

"All right. We'll deduct it from their pay," the sec man said. "Being on this road, and the end of daylight upon us, I suppose you were heading for Freedom?"

Ryan nodded. "The thought had crossed our minds."

"Then let me offer an escort," Rollins replied. "You're close, but the more people on the trail, the safer the trip. These boys have horses somewhere. They can walk in, and you and some of your party can ride, if you know how."

"Riding's not a problem."

"Mebbe not. But something is, the way you're looking me over."

"We're invited into Freedom, just like that." Ryan's tone was as friendly as he could make it, despite his suspicions.

"Just like that," the tall sec man replied.

"Your baron won't mind?" Krysty asked.

The big sec man chuckled. "No baron in Freedom, ma'am. There's Mr. Morgan, but he keeps a low profile. He's a behind-the-scenes type of leader. We're all answerable to him, but you'll never see his face unless things go bad for you once you're inside."

"Don't guess we'll be meeting him, then," Ryan said.

"Freedom is nothing but people, stores, food and sluts. A fully functioning ville under one roof. You got jack to spend? Creds? Metals and stones?"

"Yeah," Ryan answered. "We got jack. Stuff to trade, too."

Rollins nodded his bald head. "Then you got an invite. Visitors with jack and useful items are always welcome to Freedom."

Chapter Ten

After some quick debate, Ryan and Krysty had taken the reins of the disgraced sec men's horses. Dean rode behind Ryan, and Krysty saddled up with Doc. Jak, Mildred, Alton Adrian and J.B. chose to follow on foot. The two beaten Freedom sec men were allowed to plod along in the lead, where a watchful eye could be kept on them.

Rollins had told the truth. The Freedom Mall was close by. The mall came into view long before they actually reached the single, imposing entrance. A massive construction of the most redbrick anyone had ever witnessed in a single location, with inset panels of tan fieldstone, the architectural beast seemed to have thrust itself upward into the hilly surroundings from a sea of black asphalt.

All of Ryan's group had seen malls like this before. In Mildred's case, being a former resident of the late twentieth century, she had actually shopped inside quite a few before being placed in the long sleep of cryonic suspension. A wallet of credit cards with her name embossed on the faces was probably still tucked away inside her purse in a hospital storage locker somewhere.

Ryan's most recent memory of a mall near this size

was the leveled remains of the SkyHi Mall back at Bear Creek Ridge in Colorado.

Unlike Freedom, which gave off the air of being as solid as a hunk of shining, freshly hewn stone, the SkyHi facility had been hit hard by quakes and severe weather, causing entire walls to cave in upon the once spacious and well-appointed interior.

That had been many long months ago. The group had been staying in Jak's former homestead in New Mexico—until an interruption saw Dean kidnapped and Ryan forced to go after the boy alone in a desperate attempt to bring him back alive. Ryan had engaged the mat-trans unit to make a long jump high up the North American continent to Canada, where his old foe Major-Commissar Gregori Zimyanin had taken command of a series of slave mines.

The baron had stolen the boy to use as bait to lure Ryan into a final confrontation that only one of them would survive. The final battle had nearly taken them both down, with Zimyanin ultimately falling to his death.

However, Ryan had never seen the body to make sure. Major-Commissar Zimyanin had a particular habit of coming back from the dead. When pressed, the one-eyed leader would admit he still wasn't sure Zimyanin was truly wormfood. Coldhearts like the major were damn hard to chill, and even harder to bury.

"Parking lot looks clear. No junk cars, no wreckage or plant growth," Doc observed with a note of pleasure in his best baritone voice.

"Yeah, this place is positively tidy," Ryan added dryly.

"We keep it cleared," Rollins said. "First order of business each spring is to repair the lots. We towed the wags out years ago. Mall management prefers the areas around the perimeter to be unobstructed."

"What about that mess?" Dean piped up, pointing at a melted, blackened mass of metal and plastic as they headed for the front entrance.

"That's new, boy. With all of the recent stickie attacks we've been having, our group has been working overtime keeping the areas clean. Drives the stickies crazy. There's nothing close to burn, so they have to drag in their own shit to set on fire. Pieces of furniture. Small engine motorcycles. Old dried-out lumber. They even trailer in larger objects from time to time to light up Freedom's nightlife."

"They were probably looking for stuff in the old hospital when they came upon us," Alton said quietly to J.B and Mildred as they listened to the conversation from the rear.

"Stickies do love their fireworks," Ryan agreed. "I've even seen them set each other ablaze when they're really worked up."

Rollins laughed. "Right! Right! Believe it or not, one of the crazy bastards actually figured out how to use a catapult. A goddamn catapult! Don't know where they got the bastard thing. Used to be an outdoor theater presented in Old Salem where they'd reenact ancient history and stuff. Mebbe it came from there. Anyway, they were flinging flaming shit up on the roof of the mall for a few weeks. Made for some long nights for all of the mall sec men, but at least we could see it coming from a mile away in time enough to dodge.''

"What made them stop?" Krysty asked, reining her horse over to keep close to Ryan's deep-copper-colored gelding.

The sec leader shook his head with amusement. "As usual, being the scholars they are, none of the stickies seemed to realize that we could see where the flaming loads from the catapult were being launched, and high-power bullets go a lot farther than a fireball.''

"Took them out using snipers?" Ryan asked.

"You bet. We dug up some old Army ordnance in a swap with a ville, and in the trade we picked up an old bolt-action sniping rifle with a night scope. That did the trick. Started picking off muties right and left. Poor stickies had to leave their catapult behind, and the next morning a team of sec men went out with fire axes and dismantled the damn thing triple quick.''

"Doesn't sound like you have a problem," Ryan said.

"Six months ago, we didn't. Things are different now. I don't know what's been going on in the downtown area, but the muties seem to be...well, they seem to be getting smarter somehow.''

AT THE GAPING MAW of the reinforced mall entrance, Rollins and his sec men parted company with Ryan's group. Mike and the staggering Ike were led away by two of their fellows, while the others took the horses in the opposite direction. A line of people, men, women and a few kids around Dean's age were awaiting entry via the Freedom checkpoint.

"Hans will check you through. He's the gatekeeper," Rollins said as he followed his men through a second sec-personnel entrance. "No offense, but I hope not to see you again."

"Likewise," Ryan agreed as he and the others took positions at the back of the slowly moving line.

"What's your take on that guy?" J.B. asked quietly.

"Seems on the up-and-up. Could be some kind of trap, but a ville this size, all enclosed...I want to get a closer look," Ryan replied.

"Same here," Krysty said. "Feels okay to me. What it appears to be, it is."

"Then we're going in," Ryan stated. "Stay alert."

The entrance was well guarded, again by four of the Freedom Mall sec men dressed in green. All were armed with long blasters cradled in their arms. One carried a .30-caliber Browning automatic, while the others cradled M-16 assault rifles. They were bulky men, padded with what Ryan guessed to be body armor similar to what Mike and Ike were wearing. They also wore bulletproof antiriot helmets with fold-down protective visors.

They didn't smile or speak, their faces slightly bored and their eyes hidden by the helmet visors. Greetings and pleasantries were left up to Hans, an elderly gentleman with the cherubic face in the old-style three-piece suit and necktie.

"I've seen malls and such before, but never like

this one," Krysty commented. "This one is in great shape."

"Built to last, and we believe in taking care of our home," Hans replied, his eyes twinkling. "I take it you're new to Freedom, missy?"

"Yes. Yes, sir," Krysty replied, her natural good manners and breeding shining through when addressed with respect. The gatekepper was unlike most of his ilk, with no leers at her breasts or comments on how they could "work an exchange" to let Krysty and her friends enter.

"Okay, here's the spiel, for your education and enlightenment," the older man said. "Plus, since I've memorized all this, might as well pass it on. First some history. Freedom Mall was opened to the public on August 21, 1975, predark calendar. Thousands of people streamed inside to shop in the ninety-three stores that were tenants. Freedom came with 1.4 million square feet of space on a span of seventy-six acres. There were 5,200 parking spaces. In 1989 they expanded upon the design, adding another 350,000 square feet to the mall's south side and room for an additional eighty stores and a twelve-unit food court. On a good week back then, Freedom saw 250,000 shoppers. During holiday seasons, the number doubled to a half million. Today our numbers are much smaller, but Freedom is more than a mere destination—it's a ville unto itself with all the offerings of a traditional outdoor city, and then some."

"You charging a toll to get in?" Ryan asked.

The old man shook his head. "No."

"That's a switch," Dean said.

Hans held up a finger. "However, there are certain rules you have to follow once you're inside, sir."

"Such as?"

Hans used the finger to point at Ryan's weapons. "You can carry one blaster each for protection. I can already see your group believes in traveling well-heeled. That's fine by me. Only a fool travels outside without ample firepower. However, indoors you lose the extra hardware. Most people go for the pistols, but I'll leave that up to you. Check the other blasters here. You won't need any long blasters or Uzis in Freedom. You can pick them up when you go. Check them now, and you'll get a receipt. There's a fee of one mall credit per weapon storage. Pay when you leave. If you don't want to pay, or don't come back to check on your blasters in thirty days, they become mall property. Stay as long as you want, just don't forget your hardware. No returns."

"Give us a second to talk this over."

Hans nodded, even as Ryan saw him make a gesture with his left hand, an alert signal for the armed guards.

"What do all of you think?" Ryan whispered.

The Armorer didn't hesitate with his disapproval. "Think I don't like letting somebody else sit with my blasters."

"Me, neither," Jak agreed.

"And they charge you for the privilege. I, for one, have never liked being jabbed in the hand with the rip-off stick." Doc said.

"Look, this is standard operating procedure," Alton told them. "Same drill last time I was in here.

Even if you leave some of the heavy artillery behind, you people are still better armed than most. Me, I'm going in. I appreciate your company and your help getting here. But it's getting dark, and if I were you, I'd get inside, too, before night falls and the gateway into Freedom shuts down. I sure as hell wouldn't want to be out here with another pack of stickies wandering around in the dark looking for the ones you chilled.''

Alton nodded a goodbye, and went back over to the small booth where Hans was waiting for him. Since he had only the Colt, he was quickly led through the check-in process into the main entrance, where he vanished from sight.

''What other options do we have?'' Krysty said. ''Like Alton said, I don't like the idea being out at night with as many stickies that are reported to be around here. We can do our traveling by day.''

''J.B.? Go in or stay out?'' Ryan asked.

''I'm not the one to ask right now. I can't see worth a damn in the dark. Daylight, sure. Even though I don't like leaving blasters behind, I vote we stay.''

''Anybody else want to add an opinion?'' Ryan asked. No answer came. ''Then it's settled.''

Ryan strode back over to the check-in counter and unlimbered his Steyr, taking time to unload the cartridges. After doing likewise, J.B. handed over his Uzi, preferring to keep the raw force of the M-4000 shotgun hanging beneath his coat by a shoulder strap.

''That all of the extra blasters?'' Hans asked as he looked them over.

''Yeah. We're keeping the pistols, per your advice—except for my friend, there. He's hanging on to the shotgun.''

''I can take your word there's no extra hardware?''

''Unless you want to search us, and I don't have a problem with that.''

''No need. We try and limit the violence inside, but we can't fully stomp it out,'' Hans said. He reached down for a receipt book and scribbled down the makes of the weapons and Ryan's name. The receipt book had carbons, and he handed over a copy.

''Where do we get mall creds?'' Ryan asked as he folded the slip of paper and placed it in a pocket.

''Bank of Freedom, Incorporated. You'll see it on the right when you go through the second checkpoint. You can exchange your currency there.''

''Right.''

''What's the rate of exchange?'' Mildred asked.

''Varies. Never heard any complaints. Freedom Mall wants to keep your business, so we play fair with what you want to spend. When you're ready to go, you can give back what you didn't use and we'll return what's left of your funds minus a ten percent handling fee.''

''Lots fees in place,'' Jak observed.

''Welcome to a sampling of a civilization of sorts,'' Mildred said with a chuckle. ''Let's just hope there isn't a Freedom Mall sales tax.''

THE MALL INTERIOR WAS a queer mix of preservation, restoration and retrofitting. There were two floors, with the second floor having a high ceiling that stretched up to a series of clear sky panels that allowed the sun to provide interior illumination. Half of the upper level was floorless, with open walkways that allowed the sunlight to filter down below, giving room for multiple sets of wide stairwells and narrow, nonfunctioning escalators. An overblown abstract sculpture also dominated in the area they currently were looking at, the "arms" of the piece stretching skyward, graceful and long.

The populace spilled out everywhere, most walking, some on skateboards or in-line skates. A rickshaw-styled taxi service seemed to be doing well, manned by weary-looking barechested men as the two-seater carriages rolled past.

Most of the visible storefronts had kept their original signage, with new additions added below. Others had chosen to strip away or cover the names of original Freedom tenants. Mildred counted several familiar names from her previous life that were still in evidence.

"First thing we do is find a place to stay," Ryan said.

"Well," Mildred said brightly, "any mall this size I ever went into had directories to help out new visitors. Directories were also good promotion for stores. They helped steer you where they wanted you to go, not where you might stumble by accident."

"Comp terminals?" Dean asked.

"No, Dean, not that high-tech, although now that I think about it, some places did feature information banks with computers, in case someone was interested in finding out more about a store or wanted to find a particular brand of merchandise. Pretty slow, primitive stuff, though, and designed to be idiot proof to keep Joe Public from becoming frustrated and screwing up the system.''

"Could just ask somebody. Might be a lot simpler," Krysty said. "Plenty of folks to choose from."

"In a place this size?" Mildred retorted. "By the time they explained where we wanted to go, we could have already been there."

"It was just a suggestion," Krysty replied.

"I must confess to a strange feeling hovering between euphoria at having a roof over my head in a secure environment, and claustrophobia at the number of people crammed alongside us in here," Doc commented after being jostled by a passing couple.

"There it is," Mildred said, pointing toward the back of the long hall of shops past the Bank of Freedom. The group peered down at a black monolithic slab that seemed to glow with a hidden radiance from within.

Everyone approached the slab. From their earlier viewpoint, it had appeared to be rectangular, but now they could see it was triangular. The same information was on all three sides, a carefully lined map of the interior of Freedom with numbers and letters in each box or passageway of the grid. The code numbers corresponded to a long list of shops and services stenciled in below, each section with a different heading in alphabetical order.

"Upper level is split into two parts, Section A and Section B," Dean said.

"And the lower level is also divided into Sections

C and D," Doc read. "We are currently in D, according to the You Are Here arrow."

"Layout looks pretty basic, and each of the sections is split by a big store. Says here the old JCPenney is the link to either side."

Mildred whistled softly as she looked over the listings. "Impressive. Someone in here has graphic-arts skills, and we all know how unusual that is to come across. This directory appears to be completely up-to-date. At least, there were no chain stores in the 1990s called The Gaudy Boutique or Mike's Meats to my recollection."

"Why glow?" Jak asked, speaking for the first time since they had entered Freedom. The albino had been scanning the visible rail of the level above them, keenly staring at any of the passersby who chose to look down. Unlike Doc, Jak found no peace or security in having a roof over his head. A roof could hide many things. The only way in and out of Freedom was crawling with sec men, but it also made a man stay wary.

Ryan felt the same way, but was more inclined to go with what was presented to him in front of his own eye—at least, for the moment.

Mildred answered Jak's question. "The construct we're looking at has fluorescent tubes on the inside with clear glass walls. I don't know where the power source is. It could be batteries or hooked into the system somehow. All you have to do is make up your color-coded overlay on a plastic sheet of acetate— this looks like it was generated by a computer laser printer—and attach your listings to the back side of the glass so no one can get to it, and presto, you've got your very own mall directory."

Dean pointed a finger at one of the headings with the listing Travel-Lodging.

"'Freedom Center Station,'" he read. "'One night or one year.'"

"The place looks big," J.B. said. "Takes up a chunk of the far end of the mall."

"And it's close by, too. We've walked long enough today," Krysty added.

Ryan was in total agreement. "Bunks for one night seems about all we can afford right now. I held back part of our jack at the bank. My guess is some of the stores in here will take tender they don't have to worry about reporting or running through the proper channels of exchange. After what we've seen, I'm sure the mall probably hits them up for a ten percent handling charge just like us visitors."

"We've got some bartering power with the antibiotics I found. Medicine is worth a pretty penny, especially in a place like this," Mildred noted.

"We'll see about selling it or swapping it tomorrow," Ryan said. "Tonight I just want to sleep."

"And see about scrubbing that skin dye off," Krysty teased.

Dean wasn't listening to any of that. His attention was still on the inwardly lit mall directory and the maze of attractions and shops it promised.

"Hey!" he suddenly yelled. "Look at this!"

"What?" Ryan asked, a little annoyed at Dean's outburst. He'd almost drawn out his side blaster, thinking they were about to be attacked.

"Here, Dad! Dr. Michael Clarke, Eye Specialist."

"By the Three Kennedys," Doc agreed in a hushed tone. "It seems we've found a solution to J.B.'s eye problems in the timely form of this good optician."

"I don't know," Mildred said gently, not wanting to get J.B.'s hopes up until they knew more about the mysterious Dr. Clarke. Besides, a doctor wasn't needed as badly as a new pair of corrective glasses.

"Guess we can make one detour before bunking down," Ryan agreed. "Think you can find this place, Dean?"

"No prob, Dad."

Ryan gestured for Dean to take the point. "Lead on, then."

"BLUE LIGHT SPECIAL!" a dirty young man with shaggy brown hair cried out, waving his scabby arms and dancing around in a circle. As his patched long coat flapped around him like a cloak, he continued to chant, "Blue light! Blue light! Blue-light special!"

The words created a surge in the milling crowd. Every man, woman and child dropped what they were doing and followed the mall crier.

"Where?" a man demanded.

"Which front?" a woman added.

"Name the place! Name it!" a couple said, their voices overlapping, matched in strident intensity.

"Where?" was the group cry. "Where is the blue light?"

A strobe suddenly erupted into being, shimmering, flickering, calling out over and over again in a strident on-off pattern from a shop located two dozen storefronts away. The instant the light revealed itself, most of the onlookers took off at a pace between a brisk walk and a fast jog.

"Pardon me, sir," Doc said, addressing a weather-beaten man dressed in a patched red-flannel shirt and threadbare denim jeans, "but what is a 'blue-light special' and why has it caused such excitement from our fellow mall visitors?"

"It's a secret," the man replied mysteriously. "A surprise sale."

"A sale of what?"

"That's the secret. A blue light means you save big on whatever the store chooses to sell dirt cheap. You never know when a store is going to have a blue light, and you never know what is going to go on sale. But the faster you can run and get there, the better selection you'll have. Personally I've never found anything worth a damn. I've got a bum knee, so by the time I show up, all the good stuff has already been taken. It's not fair, but then again, nothing in life ever is."

"You don't say," Doc said, stroking his chin.

J.B. STEPPED OUT of the small entrance to Dr. Clarke's office. Clarke had also kept a piece of the past, retaining the Lenscrafters sign his facility originally used.

The visit to the eye doctor took only moments. The prices quoted for the man's services, including a pair of eyeglasses, were well beyond the group's current financial status. Another solution would have to be sought, but not until all had gotten some much needed rest.

Silently the group walked back to the Freedom Center Station. In a former life, the boarding hotel and apartment building had served as a "hub" store, one of the name-brand anchor shops that ensured a large crowd of excited customers would continue to come out to buy on a regular basis. Mildred recognized the logo of the place immediately.

"Sears. Where America Shops For Value," she said dryly.

Once the rate was paid, and three rooms were secured, the companions went their separate ways. Each couple got a room, with Dean, Jak and Doc getting the third.

Usually a room alone meant time for lovemaking for Ryan and Krysty, but exhaustion had combined with the still fresh memories of Pharaoh Akhnaton's mind games to still their passions. They mostly succeeded in cleansing themselves in a lukewarm shower, and were asleep within seconds of lying down together, their bodies intertwined tightly.

Chapter Eleven

J.B., now also cleansed of the skin dye, felt terrible, and his eyes hurt from the constant squinting he was having to engage in to try to bring his surroundings into better focus. The century-old adhesive of the fresh bandages Mildred had applied to his facial lesions itched, but he knew better than to scratch. The last thing he wanted to do was endure a double dose of Doc's aimless chatter before he even had a full cup of coffee sub.

The group of friends had gathered in the late morning for a meal of water and eats from their supply packs. They were sitting in one of the common areas inside the mall. Arriving early due to being awakened at dawn by chronic aches and pains of travel, Doc had scoped out a wide bench and claimed it for his own, and for the use of his companions as they began arriving at the spot at the agreed-upon time.

However, sitting with Doc at your elbow came with a price, as J.B. was reminding himself.

"Alas, friends, but the fates have provided for us while spitting upon our unprotected brows simultaneously," Doc was saying. "Normally the loss of John Barrymore's spectacles would be the cause of dire calamities indeed. Now we are within the protected walls of a virtual village of shops, including that rarest of rarities, a genuine optician."

"What wrong with this picture, Doc?" Mildred asked, her clear voice thick with annoyance.

"I was getting to that, Dr. Wyeth. No, unfortunately, we do not possess the necessary currency to purchase the needed services of the aforementioned ocular physician," Doc said, and added, "So, we are fucked. Put succinctly."

"Don't say 'fuck,' Doc. It sounds all wrong coming out of your mouth," Krysty protested.

"There's always a way," Ryan said. "We're not out of ideas yet."

Krysty squeezed Ryan's knee. "I know that tone, and you know better than to even think of trying to walk in there and take a pair of eyeglasses for J.B."

Ryan assumed a look of mock hurt. "You don't think I could get away with it?"

"Mebbe, mebbe not. First J.B. would have to take the eye exam so we'll know what kind of lenses he needs. He said the eye doc told him he needed jack up front before doing the examination."

"Makes good sense. Payment in full before you get started, otherwise whoever it is you're examining may decide he doesn't like what you've got to say and bolt."

"Even if you bullied Dr. Clarke into doing the exam, he's got thousands of different kinds of glasses in his office. No telling which set of lenses J.B. needs," Mildred added. "Besides, I kind of liked the guy."

"Shit!" J.B. snorted. "The prices he's charging are ridiculous."

"That's a carry-over from the good old days," Mildred interjected. "Us doctors always demanded top pay for our services."

"What we do now?" Jak asked.

"Pay the man what he wants, I guess," Ryan said, polishing off the last of his portion of the powdered-eggs self-heat for his morning meal.

"Still think just go in, take them," Jak muttered. "Take them all. Find a pair that works."

Mildred threw up her hands. "Jak, the going rate is the going rate. Clarke's talents—and his apparent ready supply of glasses—are rarely found. I never met an eye doctor wandering around in Deathlands, have you?"

"Can't say as I ever have," Ryan said. "Where did you get your first pair of specs anyway, J.B.?"

"I was just a kid," the Armorer began to say before a very small man stepped in front of him with an excited look

"Pardon me, yes, I overhear you have a problem, no?" the unfamiliar voice piped up. "I have the answer, yes!"

Ryan's hand shot out like a steel baton and grabbed the little man by the throat. The fellow was dressed to the nines in a tiny pair of dress shoes, green pants and matching jacket, bow tie and a dramatic black cape draped over his shoulders.

"You listening to our private conversations, runt?" Ryan said as the little man tried to pull away.

"Define listening, uh-huh. Air is free. Mall is open.

I pass by, I hear. You no want people hearing, keep mouth shut, understand?"

J.B. gave a short bark of laughter at the dwarf's logic. "Yeah, Ryan, understand?"

Jak narrowed his ruby red eyes at the struggling dwarf.

"Your white-hair no like Lucas."

"He doesn't like eavesdroppers," Mildred said. "Nor do I."

"Is okay. I no like him, either," the dwarf replied.

Ryan unclenched his hand and released the little man. "You planning on making some kind of point, Lucas? Or are you purposefully trying to piss one of us off enough to get yourself chilled?"

"Make you offer. Good money to be had. Mall credits enough to take care of any problems," Lucas replied, adjusting his cape.

"Oh, yeah? How?"

"The pit. Combat in the pit, winner take all."

"What, a fight?"

"In the pit, that's right, yes, fight, yes. One against another. Two go in, one comes out. Beat the champion and the winner gets a shopping spree, up to a thousand mall creds on anything he wants to buy in Freedom. No blasters, blades or other nonprojectile hand weapons, yes. Anything goes."

"Sounds like a bargain-basement version of the Big Game," J.B. mused.

Dean gave a barely noticeable shudder as the Armorer's words triggered the memory of the gladiator-style killing games held in the ruins in the once prosperous Las Vegas, Nevada. Until a few months ago, the youngster had been a student at the Nicholas Brody School in Colorado, where Ryan had left him for a period of proper education.

The kind of learning Ryan had paid for hadn't come cheap in the hellish world of Deathlands, but he had known his son would need some formal schooling before returning to the harsh realities of daily survival. Knowledge was just as useful a weapon as a good blaster if a man was educated enough to use it, and Ryan wanted his own flesh and blood to have the opportunity to be as culturally aware as he had been during his own childhood.

Unfortunately things had started to go wrong at the Brody School soon after Ryan left his son.

The school hadn't been able to live up to what its reputation and secure grounds promised. More and more often, Ryan was seeing that so much of anything relied on the strength of a single vision. Sometimes the vision was for the greater good, like the school and the desire to educate, but more often, the vision was yet another nameless, faceless land baron who had grabbed enough power and clout to swing his weight around.

Like the five men locked in the power struggle for the land and villes surrounding Las Vegas.

Dean and nine of his classmates from the Brody School in Colorado had been kidnapped by one of these men, Baron Vinge Connrad, to serve as young warriors in his fight against his competition.

At the same time, Ryan and his friends had been on their way to retrieve Dean after many long months of travel. He had desperately missed his son and decided it was time for the boy's studies to come to an end. Before they reached their goal, they themselves inadvertently came upon the sadistic and primitive way of settling who would be the leader of the Vegas villes for another year, having been forced by circumstances to be warriors for a different baron.

"If this is like the Big Game, I could probably handle any two-bit gladiator they throw my way with one arm tied behind my back and my other thumb up my ass," J.B. announced.

"Right. You can't even see well enough to squat down and take a proper shit, J.B.," Mildred retorted. "No way are you going in for any gladiator games."

"I don't recall asking for your permission, Millie," J.B. replied.

"She's right. I'm not having you cut down by a lucky punch from some hard-ass," Ryan said firmly. "But without your glasses, you're a definite liability to be carrying around. Got to change that triple fast."

"Thanks a whole heaping lot for the vote of confidence," J.B. said, with an annoyed sneer.

"He has fire, yes, even blind, you say? Would do well, would do well," the dwarf interjected. "First battle scheduled today for noon. Need to sign on as contender now, yes."

"Quiet, squirt," Ryan said, cutting off the little man. "Doc said it best—"

"I always do," Doc quipped.

"We could be in a lot worse shape. Matter of time J.B. broke his glasses anyway. At least there's a place here to fix them. So, I say we're not leaving Freedom without two pairs—one to wear and one to keep as a backup in case this ever happens again. And the most immediate solution to the problem seems to be this fight in the pit the shrimp's babbling about."

"I don't care, Ryan. John is not going to get himself killed over a pair of eyeglasses in some stupid hand-to-hand battle," Mildred protested. "We've got to find another way."

"I know, Mildred, I know," Ryan said impatiently. "But who said anything about J.B. being the one doing the fighting?"

BEFORE STEPPING into the pit, Ryan eyeballed the arena from above.

The walls plunging downward were sheer, with grooves cut into two sides. He guessed it was a forty-foot drop to the floor below. The actual fighting arena was open and wide, with curved walls to prevent any attempts to crawl up and out of the battle.

In the few hours since he had agreed to the challenge, word had spread throughout Freedom like prairie fire in the dry season. He'd been told all of the seats to the pit match were sold out, "seats" being a term for spots to stand around the protective railing and watch. Already a sizable sum of jack had been generated through pay-per-view sales via the mall's antiquated closed-circuit television system.

Money had even been made from Ryan himself, since he'd been forced to pay a substantial entry fee as a pit challenger. His new manager, Lucas, had kicked in additional funds to complete what Ryan needed to satisfy the demanded sum.

"Case you run. Case you chicken out, call off

match before it begins," Lucas explained. "Refunds expensive. I'm counting on you. Do good."

"Don't have to worry about my turning tail," Ryan replied, gesturing at the open hole in the center of the mall. "What the hell was this thing, anyway? I doubt any predark malls had gladiator bouts between shopping stints."

"Used to be stage," Lucas said. "Live shows. Raised and lowered from the basement for special effects, scene changes. Worked for a long time till motors gave out. Now floor don't go up no more. So, gutted most of the innards and ripped out the old floor. Sloped the walls. Made a dandy pit for the brawl. One-on-one or big fight. Doesn't matter. Sometimes stuntmen come in on cycles. Motor bikes. Ride them around and around, high up the walls. Like magic show! Fall sometimes. Best part."

"Centrifugal force," Ryan said. "Holds them up."

"Whatever you say," Lucas replied, not understanding the terminology, but wanting to keep his new warrior happy.

"Am I going to have to chill this guy?" Ryan asked bluntly.

Lucas sniggered. "You'll be the one who decides, friend Ryan. My guess is yes. To stop him, you have to put end to his feeble life. I shall meet you down there in but a moment. Must go pay more fees, see to betting, wagers. Money to be made."

Ryan turned and entered the access door that led to the backstage area of the arena, heading for the room assigned earlier to use as his place to prepare for the fight. Dean was standing in front of the door, waiting for him.

Ryan nodded to his son as he pulled on his tight black gloves. He clenched his fingers, enjoying the sensation of warmth and protection inside the comforting second skin of leather. He shrugged out of his long coat, his previously dislocated shoulder reminding him of the injury he'd suffered back in the Barrens. Ryan mentally debated keeping his long white scarf with the weighted ends, but decided to leave it behind, choosing instead to keep himself as unencumbered as possible.

Once the SIG-Sauer was unholstered and the exterior layers of clothing removed, Ryan was dressed in a black T-shirt, heavy jeans, combat boots. Simple, tight apparel—the better to keep a foe from finding a handhold with. He kept his hidden flensing blade under the back of his shirt and the deadly eighteen-inch honed panga on his hip.

"How do I look?" he asked Dean, who'd been watching. The room they were inside was once a dressing room when the stage was used for less deadly performances of music and song. The door of the room had been taken off the hinges, allowing a partial view of the site of the fight to come.

"Like a hot pipe, Dad. Aces on the line all the way down. This won't take long," Dean said. The boy seemed quite sure of this, much to Ryan's hidden amusement.

"Wish I shared your confidence, son. It's not always skill. Many a time luck plays a big role."

Ryan did a deep knee bend and frowned at the loud

pop that cracked out of his joints. "Knees aren't what they used to be," he noted ruefully. He stretched out his arms, extending them and moving them from side to side. His dislocated right shoulder twinged again.

"Nothing is what it used to be," he muttered.

Lucas walked into the room through the open doorway, followed by the tense figures of Krysty and Mildred.

"Your women, they say they stay in here, near pit itself. Boy already here. Too many. Against rules," the little man said firmly.

"Don't worry. My boy's going back up to the top to watch. The women are healers," Ryan explained. "I need them close. Might need their help triple fast after this fight."

Lucas pondered Ryan's words. "Doors will be sealed to the pit floor. They cannot help you until match is over."

"Understood."

"Boy will take females' blasters with him to top. They stay, okay, but unarmed."

Krysty and Mildred both took out their pistols and handed them to Dean, who was already weighted down by Ryan's heavy SIG-Sauer. The boy didn't complain. He accepted the hardware and departed the way Mildred and Krysty had come into the dressing area.

"Hurry back, lover," Krysty said, giving him a quick peck on the lips. "There's more where that came from."

"You can count on it."

Ryan took another deep breath and looked at a

large clock hanging on the wall. High noon. Time to go. He stepped past them to the reinforced door leading out to the pit floor itself. He lifted the handle, and the door swung out into the arena. A loud cry of excitement was ignited with his appearance as Ryan ducked slightly and strode through the opening.

Instinctively he looked up. The bright stage lights used for illumination prevented him from seeing into the upper reaches of the stands. As he moved farther toward the center of the pit, the voices above got even louder.

Across from Ryan, a twin to his own exit door was recessed into the wall.

The door opened, swinging out. Ryan continued to stare, waiting for the first look at his foe. A canopy overhang cast a dramatic curtain of black over the entryway, allowing for a resplendent entrance.

Like everyone else around the pit, Ryan was waiting. He wasn't expecting death himself to come gliding out of the shadows.

Chapter Twelve

One-on-one.

Hand-to-hand.

Man against…man?

"Aw, shit," Ryan cursed as he saw his foe for the first time.

One essential fact had gone unmentioned by Lucas when the one-eyed man had insisted on accepting the challenge of the pit to assist J.B., and that was the key piece of information about his intended opponent.

The sec droid was a familiar sight to Ryan Cawdor. He'd faced them before. Like droids he'd fought in the past, this one was vaguely humanoid in construction, legs slightly bent at the knees, arms dangling apelike at its sides. Each arm was slightly longer than a man's would be, in direct proportion to its height.

One arm ended in three fingerlike digits. Two of them were pincerlike, with deadly honed edges. The third was a stubby hammer. The other arm appeared to have been broken at the wrist, and a studded mace added in place of what once were additional appendages.

The android was bent and squatty, less than five feet tall and hunched over. Both legs were stubby, ending in flexible platforms for feet. One foot had three toes, the other two—if one wanted to call the sharpened edges sticking out "toes."

Unlike some of the other androids Ryan had seen, there was no attempt at providing any sort of "flesh" on this creation. The droid was open and bare, with a thick metal skeleton made up of rods of once gleaming but now faded and pitted chromed steel.

Perched on a flat wide metal collar serving as a neck was the robot's head, a head that looked exactly like a scuffed goldfish bowl. Small red crystals embedded in the circuitry gleamed evilly from behind the unbreakable glass dome.

This one came with the surprise addition of a narrow and open mouth beneath the clear dome, which was unusual since sec droids were known for being silent and deadly, their mouths usually consisting of nothing more than a metallic slit. Razor-sharp teeth gleamed behind the droid's metal lips.

The construct's broad chest was armored, and the first spot where Ryan could sense a weakness. There were definite repairs to be seen here, patches of flat steel soldered into place to cover previous blows. Come to think of it, the neck on the thing was all wrong, as well. Every sec droid Ryan had ever seen came with a tubular, articulated neck that let the head swivel in all directions.

No, this was no factory mint sec droid hidden away to be liberated from within the confines of a redoubt, like the band of five that Ryan had once inadvertently activated—a costly mistake where the one-eyed warrior had merely walked down the wrong hallway and sent them lurching into action with his genetic imprint tattooed on their sensors. After that, Ryan always figured he'd already had his worst experience with the killing machines.

"Hey!" Ryan bellowed into the lights. "Nobody said anything about fighting a bastard droid!"

"It's up to you. There's still time to call this off. You forfeit your entry fee, but you can back out and slink away," the appointed referee of the match yelled back from the observation box mounted high over the onlookers.

Back down below, Ryan eyeballed the robot. He knew the onboard computers and data banks that gave the commands to the head and limbs of the droid were housed in that broad chest. His job was going to be figuring out how to pry off one of the patches for a look inside without having the droid's mace crush his skull or, even worse, ending up with a bladed foot sunk up to the ankle in his crotch.

Still, those plates had been cracked open before, in battle and in the repairs he knew a combat machine such as that would have required.

Ryan debated. He knew his comrades would understand if he passed on this deadly duel. No one had expected his foe to be a sec droid. Ryan felt tricked, placed in the situation of being between a rock and a hard place. They needed the jack he'd ponied up as an entry fee. J.B. needed new peepers, or they would have to get used to running around with a near blind man in tow.

"I can take this bastard," Ryan whispered to himself.

"What's your decision? Fight or hide?" The ref's

query was amplified by the former stage's still functioning sound system.

For a second, Ryan felt the world tunneling in on him, as if a camera lens was zooming in on his own grim visage and he was also outside himself, witnessing it.

He had to make a decision.

"I'm staying," he yelled, to the happiness of all the watchers…except his companions'.

Inside his head, a voice seemed to be repeating, "Killer robot, killer bot…."

A rubber ball wrapped in a strip of white cloth was dropped down into the pit, where it bounced, up and down, up and down, and off one of the curved walls before rolling to a stop near Ryan's left boot.

The sec droid lurched forward the instant the ball stopped moving, causing the crowd above to cry out in anticipation and joy.

"Nothing like live entertainment," Ryan said under his breath as he readied himself for the endurance test to come.

One hesitant step forward, and already Ryan could sense his earlier estimation was correct. This droid had seen better days. One foot up, then down. Left foot, then the right. The arm weighed down with the mace remained motionless, but the second one telescoped outward, the scalpellike pincers opening and closing.

Yelling ferociously, getting his blood up after the shock, Ryan sprang forward, waving his arms. "Piss off, you clanking piece of junk!"

The droid stiffly hopped back in a defensive maneuver.

Odd. He'd heard these things could exhibit learned behavior, but against a single man? Perhaps the programmers had made this a fairer fight than Ryan would have believed upon first seeing the droid.

"Come any closer and I'll rip off those skinny arms and shove them sideways up your metal ass!" Ryan bellowed.

The onlookers exploded in appreciative laughter.

In response, the sec hunter again took another step toward Ryan, its glass head turning slowly from side to side as if making sure no other attacker would be coming out of hiding or from the guard rails of the pit above.

"Fuck you, One-eye," the droid said in an inhumanly flat and mechanical tone that came from a hidden speaker buried deep inside the creature's thick neck. The deadly metal teeth moved in synchronization with the words. "You're nothing to me but fresh red meat, you dumb-ass outlander."

More laughter from above, and despite himself, Ryan felt his blood start to sing in his ears at the string of insults. Obviously, in addition to the numerous repairs and replacement parts to this rusting unit, someone had decided it would be a laugh riot to give their pet techno-assassin a voice.

"Chicken-shit," the android announced to even more guffaws from the rim of the pit.

Ryan held his anger. Even the blackest of humorists would be amused at a sentient being growing angry at the prerecorded insults from a collection of circuit boards and killing metal. This thing wasn't alive. All the android was to Ryan was an obstacle, a hunk of junk dropped in his way, a mass of metal he had to remove so he could go about his business, earn his reward, get J.B. his spectacles and forget he'd ever been inside this shrine to the long dead concept of consumerism.

Now that he was closer, Ryan could hear the loud, strained whining of gears and servo motors attempting to keep the droid on both feet. The sounds told him a crucial fact. As he had hoped from his first impression, the internal clockwork of his foe wasn't meshing properly. The hunter could be toppled.

Ryan took a deep breath and examined his options. He knew from previous battles with the droids that even if he'd been well heeled with a blaster, the armor was still a deterrent. The thing was programmed to be lightning fast, but a man would have the edge in maneuverability. Plus, he could see this hunter was well along in years and use, and he'd heard Lucas say that the champion had been beaten before.

Ryan slid the panga from the oiled leather sheath and took an offensive stance, balancing himself on the balls of his booted feet.

"Come on, you coldhearted tin can. Bring it on," he said.

"Make me," the bot replied.

Ryan squatted, still keeping his back straight and his eye on the android as he moved around the arena floor. After a second or two of feeling around with his free hand, he found what he was searching for.

"Heads up, clanky," Ryan said, and threw the ball tossed down earlier to start the match. The ball hurtled toward the bot, thrown with all of Ryan's might. The rubber sphere whizzed through the air and impacted high on the clear dome of the sec droid's head, hitting with a bonk before bouncing up wildly into the air.

Interestingly enough, the droid had made no effort to dodge the lobbed ball.

Ryan was starting to feel even more confident.

Until the modified sec hunter hopped up like a frog, bounding once, twice, three times before almost landing right on top of his unprotected skull.

Ryan dodged and slashed out with the panga, aiming at an exposed metal cable in the bot's hip joint. The blade gave out a clang, but otherwise had about as much effect on stopping the sec hunter as the thrown rubber ball.

The android responded to the knife jab by swinging its monkey arms high, right where Ryan's head would have been if he hadn't already decided to go low.

Ryan stayed in motion and swung his leg to let the sec droid taste boot leather, feeling two of the toes on his right foot shatter in protest against the force of the impact from the desperate roundhouse kick. The only good the blow did was to leave a black smear across the clear dome of the opponent's observation bubble.

"No good, shit-face," the machine said, the tone still inflectionless.

Before Ryan could give a retort, his foe chose to

undertake another of the rabbitlike leaps, straight up into the air. But this time when it landed, the one-eyed man was on the receiving end, pinned down hard.

"Fireblast!" Ryan wheezed as he struggled to breathe from the droid's terrible weight. "Get off my gut."

Gritting his teeth, Ryan pushed back with his left forearm while jamming the panga into one of the small cracks in the repaired areas on the droid's chest. He worked the blade back and forth, striving to find an in. The bot whirred and clicked as servo motors gave back as good as they got. The small onboard comp analyzed the stress the android was currently enduring and chose yet another programmed quip from the select file of profane insults. Sensing a possible victory, the hunter droid came up with a classic.

"Fuck you, asshole," it retorted in a cold metallic voice.

"Fuck me?" Ryan spit, his voice rising in disbelief. He knew his mounting rage was totally inappropriate, but he couldn't help himself. "Fuck *me?*"

The android was silent as it relentlessly continued to apply pressure.

"No, not fuck me. Fuck *you!*" Ryan roared, and shoved with all of his remaining strength. The bot flew back as if it had been launched like a torpedo, rolling over on one side and using its strong steel arms to try to push itself back up.

Ryan had leaped onto the machine's back, keeping his head low as he locked his legs around its middle and hooked his arms under the metal appendages. The droid struggled in Ryan's grip as he applied pressure, using the moment to try to catch his breath as he rode the metal unit around the pit.

This avenue of attack was unfamiliar to the hunter. Usually prey tried to stay away, not come in and stay attached. The obvious tactic of lunging backward and smashing Ryan into a curved pit wall was a tactic not programmed into the device's defense comp, so all it could think of to do was spin and hop.

Ryan hung on, squeezing the droid's arms back even harder. He felt one of the shoulder sockets start to give, and a small burst of sparks flashed out from the joint. He focused renewed energy on the spot, feeling his own recently injured shoulder start to throb in reflected agony.

Then the entire arm ripped free in a spray of sparks and smell of burning wire. Ryan was flung backward when the arm gave way, carried by the momentum he'd generated.

The injury seemed to extend beyond a lost arm. The droid began to thrash and buck in place, a horrible, almost human screaming coming from the speaker that had earlier been tossing out quips.

Ryan staggered to his feet, using the broken arm as a support. Then, once he was erect, he placed the limb on his shoulder and swung it like a baseball bat, smashing it across the side of the bot's face.

The hunter fell like a cut tree to the floor of the pit.

"Hate you, you and all who made you!" Ryan

yelled as he smashed the steel rod again and again over the clear housing of the sec hunter's head. He had already decided he wasn't going to stop until the glasslike substance shattered.

Krysty came running through the lower stage door, with Mildred close behind. Dean, Jak and Doc remained in the stands with J.B., who had been unable to clearly see the battle from their viewpoint at the top of the pit. To the Armorer's dismay, Doc had provided a running commentary in the most flowery of language describing what Ryan was doing—and having to endure—in the pit.

"Thanks to Gaia. Ryan. Stop now, stop," Krysty said, her pale skin flushed a deep pink in a mix of relief and excitement now that the combat had ended with Ryan the victor. Her red, prehensile hair was coiling and moving along her skull like a living thing as she tried to penetrate the killing rage that had fueled Ryan's victory.

Not responding, Ryan brought down the arm a final time across the machine's upper torso before allowing the steel limb to fall from his fingers. He kicked out with his uninjured foot, and the toe of his boot made a dull thudding noise as he smashed it into the pitted steel of the now inert bot.

"He appears to be all right, but I need to examine him," Mildred announced in a voice tight with anxiety, helping Krysty support Ryan as they walked him briskly away from the eyes and cries of the cheering crowd. They passed twin techies, in coveralls and tool belts, who had also come out running to try to see to the damage to their own champion.

"You didn't have to rip his damn arm off," one of the two whined.

"Piss off," Krysty retorted, "before I go pick up that arm and beat your heads in myself."

Chapter Thirteen

"So, what's first on the list?" J.B. asked.

J.B. and Mildred were standing together for the second time in the front room of the tiny clinic Dr. Michael Clarke called an office. It was two hours after Ryan's battle, after the cuts had been wrapped and the broken toes taped. Winded and bruised, the one-eyed man had accepted his winnings from the pit organizers.

Ryan had passed the credit chit to J.B., and they'd agreed to meet as soon as the Armorer had obtained the two pairs of glasses.

"You sit. You wait," Clarke replied, having stepped out of the back of the establishment when hearing J.B. and Mildred enter. After J.B. had shown him the credit chit from Ryan's fight in the pit, the doctor had most anxiously instructed them "not to leave his sight."

Mildred couldn't help but be amused by the fact that Clarke dressed the part of doctor. He wore thick horn-rimmed bifocals, a long white lab coat, conservative necktie, conservative shoes.

"What if we're in a hurry?" Mildred said, enjoying the brief, satisfying rush of power. After the way they had been previously treated when entering Clarke's office the previous night, it felt good to see the little balding man squirm. Now that J.B. was flush, the self-appointed physician was eager to see to their wants and needs.

"I'm with a patient right now," Clarke explained.

"Maybe you needed to make an appointment, John—no, wait, that's what you tried to do last time we were here."

"Could be," the Armorer agreed, warming to the game. "Hey, Doc Clarke, you want me to come back?"

"No, I want you to wait."

J.B. sat down slowly. "Make it quick."

"Of course."

"Say, Dr. Clarke? I do have one question before you go," Mildred probed.

"Yes?"

"Are you an ophthalmologist or an optometrist?"

"Neither. I never could tell them apart."

Mildred smiled, feeling oddly the way she imagined Doc must feel when catching her in an error. "An ophthalmologist is a medical doctor who can practice surgery and diagnose—"

Clarke interrupted her. "I was joking. I know the difference. But working with such crude instruments keeps me from practicing surgery. I do the best I can. If you want to be smug about it, I suppose I'm nothing more than a glorified optician."

Bingo, Mildred thought, but she didn't want to antagonize a man whose services they needed, after all. "Just curious. That's all."

MOMENTS LATER, Clarke reappeared. "I am sorry for keeping you, Mr. Dix. Please come back with me."

"You want company?" Mildred asked.

"No," J.B. replied, his tone sharp.

"Whoa! Excuse me for asking!"

The Armorer's tone softened. "I mean, no. I'd rather do it myself."

Mildred looked at her lover with an odd expression. "I'll wait out here, then."

"This shouldn't take long," Clarke told her. "Usually what eats up the time is the trial and error of matching the right lenses to his eyes. I don't have the luxury of writing him a prescription and sending him on his way. We have to go through the boxes, hoping to find frames and lenses in the same package that fit."

The examining room was lined with cabinets on three sides, a salmon pink series of upper cabinets and lower cabinets. A black countertop ran along the tops of the lower. The fourth wall was cabinetless, and dotted with various eye charts and diagrams of the interior of the eye.

Some gear J.B. didn't recognize was on wheels in a corner. Four three-legged stools were lined up along one of the cluttered counters.

"You do a lot of business? With glasses, I mean," he asked.

"Sure. No matter what, you've got people with failing vision. I do some work with contact lenses, too, but those are much more troublesome to match up to an individual and finding proper cleaning fluid's a bitch," Clarke replied as he peered intently at J.B.'s open eyes. His attention was drawn to the white slashes of the various adhesive bandages on J.B.'s frowning visage.

"What happened to your face, if you don't mind my asking?"

"Cut myself shaving."

"On your forehead?"

J.B. gave the optician a scathing look. "That's why I need glasses."

"Very well," Clarke said, letting the matter drop. "But I warn you now, you're going to have to talk to me if you want my help. I have no use for a man who grunts and speaks in monosyllables. If I'm to treat you, I must have your cooperation."

"Okay. I'm used to keeping my own counsel."

"You don't have to with me, not in here. Did you know that before predark, half the population of the United States wore some kind of glasses or corrective lenses?"

"Half?" J.B. said dubiously. "Don't see that many people running around with specs anymore."

"I know. In those days, increased life expectancy was the cause for the added eyestrain. See, around, oh, I don't know, the year 1900 or so, the average life span of an American was only forty-seven years. More disease and harder work combined to kill a man much earlier then, and this was around the same time when his vision began to fail anyway due to natural causes."

"Everything's got to wear out," J.B. said.

"Agreed," Clarke replied. "However, by the year 2000, a man's life span had increased to seventy-five years."

"Really."

"Yes. So, not only were people living longer, but they were better educated, which meant more reading, and much of the technology was vision driven, which caused even more wear on the eyes. Television and comp monitors. Very bad."

"Not anymore," J.B. remarked wryly..

Clarke continued with the explanation. "Then, after we managed to take out most of civilization with nukes and chems and God knows what else, another hundred years pass and in a century's time the life expectancy rate has dropped to a dreadfully low figure."

"How do you figure that?"

"I keep my own records. No census bureau to track it anymore," Clarke said breezily. He gestured to one of the stools. "Now, please sit over there, on the edge of the stool, and face me."

J.B. did as he was told, grateful the stool was covered with a spongy yellow pad.

"I'm going to hold up a finger—"

"I'm not drunk, Doc."

"This isn't a sobriety test," the optician replied with a smile. "This is for ocular movement. When I hold up my finger, please watch it as I move it back and forth. Keep your eyes glued to the finger, but don't move your head."

"All right."

Clarke continued to speak as he moved the finger in a broad H-shaped motion. "I would daresay due to disease and malnutrition, even with today's shorter life spans, many men and women could use a pair of glasses. Children, too. But expense and ignorance conspire to keep them trapped in their self-imposed blur, squinting and straining to the see the world around them.''

J.B. thought of some of the squalid conditions of the villes and outposts he'd traveled through, and of the faces of the poor and helpless he'd seen. ''There are parts of Deathlands where lousy vision could be considered a blessing, Doc,'' he said quietly.

''Quite. When did you receive your first pair of eyeglasses, Mr. Dix?'' the optician replied, mirroring Ryan's question from earlier that day.

''Way back. I'd noticed my vision was starting to go in my early teens. I was having trouble with distance, but up close was fine. Reading wasn't getting harder.''

''Wait—you read?'' Clarke asked in a surprised tone of voice.

J.B. glared at the doctor. ''Hell, yes, I read.''

''No reason for anger, Mr. Dix. Just making sure for my records. What do you like to read?''

''Information on blasters. Rifle and pistol journals. Blaster specs. Anything I can find, use, and tuck away in my brain. Even the history of the weapons long gone and extinct. I like to know about them all, just in case I ever do see one.''

''Practical, I suppose.''

''Damn straight. But like I say, my eyes were starting to bother me, so I'd been trying to figure out how to get some specs. Then I got lucky. I got them in a trade. Rolling medicine man in a horse-drawn wag. Had pills, needles, bottles and a big steamer trunk of glasses. I sat down and started trying on pairs until I found a set that worked. The guy had been around and seemed to stay out of trouble since he was legit. Lots of bullshit artists pretending to be docs, Doc,'' J.B. said pointedly.

"Yes, I've met a few," Clarke replied, unruffled. "So, you knew even then your vision needed correcting?"

"Like I said, it wasn't so bad then. I could read fine. Needed help seeing far off, but I could shoot if I squinted down hard and refocused."

"I had wondered by your demeanor and weaponry if you might be a sec man. With your reading interests, that confirms my suspicions."

"I just try to get by, and I need my eyes to do it."

"Would you read the letters off the chart on the wall behind me, please?" Clarke stood and took a thin wooden pointer. He gestured with it to the top of the chart. "Start with the third line."

J.B. automatically squinted and said, "*Q, G, T, X.*"

Clarke rapped the stick on the chart, creating a popping sound on the heavy paper. "Without squinting, please."

J.B. had to make himself not follow the reflex. "*Q, G, T, X,*" he said, as much from memory as actually being able to see the printing.

The optician lowered the pointer. "Fourth line."

"*E, D, O*—no, wait, *Q, P.*"

"Fifth line."

"*B, U,* or is that a *V?* Shit, those letters are tiny."

Clarke didn't respond. He lowered the pointer to the next level. "Sixth line."

J.B. didn't reply. He squinted, waiting for Clarke to tell him to stop. Not that an admonishment from the doctor would have mattered since the squinting didn't help.

"I can't see the sixth line," J.B. admitted.

"Very well." Clarke stepped to one side and wheeled over a large device that appeared to be a high-tech pair of binoculars mounted on a bracket between two enormous steel drums, one per side. He rolled the unwieldy apparatus up to J.B.'s face and lowered the binocular section until it was even with the Armorer's eyes.

"Is that bad, not being able to see that line?" J.B. asked.

"No. I wish you still had your other pair of spectacles so I could compare your vision with and without them, but we'll have to make do."

"What's this hunk of metal I'm peeping through?"

"This is a corrector, Mr. Dix. I am going to switch by hand various kinds of lenses inside this device until you are able to see the eye chart more clearly. This is a much quicker way and can be handled without putting on and taking off a thousand pairs of glasses. We'll start with the right eye. Each time I change the lenses, let me know if you can see better, or if the lens has decreased your vision even further."

Several minutes passed, with J.B. informing Clarke which lens worked best. The small man made notes on a sheet of paper as he worked. Finally he opened both sides of the binocularlike device and allowed J.B. to peer through at the same time.

"This is great," the Armorer said enthusiastically.

"I can see even better than I could with my old glasses."

"I'm not surprised. Vision changes over time, Mr. Dix. Still, twenty-forty vision in one eye and twenty-thirty in the other with corrective lenses isn't very good eyesight."

"Good enough for me."

Clarke wheeled the correction mechanism back to the corner and took up his seated position in front of J.B. once more.

"Now comes the hard part," he said. "I have to find an existing pair of lenses and frames. I have no way of manufacturing or cutting the glass myself."

"Actually I need two pairs. How do you get glasses, anyway?"

"I buy them. I have a standing offer of jack for any pair of prescription glasses in decent condition. One fellow brings in pairs by the dozens." While talking, Clarke picked up an eye patch from the table.

"What's the patch for? I thought we were finished," J.B. asked.

"It's not a patch, it's an occluder. I'm going to run an accommodative and convergence test. At your age, you need to know what kind of physical shape your eyes are in, and a few more tests will give you a complete exam," the optician replied. He paused and shrugged. "Well, as complete as I can do anyway. We might as well finish. You *are* paying for the package."

"Guess so. Go ahead, then."

A reader card was moved up to each of J.B.'s eyes while the test was conducted. Clarke then used a

pocket pencil flash to see if his patient's pupils responded properly by constricting.

"Mmm," Clarke said. "Your left eye, which is your strong eye, isn't responding according to procedure."

"What does that mean?"

"I want you to be honest with me. Your future eyesight may depend on it. I need to know when you first noticed that your glasses perhaps weren't as effective as before. Take firing with your blaster, for example. Are shots you were making previously now taking longer to line up? Are they as accurate as before?"

"Well, I suppose I noticed some vision loss a year back. Mebbe two. Hard to say."

"I understand. On a day-to-day basis, one doesn't notice such things," Clarke replied. "Describe what you are seeing right now."

J.B. snorted. "Well, I see you."

"You're looking directly at me. Use your peripheral vision. What's to the left? No, dammit, don't move your head!"

J.B. froze, angered by the doctor's outburst, and angered by what the optician had stumbled onto, a deep secret the Armorer hadn't even dared admit to himself.

"I—I— Doc, I don't know," J.B. whispered. "I can't see to the left all that well."

Clarke kept his voice modulated, professional. "To the right?"

J.B. hesitated before answering, "Even worse."

"Yet straight on?" Clarke stepped out and faced him.

"I see good. Perfect with those lenses you tried out."

"The loss of some of your peripheral vision, is it like looking down a tunnel at times, Mr. Dix?"

"Yeah. Exactly. Some days it doesn't bother me at all. Other times I have to be careful. Hasn't been life-threatening yet."

"I fear it will be depending on when it flares up and what your situation entails. Have you told anyone about the problem? Your lady companion?"

"No."

"Why not?"

"Why worry her? I use my eyes constantly. Last thing my friends need is a half-blind buddy doggin' their heels," J.B. said, and then he glared at the blurry image of Clarke he could see before him. "You know what this is, don't you?"

The doctor hedged. "Without proper testing, I can't be sure—"

"So, do the test!" J.B. snapped.

"I can't. I would need a measurement of the intra-ocular pressure of the eye to be able to say for sure. The process is called tonometry, and it involves a special probe and I don't have the device. Even if I did, I'm not sure how to perform the test correctly. Your cornea would have to be anesthetized, for one thing, and such procedures are beyond me."

J.B. sighed deeply, dreading what else the optician had to say and needing to hear it all the same. "So, what's causing the problem?"

Clarke stood up and opened a cabinet, removing a well-worn green hardcover book with full-color illustrations of the human eye. He pointed to various ones as he explained. "High pressure inside the eye causes damage to the optic nerve, Mr. Dix. Understand, your eyes, all of our eyes, have a remarkable drainage system. Fluid comes in and goes out from within the eyeball, keeping the pressure consistent and higher than that of the outside atmosphere so the eye doesn't collapse."

"Like diving, when you're underwater. Come up too fast, you get the bends."

"Yes. Like that. What has happened here is that your drainage system has gotten clogged. Continual pressure creates a subsequent loss of the visual field, which is what is creating your 'tunnel vision.'" Clarke hesitated, and licked his lips. "This condition is called glaucoma, and it sounds like you've progressed beyond the early stages."

"Dark night." When J.B. spoke the words, even he was aware of the black humor the epithet now held.

"It's not your fault, Mr. Dix. The process is gradual and insidious. You might have decided your continual loss of sight was due to age or old glasses. It's not like you woke up one morning completely blind and had to deal with the problem that way. From what I've read, and the other cases I've encountered, there isn't a damn thing you could have done to stop it from happening."

J.B. stood up, pacing the room. "No cure?"

"There were medicines once. Eye drops. Even surgery. All lost. I can tell you what needs to be done, but I can't help you in doing it. New glasses, yes. Those, I can find. Surgery or medicine, no. I'm not trained and I don't have the drugs.''

"Yeah, pulling the glasses off a dead man's eyes doesn't take much in the way of brains," J.B. said angrily.

"I perform a service," Clarke said. "You don't have to get nasty about my methods. There are no longer any one-hour eyeglass-manufacturing stores. I'm telling you like it is. Without more tests, I'd still be guessing to the extent of the damage. From the journals I've studied, this disorder is so highly individualistic that treatment had to be specifically tailored to each patient's condition.''

"There's got to be something I can do to stop this," the Armorer said.

"Well, there is to a small degree. Existing nerve-fiber damage is irreversible, but you can try and slow down any further injury. Some people have higher than normal pressure in their eyes due to their blood pressure, alcohol abuse and stress. You need to keep the pressure down as best you can manage.''

"My blood pressure is okay and I'm not an alky, but I tend to spend a lot of my life under stress," J.B. stated, still standing and pacing.

"I can tell you that one characteristic of the disease is that pressure within the eye is caused due to changes in the rate of aqueous-humor formation—''

"What's that?" J.B. asked, cutting the man off.

"The fluid buildup, Mr. Dix," Clarke said patiently in the warmest vocal register he could summon up.

"It fluctuates during the day, usually high in the morning, less as the day goes on and it declines during the night. When you're sleeping, it declines even more."

"Guess I should look into joining the freezie program," J.B. remarked bitterly.

"Temperature doesn't affect the pressure one way or the other," Clarke said, misunderstanding the reference.

"How long? How long until I go completely blind?"

"There's no way of knowing. A year? Ten years? Twenty? All cases are different. With treatment, we could end this immediately. Without it, who can say?"

J.B. pondered this for a long moment.

"Well, a man I used to know once told me, 'If it ain't broke, don't fix it.' I'm still one of the best shots in Deathlands and by God, that's something. And I still see pretty damn good, too, or I will once you fix me up with some new specs."

"Yes. I can do that."

The Armorer pulled out the twisted remains of his other pair. "Why don't we find some that look like these."

"I'll do my best."

J.B. reached out and caught the shorter man by the shoulder, turning him.

"And Dr. Clarke? This is our little secret."

The doctor shrugged. "Very well."

Chapter Fourteen

The wooden sign that ran along the length of the storefront was painted in bright hues of orange, green and blue, with cutout sound-effect icons such as Pow and Biff and Zonk decorating the corners in a three-dimensional effect.

"Kollector's Kloset," Dean read.

"Yet another example of the wretched spelling to be found across Deathlands." Doc sighed from his vantage point next to the boy. "Eventually I fear the human race will ultimately regress to painting pictographs in dyes made of blood and dung on dank cave walls."

"And fighting with clubs and stones, eh, Doc?" Krysty said.

"Why not?" Ryan said thoughtfully, allowing himself to see the philosophical side of life after his pit battle. "The world's got to run out of ammo sooner or later. Then we're all reduced to fighting in bearskins."

"Indeed," Doc agreed.

"I don't think the guy who runs this place is that stupid, Doc. I think the owner is trying to make some kind of statement," Krysty said.

None of the group could see inside the store very well, since the front display windows and door were covered in layers and layers of old faded paper posters, featuring drawings of colorfully attired characters with names like Wolverine and Batman. It was hard to fully read any of the advertisement in the collagelike display. It seemed that once one poster had served out its time in the shop's display, the owner merely pasted up another on top instead of taking down the earlier one, giving the windows a curious checkerboard pattern of overlapping designs.

"*The X-Men,*" Dean read off one poster. "Mutant Hope In A World Gone Mad. Twenty Monthly Titles For Your Reading Excitement, Only From The House Of Ideas. What a load of crap. Those guys in the funny suits are norms. They sure aren't like any muties I ever saw."

"Nor are any of those women," Krysty added.

"Mutant tits," Jak said.

"Wait, I have heard of this Batman," Doc said. "He was what they once called a superhero. His costume was worn to strike terror in the hearts of evil men."

"No kidding?" Ryan said. "Was he a fancy sec man or what?"

"No, no, Ryan, you misunderstand. Batman was a fictional creation who appeared in comic books for the delight of the under-eighteen set."

"Meaning?"

"Children's entertainment," Doc said succinctly.

"We've got time," Ryan mused, glancing at his wrist chron. "You want to go in for a look, Dean? Better than standing out here in the mall with our thumbs up our asses waiting on J.B."

"Yeah! All right," Dean eagerly agreed, "That would be a hot pipe, Dad!"

Before the boy could open the door to the store, Ryan held out a hand. "Hold up. The window's so crowded, we can't see in. Let me take a quick look first."

He pulled open the glass entrance and stuck his head through. He felt half-silly doing a recce inside a place obviously designed to be a spot for what Doc had told him was the entertainment of half-wits and children, but he knew from hard experience that nothing was ever as it seemed in the Deathlands.

Still, his eye wasn't ready for a sight such as this.

From floor to ceiling were off-white cardboard boxes filled with magazines, wall pegs adorned with packaged miniature toys and games, racks of compact discs and black vinyl LPs, and an array of other colorful debris that Ryan didn't even pretend to recognize. Even the surface of the drop ceiling was adorned with more of the posters as seen on the front of the establishment. As Ryan stepped through the glass door into the morass, a tinkly bell jingled overhead to announce his arrival.

"Wasn't kidding about the closet part in the name of this place, lover," Krysty said, walking in close behind him. "Going to be crowded in here."

"Feel anything?" Ryan asked, hoping Krysty's latent psi abilities might pick out any dangers hidden behind the crowded piles of boxes.

"Just claustrophobic. Only danger here as far as I can tell is mebbe having something fall on you."

Ryan glanced back and grinned. "You break it, you bought it, darlin'."

"Wow," Dean breathed, his eyes open wide. "Look at all this stuff!"

Ryan pressed forward, allowing the others to come inside the small pathway that wound its way along the store's contents to the back counter.

"That smell," Doc whispered. "Wait, let me place it in the proper context!"

Jak wrinkled his nose. "Stinks. Smell sweat."

"Yeah, somebody needs to wash their ass," Dean agreed.

"No, I speak not of the stench of unwashed flesh, young Cawdor. I'm talking about the heavenly aroma of old paper. Rotting pulp."

"Dust, you mean," Krysty said, running a finger along a box top and bringing it up coated with fine dirt.

The smell was unfamiliar. In the Deathlands it was quite unusual to find much in the way of printed material, new or old. The larger villes might have their own little news sheets run off on antique printing presses—Doc had spied a version of this in Freedom and had happily grabbed one up in search of any printed information, only to find it was a series of advertisements for the endless array of mall stores—but in the poorer sections, more often than not paper was viewed as nothing more than useful kindling or toilet tissue.

As for older, predark vintage books and magazines, most of the paper goods had long since crumbled into dust due to the abnormal weather conditions around the globe or vanished into nothingness in the long nuclear winter immediately following skydark. There were rare exceptions, the odd baron and a hoard of books.

A fair estimate of the general populace of Deathlands would probably put most men and women in the category of the functionally illiterate. There was no time for reading for the enjoyment of books, nor was there a viable system of delivering written letters or messages. Written contracts with signatures were a thing of the past, except for barons who delighted in thrusting papers down for hired help to make their signature mark without even knowing what agreements such contracts contained.

Kollector's Kloset contained the most pulp paper any of the group had ever seen. One wall was devoted to bagged examples of horror magazines. Ryan's eye traveled over the lurid covers before one caught his complete and undivided attention.

As he sighted the predark magazine, everyone heard a sound that was familiar yet disturbing all the same.

Ryan was laughing, a deep-from-the-gut laugh followed by a few guffaws and chuckles.

"You okay?" Jak asked carefully. The albino hadn't cared much for this shop from the beginning, and now Ryan's mirth was starting to set him more on edge. Ryan rarely laughed, unless it was in irony or bitterness.

This laughter was genuine, the kind that came without conscious thought or warning, the kind of natural laughter few people were able to give of themselves.

Ryan nodded toward the wall of monster magazines. "Check out the one on the bottom left there," he said, still amused. "Does the ghoul on the front in the fancy knee britches look familiar to anybody besides me?"

Dean's young voice was the next to ring out in laughter, followed in turn by Krysty's chuckling, then Jak's bark of surprise and amusement. Unable to contain his curiosity, Doc bent over and peered intently at the indicated magazine cover. The colors were lurid green on mustard yellow. The center of the cover was dominated by a tall, spindly man dressed in a long greenish coat with a lean face, hawk nose and thinning white hair. The man was waving a hand in a gesture of entry into the magazine's interior.

"*Creepy,*" Doc read off the top of the cover. "*Creepy Magazine.*"

"You forget the rest, Doc," Ryan added, reading the blurb next to the figure. "Says here that Uncle Creepy Welcomes You Inside."

"Yes, yes, I see that. What I am missing is the implied humor."

"That Uncle Creepy…he looks just like you, Doc!" Dean piped up, in a gale of giggling.

Doc frowned. "Nonsense! This fellow looks nothing like the proud countenance of—"

"Quiet!" Ryan whispered. "Somebody's in the back. I guess the guy who owns the place finally decided to make an appearance."

Ryan's words were proven true when a fat, bearded man-child waddled out from a back room and took up a stance behind the long row of glass showcases.

He looked to be carrying about three-hundred-plus pounds on his five-foot-four-inch frame. His hair was long and greasy, and appeared to have been dyed a phony jet black that never existed in nature. His beard was also the same unnatural color of night. He wore a T-shirt two sizes too small. On the shirt was a picture of a tall man with pointed ears spouting the command Live Long And Prosper.

Some dark brown gravy stains also adorned the shop owner's attire above the moon white expanse of flesh visible between his shirttail and waistband.

Ryan kept expecting him to knock over one of the many precariously stacked piles of books, toys and junk with either his wide ass or wider stomach, but he was nimble and seemed to possess an uncanny sense of grace when it came to navigating the store's many possessions.

"Greetings and salutations. My name is Chet. I am the proprietor of this, my humble establishment," the bearded man said. "Welcome to the finest array of predark comics and collectibles on the East Coast. If we don't have what you're looking for, we can find it for you with our search service for a small fee."

"More fees," Jak sniffed.

"Pardon me," Doc said, moving to the counter. "I cannot help but notice you deal in paper goods."

"Whoa, you are quite the elder," Chet said, staggering back and holding a hand over his heart as he got his first clear look at Doc. "Hey! Anybody ever tell you that you look just like Uncle Cree—"

"No! No, they have not."

"Oh, okay. Man, a guy your age, I bet you've got a bitching collection."

"Only of memories, my rotund friend, and those are getting harder and harder to find as time goes on," Doc said wistfully. "Alas, I now have no place to call home to keep my possessions. All I have is what I carry."

"Say, that's a real flashback of a mack daddy jacket you're wearing," Chet said, pointing at the lapels of Doc's frock coat. "Very retro. Need to get you an ascot or neck kerchief and you'd be humming."

"Before you ask, no, my coat is not for sale, especially to one such as yourself."

Chet didn't get the implied insult. "Suit yourself. I wouldn't give it up, either. My problem is finding apparel that will fit my ample girth," the fat clerk said.

"That's what tailors are for, my good man," Doc noted.

"Tailors cost jack. Any jack I get I spend on collecting," Chet replied, nodding his three chins as he spoke. "All the good stuff is going up in value. Used to be, I put the word out for baseball cards or comic books and within a month I'd have more than I could handle from outlanders and wanderers going back and forth across Deathlands. Now, my best pickers can't find dick anymore. Everybody thinks this stuff is worth a fortune, and I can't afford to pay top jack to have to then turn around and resell it and make a profit anymore."

"Supply and demand," Krysty said.

"Exactly!" Chet replied. "All the stores in the mall are occupied. I cannot demand a break in my rent. Instead, I must weather the annual rent increases! Do you know what rent goes for in Freedom?"

"I've seen enough," Ryan said, already bored with the sales pitch. "Let's go."

"In a minute, Dad," Dean replied, his attention drawn to a rack covered with old-style wire coat hangers. An array of T-shirts was hanging from the rack.

"They got any black ones?" Jak asked, stepping over next to Dean as carefully as possible.

"They're all black," Dean replied, looking at some of the small white size tags in the collars. "All XXL, too."

"That's good," Krysty said. "Allows you to grow into them."

"I don't know," Ryan said, holding up one of the huge shirts. "I think a boy Dean's age could pitch a tent with one of these things."

"So what's your reading fancy, mister?" Chet said to Doc.

"So many choices," Doc said, searching his mind for a book he desired.

"I know. And you want to know why?" Chet asked.

"Why?"

And then the portly salesman launched into a dissertation the likes of which Doc had never heard before. Unlike most common reading material such as paperbacks or hardcover books, the mass-published glossy magazines or hundreds of daily newspapers on newsprint, comics had the quantum edge in survival. Starting in the mid-1950s, comics were no longer being seen as just childish diversions to be read and disposed of, but also as pop-culture collectibles to be hoarded.

As the years passed, more and more comics were kept stored away until finally, by the late seventies, practically every comic book sold off the stands was read once—or not at all—hermetically sealed in a plastic bag, kept flat by a specially cut piece of coated card stock and stored upright in a specially designed box to avoid any damage.

Millions of comics were kept safe in this fashion, with the more valuable examples receiving extraspecial care. Those were put in stiff Mylar snugs, which were then placed in acid-free archival boxes. Larger collectors even built their very own comics vaults, some aboveground, some below. All were airtight.

Compared to all their paper brethren, comic books lasted because of the extra care taken in the decades before skydark to keep them from deteriorating due to natural causes.

"Yes, well, that's all very nice," Doc said, taking the time to speak while Chet gasped for air after his verbal history of the comics. "But I was actually hoping to find a volume of Chaucer."

"What issues did he draw?" Chet asked. "Did he work for Marvel? D.C.? Dark Horse? Image?"

Doc gave up. He'd had enough. "He's not an artist, he's a writer, you overstuffed cretin."

"Sorry, I get those guys mixed up sometimes. Artists, writers, inkers, letterers—too many names. Got a title for this book?"

"The Canterbury Tales," Doc said respectfully.

Chet looked blank for a few seconds, then reached behind him and plucked a chipped brown clipboard from a stack of papers and consulted a list.

"Got *Marvel Tales, Weird Tales, Tales from the Darkside, Sonic's Pal Tails, Tale Spin, Shirt Tales* and *Tales Guaranteed to Drive You Bats,* but nope, no *Canterbury Tales.* Sorry. Hold up, I missed one. *A Tale of Two Cites.*"

"Dickens!" Doc cried. "Let me view it, please!"

Chet consulted the list a second time. "Box 63-A, Row F," he read before wading out and pulling down a box from a wooden rack. He removed the lid, and inside were bagged and boarded comics. He pulled one out and handed it over with a flourish to Doc.

He stared down at the cover. *"Classics Illustrated?"* he snorted.

"Don't get a call for those, anymore. You are a man of taste."

"Wait, wait a moment," Doc said, struggling to communicate. His entire skinny frame nearly shook with frustration. "I don't believe we're on the same page, to coin a phrase. I see all of the men's magazines and juvenile antics of the comics, and I appreciate your discovery of this crudely drawn mockery of the good Charles Dickens, but I wonder…dare I ask…if you have *any* books at all?"

Chet looked insulted. "Of course!"

"Splendid," Doc said with relief in his educator's voice. "What kind?"

Chet started counting down on his fingers again before launching into a litany of selections in a merry singsong voice. "What kind? We got Big Little Books, Golden Books, Tell-Me-a-Story books, black-and-white *and* color Graphic Novels—both original and reprints, Whitman Tell-a-Tale, Wonder Books, talking story books, but I'm afraid they no longer talk when you pull the string, and a near complete line of every TV-paperback tie-in known to the historians."

"Really."

"You bet! What kind you wanting?"

"I believe I'm in need of that rare animal—a *book* book."

"A *book* book? Never heard of it."

"I'm not surprised," Doc sniffed, and turned on his heel to exit.

Chapter Fifteen

According to the locals, the best place for food in Freedom where the food was worth a damn was a former eatery, one of a chain specializing in Southwest cooking. The exterior and interior of the crowded former fast-food restaurant had been repainted in shades of green, but there was no disguising the faux-Tex-Mex building facade and architecture.

Mildred and J.B. were seated at a black metal mesh table with a wooden top, watching the people and waiting for their friends to join them.

"Make A Run For The Border," Mildred quoted, a fragment of cultural memory floating up, untethered, to the surface of her conscious mind. "That used to be this place's advertised motto."

"Skipping borders is bad news. Why would they want you to do that?" J.B asked. "They some kind of food smugglers or what?"

"I always believed it referred to the eventual run to the bathroom," Mildred replied with as straight a face as she could manage. "Tacos could be hard on the stomach of the uninitiated."

The Armorer glanced down at his wrist chron. "I'm hungry. Wonder where the others are? Not like Ryan to be late."

"We're in a shopping mall, J.B. No man, woman or child ever made it on time to a meeting place in a mall, especially one as huge as this," the woman replied lightly. "Ryan'll be along. He's probably being held up by Dean and Doc wanting to go into every store they pass."

"And Krysty and Jak," J.B. agreed. "Something in this gussied-up warehouse for everybody."

Mildred reached up and took off the new pair of glasses. "How are your eyes feeling, John?"

"Good," he replied. "Real good. That eye doc was true to his word in finding me a new pair similar to my old ones. These feel a bit thicker than my other pair, but other than that, my vision's as good as it ever was."

"The glass is thicker because your eyes are getting weaker. Comes with age."

"Bullshit," the Armorer replied. "If losing your eyesight comes with age, Doc would be tripping and falling on his skinny ass everywhere we went."

"I heard that, John Barrymore!" Doc boomed out in his most able educator's tone of voice. "I will have you know my skinny posterior remains upright, thank you very much."

"Age sure as hell hasn't affected his hearing," J.B. groused, causing Mildred to laugh as the rest of the group took up positions around the ornate bench.

"Look same," Jak said, peering at J.B.'s glasses.

"They are, practically. Got a backup pair, too."

"Let's see the backups," Ryan said, rubbing his still aching shoulder. "I want to know what my duel with a bot paid for."

"Bot?" Doc echoed. "Ah, yes, the killer robot."

J.B. had hesitated, and now Mildred spoke for him. "Well, Ryan, the backup lenses and frames are much larger than this pair."

"So?"

"So, he doesn't think his backup pair of specs are very becoming to a man with his features."

"Oh, now I've got to see them," Ryan said.

The rest of the group voiced their agreement.

Sighing loudly, J.B. made a show of searching through each and every pocket of his leather jacket before removing a black padded case.

Off came the wire spectacles, which he placed gently on the tabletop.

He snapped open the new black case and removed an oversize pair of purple frames and tinted lenses, which he angrily thrust on his frowning face.

"There. Happy?"

"You bet," Ryan replied, trying hard not to laugh. No one else looking at the bizarre sight shared Ryan's tact. The rest of the friends broke out in guffaws of amusement.

"Laugh all you want. I think he looks like a rock star," Mildred stated proudly, taking J.B.'s arm.

"Oh, hell," J.B. said from between clenched teeth.

The Armorer's discomfort was eased when Mildred noticed Dean's new attire. The boy was wearing a black T-shirt featuring a mass of silvery storm clouds and lightning superimposed over a large, unblinking single eye. The Truth Is Out There was at the bottom of the shirt's hem, and on the back, in a broken-typewriter font, another slogan read Trust No One.

"Krysty and Dad liked this one," Dean said, turning and modeling for J.B. and Mildred.

Krysty shrugged. "What can I say? The message struck me right funny. Guess if you keep looking long enough, you can find anything."

"Well, I liked the back," Ryan said, picking up the lull. "Trust No One might seem paranoid to some, but I decided that was a sentiment I could agree with without any debate."

J.B. agreed. "Damn good advice for any halfway intelligent citizen of Deathlands."

Mildred wrinkled her nose. "True, most of the time. Otherwise it's kind of negative, don't you think?"

"Hell, it beat the other shirts that fat guy was selling. What were they, Dean?"

"Um, most of them had a yellow mutie with a spiked head saying Eat My Shorts. He had a lot of those. None of them had ever been worn, he said. Had a few with a man dressed like a bug. Some with guys playing predark sports, like basketball. Triple dull. This was the best of the bunch."

"I can attest to that," Doc agreed. "That store owner was an idiot, and his collection of moldy paper useless."

"Tried to get Jak to take him a shirt, but he wasn't interested."

"Like clothes no message," Jak replied. "Wanted black shirt. All had stupid shit pix."

THE INTERIOR of the eatery had been designed to replicate what some predark advertising executive had distilled into being a Mexican dining experience. There were no primary colors to be seen. The dominant hue was brown. All shades of brown. Dark brown walnut. Light brown walls hinting at adobe stone. Off-white flooring with a grit pattern of brown dots broken up by horizontal and vertical chestnut brown lines.

The tables matched the decor, but the chairs, which were standard-issue steel folding chairs, had obviously been replaced at one time or another. The front counter was made of stainless steel, low slung, with indentations where automated cash registers once rested. Now hungry patrons waited in line to verbally give their order to a single cashier.

Both cashier and her small comp console were encased inside a massive armaglass sec booth.

A slot allowed the passing of jack. After payment the order was called back to the hidden cooks in the rear. Once the order was given, a customer then was allowed to go down the counter to await his or her food.

"This damn well better be good. I hate waiting in line," Ryan announced.

"Where are the menus?" Doc asked.

"Up there. Above the woman taking the orders," J.B. said, pointing out the hand-lettered displays hanging from the ceiling. "Nice to be able to read fine print from a distance again."

"At least the selection is generous," Doc remarked, his lips moving as he read off some of the offering on the day's menu.

"Hey! Glazed ham!" Dean said eagerly.

"Pricey," Ryan said, reading the listed amounts for various meals. "Still, I guess we're entitled to one good meal. I know I am. Order what you want."

"Bless my fragile soul, but is that a listing for a bowl of pinto beans?" Doc asked.

As the group looked over the menu, Ryan took in the rest of the restaurant. The interior was crowded to near bursting, and filled not only with a wide variety of customers, but with their overlapping conversations, as well, all of which seemed to blur together into a single mass hum that phased in and out between being uncomfortable and unnoticeable.

There wasn't an empty seat in the house. Older men seemed to have claimed the long metal countertop bar that ran along the left windowless wall, all of them busy at their plates, shoveling forkfuls of food into their mouths. The tables and booths were also all occupied with people of all races. While the food appeared to vary, the only beverages being offered seemed to be water or coffee sub.

Unlike any other ville Ryan had ever visited, none of the inhabitants had paid attention to a new group of seven walking into the eatery. Jak got a curious glance or two, and that was all.

A table filled with the forest greens of the mall sec force occupied a corner table, a good location Ryan would have chosen for himself if there had been room. From the vantage point the sec men had chosen, they could see anyone who came into the place, as well as having a good view of the dual kitchen doors to the back. Two of the men stared back at Ryan as the one-eyed man gave them the once-over.

"No good, this," Jak griped. "Many people. Hard see, hard hear. Dangerous."

"My daddy always used to tell me, the more people in a restaurant, the better the food was," Mildred said. "And I'm starved."

"So let's eat," Ryan stated, striding across the floor to the line waiting for service at the counter.

WHEN THEIR ORDERS were delivered, the friends decided to go into the central food court outside. Carrying their trays carefully, they looked for a place to sit. Ryan chose a table near a wall so they could be guaranteed of having one section safe. J.B. sat on his left and Dean on his right. Krysty took the chair next to Dean. Jak, Doc and Mildred completed the circle.

Their meals showed off variety. All of them drank coffee sub or water or both, but they differed in food selections. Ryan had gone for a hunk of steak smothered in thick brown gravy, with mashed potatoes and green peas, while Krysty asked for and got a massive salad covered in dressing and bread crumbs. Dean had selected his glazed ham and fried apples. Mildred chose breakfast—scrambled eggs, strips of bacon, spicy hash brown potatoes and dark toasted bread. J.B. also got eggs, but had his fried, with a side of chewy sausage patties and more of the bread.

Nothing elaborate, but it was all good, filling food.

Doc—for some reason—had selected his bowl of pinto beans smothered in onions with a generous helping of corn bread on the side.

"I've never had a tastier platter of beans," Doc said with relish once his meal was done. "This reminds me," he started out, "of another fine occasion—"

"No, no reminders," Dean said hastily. "Doc, I like it fine here. Let me enjoy it!" he pleaded.

"Are you saying my company is less than stellar, young Cawdor?" Doc responded haughtily over the rim of his coffee cup. "And I thought I contributed to the boy's education," he added with a hurt air to Ryan.

Krysty spoke up quickly. "Dean's a growing boy, Doc. He needs more in the way of nightly entertainment than another discussion of the Crusades or the finer points of whether that Poe fella's poetry was as good as his short stories."

"They were. Perhaps his verse was even superior to his prose," Doc said crisply through sips of the brew. "The good Mr. Brody only started Dean's education. Alas, I fear the majority of the knowledge he needs to be well-rounded must come from within our merry little band of rogues. As the only educator here, I must accept my responsibility for his future development."

"Wish I had another cup of this coffee," J.B. said, looking down through his new specs at the bottom of the empty mug. "But I sure as hell don't feel like getting back in that line for a refill."

"Me, too. Times like this, I miss having a waitress," Krysty mused.

"Yeah, like that Sandy girl. The one we ran into back in Florida at that weird-ass Tuckey's roadhouse," J.B. said.

"Don't remind me," Mildred said with a laugh. "I still carry visions of that horrible orange decor."

"And of the mysterious pecan-nut log," Doc said wistfully. "If only I'd been allowed a taste..."

"One bite and you'd probably still be back down in Florida, six feet under," Mildred told him. "I told you those damn things were probably over 150 years old."

"But preserved, perfectly preserved in their shiny red-and-white-plastic wrappers. I still wonder what treasures were hidden inside."

"A salty brown lump hard enough to bash a man's skull in—or break out a few pearly white teeth."

"Good ol' Tuckey's! Yum! Real stickie meat!" Dean added, getting caught up in the humor. "Visit Our Pettin Zoo—Real Live Mutents!"

"I see it left an impression on one of us, anyway," Krysty commented.

Still riding the high after the stress of the pitfight, Ryan gave in to a streak of humor and irony he didn't often indulge in. "Okay, okay," he said, raising a hand. "So the place was lacking in some of the refinements. But the food was good and we'd gotten off without any trouble if those four clowns in the fancy Western duds hadn't come in wanting to pick a fight."

"Still say you should have let me pet the muties, Dad."

"Pet a mutie and you come back a few fingers shy of a hand, Dean."

USING HIS NEWFOUND STATUS as the big winner of the day, Ryan decided to go ahead and stock up on as many supplies as their line of Freedom Mall credit would allow. He imagined it would be some time before they encountered a ville with such a wide variety of choices. At Krysty's suggestion, after their gutbusting meal, they went in search of some food that was practical to carry around in the less-than-ideal conditions of the Deathlands.

"Save some worry if we buy now," Krysty said. "And it's not often we have such choice."

First off was a stop at one of the numerous markets that lined the interior corridors of the mall in search of supplies that would travel well, like jerky and dried fruit, and Ryan even allowed himself the luxury of buying a box of ribbon-striped stick candy for special occasions. Doc was big on banana chips, and Ryan had to restrain him from stuffing his pockets to bursting with the yellowish crispy treats.

Some potato chips for immediate consumption, a few pull tabs of water, a canvas bag of coffee sub and a box of crackers divided among the group ended the food-shopping spree. All wanted to take along more, but knew overloading themselves with more than they could comfortably carry would prove wasteful in the long run.

Besides Dean's new shirt, which was an admitted impulse buy, the only clothing any of the group really needed was fresh socks and underwear. A shop called Under the Covers provided long tables stacked high with plastic-wrapped supplies of socks.

"North Carolina used to be big on textiles," one of the shop clerks explained. "There was a small ville up north from here called Mount Airy. All they did was have factories churning out boxes of socks. I'll bet there's more socks in this part of the world than in all of Deathlands. The thing is, you take what sizes are left.''

Ryan eyeballed the chirpy salesgirl. "Will do,'' he said, and moved away as she pressed too close for comfort.

Underwear took some extra looking, and there were no bras to be found for the women. Trying to help conserve funds, Doc made a show of announcing he was sticking with his genuine one-of-a-kind long johns.

"Keep wearing those moldy old drawers, and they're going to adhere to you like a second skin, Doc,'' Mildred retorted. "One of these nights, I'll have to surgically remove the smelly things!''

"Smelly? You dare cast aspersions on my cleanliness, woman?'' Doc boomed in his best outraged tone of voice. He struck a lecturer's pose, one hand on his hip and the other tugging at the lapel of his frock coat.

"Now you've gone and done it,'' J.B. said sadly.

"I will have you know my personal hygiene is beyond reproach! On occasion, this extra layer of clothing I wear might be a burden during times of warmth, but who is the one enjoying the insulation when a brittle chill settles down around us at night? Dr. Theophilus Algernon Tanner, that's who!''

"Alas,'' Mildred retorted, sarcastically lifting the back of her hand to her brow and striking a shrinking-violet pose. "Once again I, Dr. Mildred Winona Wyeth, have been struck down by the irrefutable logic of a doddering old fool in a threadbare pair of long johns! What can I do but admit defeat! Defeat!''

Doc gave Mildred a withering look. ''At last she admits it. I have witnesses. Witnesses! Ryan, we must race posthaste to a notary public so that I might have this moment legally documented and signed!''

''No can do, Doc,'' Ryan said, shaking his head. ''I'll pony up for a pair of black socks for your feet, though.''

Doc bowed at the waist. ''You are a kind man, my dear Ryan. Much too kind.''

The place was wearing on everybody, and once the needed items were located, Ryan plunked down the charge chit for all.

''Another thing,'' J.B. said. ''We need to stock up on some ammo if prices aren't too high.''

''Only one way to find out,'' Ryan agreed.

Strangely enough, when they reached the designated area for blasters and ammunition, the storefront was abandoned. Closed. Empty. J.B. checked with the shop's neighbors and discovered it had sold out the inventory over a month earlier. The owner hadn't been seen since.

''What you think happened, Dad?'' Dean asked after the Armorer returned with the bad news.

''Don't know, son,'' Ryan replied. ''I do know one thing, though.''

''What?''

''We're going to have to continue to conserve on bullets.''

Chapter Sixteen

Upon his return to Freedom Center Station, Ryan had gratefully stripped out of his clothing and stepped into the shower stall to examine his injuries: minor cuts and contusions; two broken toes; a lump the size of a robin's egg on the back of his skull; a shoulder turning even darker colors of blue and purple. Even his tongue hurt, where his teeth had slammed on it when the android threw him into the wall of the pit.

Ryan turned the faucet, praying for a long hot shower.

What he got was a trickle of water that wasn't exactly cold, but sure as hell wasn't piping hot. The temperature was as tepid as it had been on the previous night. Ryan quickly washed his hair and body, wincing when he had to raise his twice-injured shoulder. The shower wasn't at all what he had hoped for.

He kept his face under the stream of water as long as he could stand it, then dried himself, taking extra care with the open socket where his ruined left eye had once been. Ryan slid the scuffed eye patch back on and stared at his reflection.

"I need a shave," he muttered, "but the hell with it."

Nude, he stepped out into the small bedroom adjoining the bath. Krysty was flipping through a small book with a cracked red leather binding she'd found in the drawer of the nightstand.

"What you reading?" he asked.

"*Holy Bible,*" she replied. "Been a while."

"Sure."

"'Placed here by the Gideons.'" Krysty read from the cover. "Wonder who they were? Some kind of traveling-preacher show? Mebbe they went from hotel to hotel, leaving Bibles all around to spread the word of God."

"Leaving behind the word of God instead of paying the bill, you mean," Ryan corrected.

"No, no, my Uncle Tyas McCann told me about missionaries back when I was a girl in Harmony. Went everywhere to spread the word. Good men and women who believed in something positive, not like those sick flagellants beating themselves to death hoping for heaven," she replied. "I think these Gideons must've done the same thing as missionaries."

Ryan shrugged. "Mebbe. Ask Doc, if you dare."

"No shave, lover?" the green-eyed woman asked softly as she ran the back of her hand along of one Ryan's sandpaper cheeks.

"Too tired," Ryan said, falling back on the mattress. "There's no hot water, either. You might want to run a bath and let it sit for a while. Least then you can bathe at room temperature. If this joint is the best the wondrous Freedom Mall has to offer, I'd hate to see the worst."

"I don't mind the stubble," the redhead replied, sitting down at the foot of the bed. "I'm used to the rugged look. Your toenails could use a clipping, however."

Ryan raised a leg up from the bed. "That damn sec droid took care of two of them. Got any scissors?"

"I think J.B. does, in one of his pockets. I never know what he's going to be pulling out to show off next. Don't want to bother him now, though."

Ryan and Krysty shared a knowing grin. Having a room with sheets, pillows and a real bed was a luxury, especially for a man and woman used to having to grab brief moments of lovemaking in roadside camps. And rarely did the chance arrive where the group felt secure enough to divide themselves up to allow the privacy needed for intimacy.

The previous night the pair had been too wiped to even think of sex. This night, however, even with his head still ringing from the droid battle, Ryan was more than ready for some loveplay.

And Krysty's own sexual appetites were even greater than his own.

"Close call, us being able to find an eye doc with lenses for J.B." Ryan said. "Can think of a thousand other places where we'd been up the creek, him breaking his glasses like that."

"I know."

"A man with poor eyesight doesn't have much of a chance when he's trying to stay alive in Deathlands. Get himself—and the ones around him—chilled in a triple hurry."

"We dealt with it as it came down, lover," Krysty replied. "Like we always have."

"Trader would've cut J.B. loose to find his own way."

"So what? As I've told you before, you're not Trader. You're better than he ever thought about being."

"Am I? Am I really?" Ryan asked. "In his own way, Trader was the most honorable man I ever met. Never did anybody wrong on a deal. Never traded some of the more deadlier stockpiles we found in those hideaways he was always so good at sniffing out. Hell, he could have earned enough jack to set up his own private little barony if he'd sold that supply of nerve gas we found."

"I never said he wasn't a man with some honor hidden away in a dark corner somewhere," Krysty replied. "I said you were his better, and nothing you say is going to change my mind about that, Ryan Cawdor."

While speaking, Krysty began to examine Ryan's offered foot and calf carefully, lightly running her fingers along the body hair growing there while looking at his toes. To Ryan, the sensation was akin to having five feathers run gently up and down his weary six-foot-plus frame. The woman at his feet turned and placed the lifted leg on one side of her hips, allowing herself full, unencumbered access between Ryan's legs.

"I must be slipping," she observed, staring at Ryan's crotch.

A timely fragment from Ryan's dream from the mat-trans jump popped into his mind. "'Not a creature was stirring,'" he said.

Krysty gave a lusty chuckle.

"Told you I was tired," Ryan added.

"Bullshit, Ryan. I've never known you not to be...up to satisfying our mutual sexual desires. What you need is a more direct approach." And on that statement, Krysty scooted back even farther, bending her head and allowing her full mane of red hair to obscure Ryan's view of what she was doing.

Not that he needed to have a picture drawn for him. His senses began to ignore his aches and pains from the sec-droid battle and devote their attentions to a new manner of bodily caress.

Krysty took him in her mouth, gently, softly lolling her tongue around and around the swelling corona of Ryan's rapidly extending manhood. He groaned. A gentle suction pulled at him as Krysty inhaled, while still keeping her tongue in rapid motion like a trapped hummingbird.

Such a move would raise an erection from a dead man, and even though he was beaten around the edges and his back had felt better and his shoulder hurt like a viper had bitten into it, Ryan was far from being deceased. Thanks to Krysty's ministrations, he was feeling more alive by the minute.

"I thought you were taking a bath," Ryan breathed, his own carnal desires starting to fully awaken. There was no hiding his interest.

"Later, lover. After we're done," Krysty said, her voice thickening as she stood and removed her outer shirt. She then playfully unsnapped her bra from the back, releasing the twin cones of flesh previously housed inside. "You like the topless look?"

"Come here and I'll show you."

Ryan allowed his eye to feast on the sight. He followed each indentation left in the sensitive skin where the straps of the bra had bitten into her voluptuous upper body. He wanted to trace each groove with his mouth and kiss away the reddish lines left in her pale flesh.

Krysty posed provocatively under his gaze.

"Why, Mr. Cawdor, I do believe you intend to take indecent liberties with me."

"That's the plan."

Krysty pouted, then strolled over, her boots gliding sinuously along the thick pile of the room's carpeting. She crossed her arms and placed her hands over her breasts, hiding the pink tips of her jutting nipples, but allowing some of the large areolae to peep through her splayed fingers.

"Think you can handle both of these?" she asked, bending at the waist and using her hands to create a plunging cavern of cleavage.

"I prefer to take one at a time," Ryan replied. "Like this."

He nuzzled her neck, working his way down to the tops of her bare breasts. He flicked his tongue along one nipple while using his fingers to lightly stoke the other. Fast, then slow.

"Mmm," Krysty breathed. "You ambidextrous little devil, you."

Ryan didn't respond. His mouth was busy with other, more-important tasks.

Krysty felt his hands at her waist, feeling around her belt and the snap of her pants. She was about to reach down and assist in their removal when Ryan was able to unlatch the buckle one-handed and flick the snap open in an easy, fluid motion. She squirmed out of the jeans and panties as he held on to their waistbands, pulling them down as she moved.

"I'm ready, lover," she breathed, looking down at him through half-lidded eyes glowing a dusky green. "From the looks of things, I think you're ready, too."

And then she was on top of him, joining him as their lips and genitals met in a lusty embrace of passion that began as a slow, steady rhythm. Soon, however, the motion broke out into a whiplash ride of thrusting that brought them simultaneously to the peaks of paradise.

RYAN WAS AWAKENED from a gentle doze by a light knocking at the hotel door. Instantly his senses came to full attention. Trouble normally didn't come with a knock, but one never could be too careful.

"You order room service?" he asked Krysty.

"No, but that's not a bad idea," she said drowsily. "Breakfast in bed."

"Still night," Ryan said, glancing at his wrist chron. "Not even eleven yet."

The big man reluctantly untangled his arms from around Krysty's sumptuous body, his bad shoulder drawing a wince across his face. He stood up carefully, pulling the covers over her splendid nudity.

"Who is it?" he called while picking up his SIG-Sauer from the nightstand. Ryan crouched at the base of the door and cocked the handblaster, waiting for whoever might answer.

"Me, Dad. Sorry to bother you."

Ryan relaxed and stood up. "Just a sec, Dean," he said. Ryan looked around the room, spotting and inventorying his shirt, coat, boots, then remembered he left his well-traveled trousers in the tiny hotel bathroom. "Let me pull on some pants."

Once he was partially clothed, Ryan opened the door and stepped out into the hallway. "Hey, Dean. Jak," he said in greeting to the pair. "I'd let you in, but Krysty's sleeping."

"Okay, Ryan," the albino said. "Come by too late? Wake up?"

"Nah, I was just resting. Been a triple-long day. What's going on?"

"Well, Jak and me are bored listening to Doc. He's started going off on something about the crazy-ass theories of some Dutch guy named Von Daniken and how we were all put here by aliens from another planet and he just won't shut up about it," Dean said, rolling his eyes.

"Yeah, I've been on the receiving end of Doc's lectures before," Ryan replied sympathetically. "He'll fall asleep soon enough once he gets tired of listening to himself ramble on."

"Until then, we wanted to go out and see the mall. Get away from him until he talks himself out or something," Dean continued.

"Got a destination in mind?" Ryan asked.

"There's a place for guys our age in here, Dad. Called a vid arcade. Supposed to have games and stuff. All kids—no oldies allowed."

"I've heard of them. All the rage in the predark

days.'' Ryan grinned at Jak. ''Surprised at you, Jak. Thought you didn't like being called 'kid.'''

''Don't,'' Jak said flatly. ''Have to keep watch on Dean.''

''I read you,'' Ryan said. ''And I appreciate that.''

''If the vid arcade sucks, we can still look around. Me and Jak figured we could recce this mall, find out where the good times are for guys our age.''

''Find Dean hobby horse. Let him ride,'' Jak teased.

''You're not that much older than me, Jak,'' Dean replied.

''I don't care where you go, as long as you stay out of bars and gaudies. I don't need you coming back here drunk or infected.''

''Oh, Dad. We just want to look.''

''Keep eye on him,'' Jak said.

''You do that.''

''I can take care of myself, you know,'' Dean protested, his face darkening at the thought of being too young or inexperienced to go out into the mall alone.

He turned to Jak. ''You want to sit in the room and chat with Doc, you go right ahead. Bore your white ass into a coma triple quick.''

''Mebbe knock you both into coma,'' Jak said. ''Shut both up.''

Ryan mulled the proposed jaunt over in his mind. Other than the battle he'd entered into in the pit—a battle he'd gone into of his own free will—he'd seen no signs of trouble in Freedom. The mall was run tighter than most villes he'd been through, and people seemed to want to mind their own business—blue-light specials or not.

He'd never allow Dean to go out alone, but with Jak at his back, Ryan knew they'd be as safe as one could be in Deathlands.

"Be safe," Ryan said.

"Count on it," Dean replied.

Chapter Seventeen

"That big lit-up map directory says the vid arcade is supposed to be down at the end of this corridor past the fruit stand," Dean mused as he and Jak turned a corner past a former men's-clothing store that now served as a combination private residence and produce shop. A few scruffy apples and some dried-up broccoli were in a cart near the proprietor, who sat in a wooden rocking chair with a sleeping child and waited patiently for someone to buy, even at that late hour.

As they walked farther down the indicated corridor, both of them noticed increasing numbers of children and teenagers, varying from eight-year-olds to girls in their early twenties. A few openly gawked at the duo, their attention on Jak's milky white skin and fine whiter hair. The albino, used to being stared at, hardly noticed the rude scrutiny.

"Whoa, whitey. Hold it. You, too, kid." A tall, wide youth dressed in matching denim pants and jacket about Jak's age stopped them at the arcade entrance. A .44 Magnum blaster was strapped to his right leg. "Don't recognize either of you, and I don't see proper ID. Visitors, I take it?"

"Right. What was your first clue? " Dean agreed,

already bristling at the young guard's arrogant tone of voice.

The sarcasm went unnoticed. "Got friends?"

Dean and Jak exchanged brief questioning looks. What a stupe question.

"Of course. Lots."

The guard looked as though he thought the pair facing him were retarded. "Let me rephrase the question. Got friends here in the mall?"

"Yeah, back at the Freedom Center Station complex."

"No, no. I mean friends who have played in here before?"

"In the vid arcade? No."

"Then you don't have memberships."

"No, I don't suppose we do," Dean said. "How do we go about getting one?"

"You got the jack, you get the membership."

"Why doesn't that surprise me?" Dean asked, glancing over at Jak. "Everything in Freedom costs money."

The guard nodded. "For a new boy, you wise up fast."

"Come on," Jak said, tugging at the hem of Dean's new T-shirt. "Fuck him. We got jack, you see."

"We'll be back."

"I'll be here. My shift goes on all night till closing."

JAK SAT DOWN on the dirty toilet seat and tried to ignore the pungent odor that had taken up residence in the grimy bathroom located at the far end of the mall corridor past the vid arcade. For all of the technological marvels that were encased and preserved within Freedom's walls, working public toilets weren't among them.

"Smell worse Doc," Jak said.

"Sorry, didn't know you were going to take a dump," Dean noted, holding his nose and backing away against the dirty mirror over the nonworking sink across from the open stall. "Here's a helpful hint, though. I think you're supposed to pull your pants down first and then go about your business."

"Smart ass. Keep watch," the albino youth said.

Dean leaned back against the bathroom door with his full weight. "No one's coming in. The smell would keep them out."

"Like you stop them."

Dean half watched Jak and half read some of the graffiti scrawled on the back of the bathroom door he was guarding. Most of the comments were sexual in nature involving male-female, male-male, male-mutie and, most disturbingly, male-animal. He was about to ask Jak to voice an opinion on how he'd personally dealt with the subject of interspecies romances back in Louisiana when the albino suddenly earned his full, unwavering attention.

Jak had crossed one leg over his other thigh so he could reach out and touch the bottom of his right combat boot. He now ran his nimble fingers along the edge of the boot near the heel until he felt what he was obviously looking for.

"Feet hurt?" Dean asked.

Jak's fine white hair swung as he moved his head

down for a better look at the sole of the boot. "Not yet," he said. "Will kick shit out you, asking questions."

"Hell of a place to do a boot repair," Dean muttered, turning back to reading the pornographic messages on the door.

"Boot's fine."

"Doc would hate these," Dean mused, gesturing to the door. "Dumb asses can't even spell *girl* right."

Finally Jak got fed up with trying to accomplish his feat by hand, and took out one of his throwing knives from a hiding place in his camou jacket, running the sharp blade along the sole of his right boot, barely cutting back the surface. The layer of black rubber peeled away like a piece of masking tape. Putting the knife back in its hiding place, he took one edge of the tread and pulled back until he revealed a second layer.

Hidden between the layers were four thin, flat golden wafers. The pale-skinned albino flashed them at Dean like a hand of playing cards.

"Jak! I didn't know you had a stash," Dean breathed, all of his swagger gone. He was seriously impressed by Jak's revelation.

"Weren't supposed know," the older boy replied. "Not much stash, unless kept secret." Jak went on to explain that he'd thought he'd have to give the cash up when they entered Freedom, but Ryan's victory over the sec droid had taken care of all the immediate financial worries.

"Have these long time," he said.

"More willpower than me. I'd have spent it when I got it," Dean replied.

The albino used a fingernail to flick the four wafers into the palm of his other waiting hand, stacking them into a thicker whole. He looked up at Dean and smirked as the gold glinted in the bare white light bulb of the bathroom.

"Now, let us in to play," Jak said. "Fuckers."

THE DISPLAY OF THE GOLD was effective. The insolent guard stepped aside and pointed them to a back office, past the many working vid games crowded into the arcade.

"Boss is back there. Name's Templeton. He'll fix you up."

As true children of Deathlands, both Dean and Jak had never seen anything like the darkened chamber. There was no interior lighting to speak of. All illumination came from the many vid screens. The noise they had heard coming out into the mall passage was busy and louder inside; electronic bleeps, boops, explosions and screams mixed with each machine's dozen digitized soundtracks for a staggering variety with differing intensities.

"Used some comps back at school with games, shoot-'em-ups, wag-driving simulations, mystery hunts, but they were nothing like this," Dean breathed.

"You forget—seen these kind games before," Jak said, speaking as loudly as he could in order to be heard over the noise.

"No way. Where?" Dean asked.

"Redoubt. Western Islands. When Trader and Abe still with us," the albino replied.

Dean looked at his friend curiously. "You funnin' me, Jak?"

"No."

Dean scratched his head, eerily mirroring the motion and posture of his father when puzzled. "I swear I don't ever recall seeing a vid arcade in a redoubt. Seems I'd remember a hot pipe like that."

"I know. Specially since one game blew asses sky-high."

Now Dean was truly perplexed. "What are you talking about?"

Jak sighed. He wasn't much for talking under the best of conditions, and the last thing he wanted to do was to try to enter into a detailed description about the past in the middle of a electronic maelstrom like the Freedom Mall's vid arcade. How to summarize one of the stranger redoubts the group had ever visited?

The underground installation had been small, tiny even, with only a mat-trans chamber and an upstairs series of rooms containing administrative offices, a small cafeteria, smaller armory, stripped-down living dormitories and secured nuke power plant. No elaborate maze or top secret labs, just enough in the way of supplies and room to house a staff to keep the mat-trans gateway open and properly functioning.

The redoubt's setup didn't even possess the usual military design. There was no sense of permanence in the evacuated rooms.

Adding to Doc's voiced theory of rotating shifts in

charge of operating the redoubt—with living quarters located somewhere outside—was an amusement center, filled with a dozen sophisticated arcade-quality video games. Jak remembered Dean being so excited, the boy had to be physically restrained by Ryan when the arcade was first discovered.

In fact Dean and Ryan both were as physically and mentally exhausted as could be at the time, what with having to endure three mat-trans jumps in a row....

"That's it!" Jak cried.

"What?" Dean replied, struggling to make himself heard over the noise.

"You and Ryan took triple jump. First, all came to Western Islands from Maine. Then you stuck in chamber, door accidentally closed. Activated cycle. Jumped back to Maine. Ryan used LD button, went after you. Then, both jumped back to Islands. Triple-fried brains, make you forget arcade. Memory loss caused by jumps," Jak said excitedly.

"Makes sense, I guess. I do remember something about jumping...and Dad coming back to get me. Yeah, you're probably right, Jak. Good thinking."

The albino was pleased. "Thanks."

"Still don't explain how our asses almost got blown out of our britches," Dean added.

Jak had an answer for this, as well. "Happened later, when you and me went to play games—just like this time, only nobody else in arcade."

The games in the redoubt had been set up for quarters, twenty-five cent pieces, not game tokens. Luckily some of the brightly decaled consoles had several spare quarters in their coin-return slots. What appeared to be a broken paper roll of coins had been dropped on the carpet. Dean's eyes fell on a garish oversize console half-shaped like an Indy racing car molded out of brilliant crimson plastic.

"Grand Prix," Dean read off the brightly lit glass housing, pronouncing "Prix" as "Pricks."

"Some kind porn game?" Jak mused, until he realized it was a race-wag simulation.

"Never been behind the wheel of a souped up wag like this," the younger boy said.

"Never been behind wheel of wag at all."

"Want to give it a spin?"

"Okay."

After an unsatisfying racing adventure that resulted in their crashing of the comp-generated automobile, the two boys quickly went through the other games. While Dean enjoyed each of the challenges, finding the situations both challenging and fun, Jak became less and less enchanted as they took turns trying the systems out.

By the time they reached a gaily decorated red, white and blue console emblazoned with a banner announcing Shield Of Freedom, Jak totally lost interest in make-believe and was sitting by the console on the floor, leaning his back against the wall and idly watching as Dean carefully read the game instructions.

Jak turned his head to stifle a wide-mouthed yawn when he saw that the lower panel of the back of the machine had been removed, and wired into the game's starting mechanism were two scarlet-and-blue implosion grenades.

Two implode grens in a confined space.

A booby trap, left behind in the redoubt for the supposed Russian invaders to come after the holocaust. The soldier or self-appointed patriot who'd set the trap up had indulged a twisted sense of humor by placing the bombs inside a patriotic, flag-waving type of game.

The albino moved in a white blur, his fine hair swirling out like a wispy fan as he leaped to his feet and snatched Dean away, pulling the boy behind him and out of the constricted interior of the game room, pulling the boy from the vid controls even as Dean pushed down on the red Start button to begin playing.

A startled "Hey!" was all Dean had a chance to utter as they half jumped, half fell out of the room and into the corridor outside the arcade. As they hit the floor, the interior of the redoubt's game room flashed once with a bright artificial light, and gave off a muffled crumping noise as the dual gren implosions tugged at their clothing and tried to pull them back inside the vortex.

Both were lucky. Jak's forehead was cut by a piece of flying glass from the vid game's shattered screen, while Dean suffered from a brief bout with temporary deafness when his eardrums were injured by the blast.

"Damn," Dean said after Jak related all of the particulars of their previous encounter with arcade games, "I don't remember *any* of that. Not even being deaf."

"It happened," Jak said firmly.

"Don't doubt it," Dean replied. "Dangerous stuff."

"Dangerous enough to stop playing more vid

games?'' Jak asked, half-hoping to get back to their room before it got much later. Doc would be sleeping, and his slumber was usually deep.

"Hah! I don't think so,'' Dean retorted. "We had some creaky old stuff on a Commodore 64 back at Brody's. Educational shit mostly, but there were some okay arcade simulations. Still, they were like fighting with wooden sticks instead of hand blasters compared to these games.''

As the boy tried to make a decision among the few unoccupied games, Jak decided to make the best of it. The albino went directly to a three-dimension target console with the unlikely name of Bloodhunter in Dimension 2000. He gripped the stock of the rifle bolted to the control console of the simulator and sighted a phosphor-dot target.

He looked down for the coin box, but the front of the console was smooth. He decided these games didn't need jack to function.

"Don't work,'' he announced after a moment of pulling the trigger and examining the rifle. "Sights off, too. Not shoot shit with this blaster.''

"Push one of those buttons. The one that says Fire,'' Dean suggested.

Jak did so. "Nothing. Game busted.''

"It's your brain that's busted, dickwad,'' a new voice said. "You need tokens to play.''

"Good one, Brack.''

A boy all of twelve years old, with close-cropped blond hair and an orange-and-brown pullover knit shirt and jeans, was standing behind Dean and Jak. At his side was an older boy, closer to Jak's age.

The older of the two was dressed in a pair of green cutoff denims with a yellow shirt. Long, lank black hair hung down across his eyes. His sartorial splendor was topped off by a yellow-and-purple baseball cap—worn backwards—with a patch on the front that read Pac-Man Fever.

"Tokens. Right. We need to get them back in the office, like the guard said," Dean stated.

"No slots," Jak protested, glaring at the boys who had broken into their conversation.

"Yes, slots, on the side, not on the front, see?" The older boy pointed at the side of the controls.

Jak looked and indeed, the console had the activation controls on the left side instead of in the front at crotch level like the vid games he'd encountered in the redoubt.

"Different. Not on front," the albino said.

"No shit, genius. Now, if you're not going to play, move," the twelve-year-old said. "Dex and I got better things to do than stand and watch you and your little buddy figure out how to put the tokens in the games."

"You got a mouth, don't you?" Dean retorted.

"So do you, and you can use it to kiss my ass if you keep bothering us," snarled the older one identified as Dex.

"How about I stomp head?" Jak asked. "Not take long."

Neither of the boys appeared impressed. "Big talk, Spooky. Try it, and mall sec men will show up and kick the shit out of you," the younger boy said. Jak spotted a telltale bulge under Brack's shirttail. The boy was heeled, a blaster close at hand.

Jak had his own Colt Python, but left it holstered. "Might be worth it," the albino said, considering the risks and developing a mental picture of the pair of snide punks on the ground, broken and bleeding.

"I ain't scared of you," Brack said.

"Me, neither," Dex agreed.

Jak abandoned the mock friendly tone. Playing nice wasn't in his nature anyway. "Should be. Should piss pants right now."

Dean took Jak's arm. "Smoke it, Jak. You're supposed to be keeping me out of trouble, remember?"

"Next time talk shit, chill you," Jak said to the insolent pair, his ruby eyes blazing as he allowed Dean to lead him away. To their credit, Brack and Dex kept their mouths shut.

The door of the office was open. Dean and Jak walked in and waited for the seated figure in the dress suit to look up. That was, if he could be bothered to stop his rapid writing of numerals in a thick ledger book to notice their presence. The man was doing his mental computations in pen, and by the light of a single oil lamp.

"What?" he barked.

"You Templeton?" Dean asked.

"That's me. Who are you?"

"Clients, I guess. Need memberships and tokens. Guard said you'd take care of us."

"Prices are on the board." The jowly man pointed at a chalkboard hanging on the wall behind him. Prices were listed in different colors of chalk inside a preprinted grid. The numbers were hard to read in the low lighting, but not impossible.

"Why do you keep it so dark back here?" Dean asked.

"Saves money," Templeton replied. "Juice costs jack. Vid games take a lot of juice. I can use candles and oil lamps ten times cheaper."

"What do you think, Jak?" Dean asked softly, wanting to know what his friend's opinion was of the prices on the board. Since Jak had the gold, he'd be the one paying for the entertainment. The least Dean could do was to get his input.

The albino shrugged. "Don't know. Not good with figures."

Dean studied the board some more, calling up his own knowledge of mathematics from both his time spent in school and what his mother had taught him at night when he was still a toddler. A handy mall rate of exchange with the official silver logo of The Bank of Freedom printed on top was also thumb-tacked next to the cluttered blackboard.

"What do your gold wafers weigh, Jak?" Dean asked, doing computations in his head.

The albino stuck a hand in his pocket and caressed one of the pieces. "Tenth ounce, mebbe."

"Don't let him know you've got more than one," Dean whispered. "The way this chart reads, we should be able to get out of here with a membership and ten free vid games each. Mebbe more games if he's really honest, which I doubt."

"You two ready to deal, or what? We don't like loiterers in here," Templeton said, looking up from the book where he was scribbling in more numbers. "Get enough of that outside, people waiting, watching. That's why we have the membership fee. Keeps out the riffraff."

"What's hurry?" Jak said, taking out a single golden wafer, just as Dean had suggested. "Here's jack. Buy us membership and games, right?"

"Let me see that," the owner said, reaching out a chubby hand. Jak dropped the light piece of metal into the fat man's palm and waited. Taking the golden wafer, Templeton weighed it, deciding by feel and texture how much gold was there. He then held it between thumb and forefinger up to his face and surprised the two friends by sticking out his tongue and licking the surface.

For a brief second, both Jak and Dean feared the man might decide to swallow the gold, but as a finale, he followed up the oral caress by biting down gently on the wafer and removing it before nodding his approval.

"Slice it thin, don't you?" he asked pleasantly.

"Last longer that way," Jak told him. "Still enough to buy you new suit."

"What's wrong with my suit?" Templeton asked as he put the wafer on the desk, where it glinted in the lamplight. "Your metal, boys—it feels real enough."

"Is real."

"So you say," the arcade owner said.

"How'd it taste?" Dean asked.

"Tasted good."

"So, is there a problem?"

"I don't know," the vid arcade owner replied. "Is there?"

"Think we try cheat you?" Jak asked with a hint of annoyance, beginning to reach out for the thin piece of gold on the desk. "Mebbe go elsewhere."

Templeton moved incredibly fast for a fat man and snatched up the gold. Dean knew Jak had purposely let him do so—no one on Earth was faster than the long-haired albino when the teen put his mind to speed.

"Hell, boy. Nothing personal," he protested. "I think everybody under thirty tries to cheat my ass. You wouldn't believe some of the kinds of counterfeit jack punks your age have tried to pass off on me. Thick or thin, coins or nuggets, paper currency or fake charge chits. I've seen more bootleg precious metals than you'll ever know. More fake jack floating around Freedom than the real thing."

"What's your deal?" Dean asked.

"A good one. Your gold tastes right to my teeth and tongue, so I'll give you what you need."

He took out two red lapel pinback buttons and held them out to the waiting Jak and Dean. They took the offered pins and looked at them with puzzlement.

"Wear these at all times while in the arcade. If you lose your button, you have to ante up for a new one. Buttons are coated with some chemical. I've got a sec screen that can read it. You won't be able to get in my arcade without wearing the pins, or an alarm goes off and you're escorted to the front to leave or to the back to pay."

"What about the tokens?" Dean asked.

"I'm getting to them." The man reached down to a silver device attached to his wide leather belt and pressed a thumb trigger rapidly, releasing a series of small, flat, round metal coins.

"Ten tokens each," he said with a flourish.

"Bull-shit." Jak said, stressing each of the syllables.

The token salesman shook his head. "There you go again. You albinos make it hell to do business with any sort of wit."

"Want twenty," Jak said, gesturing to himself and Dean. "Each."

"Don't try and rogue us, mister," Dean added, wanting to know where Jak was going with his request to double the deal, since he knew they'd already decided that an offer of ten tokens and membership was fair.

The larger man shook his head with a pained expression. "Damn. A haggler. Christ save us all from hagglers. Okay. Fifteen. Each."

Dean glanced over at his friend, ready to back the play if things went south.

"Eighteen," Jak countered.

Templeton looked as though he were about to succumb to a heart attack. "Goddamn, boy, this ain't no roadside carny! Things are more cut-and-dried here! You want deals, go to a ville flea market! Find a street peddler! Dig in the graveyards! But don't hassle me with trying to skim a better deal than retail price!"

Jak didn't reply. He just waited.

Dean decided to play along. "When he gets like this, mister, he'd rather cheat himself out of having a good time than spend extra jack on entertainment he thinks is a rip-off.''

"No refunds," Templeton said icily, wrapping his hand around the gold.

"What you think." Jak allowed himself to smile a feral smile, his lips peeling back and revealing his sharp canine teeth.

The owner frowned. "Seventeen. My final offer, otherwise we can get as nasty as you want to be, son."

Jak turned off the evil disconcerting grin. "Deal."

"Excellent!" Templeton crowed, and thumbed the coin changer at his side rapidly, spitting out the rest of the needed tokens to activate the vid games.

Jak and Dean left they way they came and entered the arena of noise and light.

"Didn't know you knew how to haggle, Jak," Dean said.

"Sure. What first?"

Dean looked around carefully. "We wait."

Jak shot him a look of sheer exasperation.

"Hang with me, Jak. If we play some of these games nobody else is on right now, we're wasting tokens. I got a theory. See, they're punk games. Shit vids that regulars stay away from. I think the most popular games are the ones you have to wait a turn on."

Jak nodded. "Makes sense. Which one you want wait for?"

"That red-and-black game," Dean said firmly. "The one called Mortal Kombat."

Brack and Dex were playing MK. They had their

backs to the two newest members of the arcade as they busily worked the joysticks and buttons to the game Dean had pointed out.

"One of assholes from earlier messing with?" Jak asked.

"Uh-huh."

The albino grinned. "All right."

Dean and Jak stepped past Mortal Kombat and stood behind another game, but that one hadn't even earned a passing glance from any of the young people in the busy arcade. The game was called Space Invaders, and even to Jak's untrained eye the unit's graphics and controls looked primitive.

"Rather wait for something good than rush into a bad game." Dean said.

"Uh-huh," Jak replied, tuning out the racket of the many games and voices as best he could, while thinking to himself that Doc's verbal jousting might not be so bad after all.

Chapter Eighteen

Ryan hadn't been flat on his back more than five minutes when another knock came from the flimsy hotel door.

"Want me to get it, lover?" Krysty said sleepily.

"No, I'm on it."

Ryan swung open the door, expecting to see Dean and Jak.

"Now what?" he said, his voice annoyed. Before him stood a freshly showered and shaved Doc.

"Ah, Ryan, might you be interested in joining me for a nightcap to celebrate today's victory of man over machine?"

"No, thanks, Doc. I'm whipped. Just want to get some sleep."

Doc assumed an understanding look as he pushed away a stray white hair that had broken loose from the rest he'd combed back from his high forehead. "I can certainly share agreement with your exhaustion, friend Cawdor. Indeed, you have earned your rest."

"Great. Well, good night," Ryan said, turning his back and moving to step into the hotel room.

"Ah, you do know young Dean and Jak both have ventured out?" Doc asked in a conspiratorial tone.

"They dropped by," Ryan replied, keeping his back to the old man, mentally willing him to leave.

Doc wasn't picking up on the mental vibrations. "I was convinced you were aware of their absence, but wanted to let you know, all the same. Growing boys are growing boys. Well, Jak really isn't a boy anymore, but you gather my meaning."

"Right," Ryan replied tightly.

"Well, if needed, I will be in that smoky little pub located on the upper level of this mammoth monstrosity, next to the front entrance of the lobby to our humble abode. I think a stiff drink of good whiskey might settle my sleeplessness."

"Right. Good night, Doc."

Ryan closed the door. "Next time, I swear, I'm not telling anyone where we're staying."

"That's okay," Krysty told him. "Why don't you come back to bed and we'll see what comes up next?"

RYAN WOKE UP in the dark bathed in a fine sheen of sweat. His recently reinjured shoulder throbbed dully in time with the pounding in his head.

"You felt it, too, lover?" Krysty's voice came from next to him in the bed.

"Felt...something," Ryan replied. "Got a triple-bad pain in my shoulder."

A rustling sound came, followed by Krysty's hand on his face. "You're burning up, Ryan."

"Not a fever," he said. "Just a headache."

"What time is it?"

Ryan reached out and felt around on the small end table next to the bed for his wrist chron. He thumbed the button, and the glowing dial revealed the time to be 4:17 a.m. "After four," he said.

"Do you think anything is wrong?"

"Mebbe." Ryan stood. "You stay put while I check the other rooms. I'll start with Doc's. Dean and Jak were supposed to be going out for some fun at a vid arcade tonight. Won't hurt to make sure they're snug in their beds."

Ryan lit a small candle on the nightstand and hurriedly dressed in the flickering light. Krysty was sitting up, watching him.

"You're sure you don't want me to come?" she asked.

"No need. Not yet. Let me see if anything's going on first," Ryan replied as he strapped down his holster to his leg. "Keep the door locked."

"Don't worry," Krysty replied, rolling out of bed and starting to rummage around for her own clothing. "Door'll be locked and I'll keep a blaster in my hand. No way I'm going back to sleep now."

Ryan leaned over and gave her a quick kiss before stepping out into the dingy hotel hallway. He closed the door behind him and heard the lock slide home from the other side. Ryan then turned left, striding down to the end room that Doc was sharing with Dean and Jak. He softly rapped his knuckles against the door once. No answer came. Then he started to pound on the side of the frame and still got no response except from the room next door.

"You looking for somebody?" A plump woman in a revealing gown that rose partially above her naked hips stood there, looking Ryan up and down with a saucy eye.

"Not tonight, but thanks," he replied, and headed for the hotel lobby and admitting desk. He knew where he was going to search next.

WHEN RYAN ENTERED the pub, he had no trouble spotting his quarry.

Doc appeared to be staggering, stupefied drunk. He had removed his frock coat and hung it over the back of the spindly wooden chair he was slumped in. His shirtsleeves were rolled up, showing his lean arms down to the elbow. Still, even in his vaporous good cheer, Ryan noticed that he hadn't let his swordstick go far from within quick reach, and the snap on the holster of the unwieldy Le Mat was unsnapped for fast removal.

"Doc, you look crocked," Ryan said.

"I am, my dear Ryan Cawdor, I am," Doc crowed back happily, his breath a pungent mix of rye and gin and only the bartender and the empty bottles on his shelves knew what else. "Come, sit! Drink and be merry—and you will sip for free! Everybody loves a winner! I have been the recipient of free bourbon all the night through thanks to our proud association! They have been playing a vid tape over and over on the pub's television of you smiting the steel dragon. You might yet have found your calling as slayer of androids."

A waitress came over, winding her way past the other tables and pub junkies. She was dressed in a short black skirt of faux leather, near sheer white hose, green shirt and matching green-and-white neckerchief. The subdued lighting in the pub helped shave years off her features and contribute to the illusion of a thirty-year-old temptress hoping for a tip.

"Nice eye patch," she said dryly. "What are you drinking?"

"Nothing."

"Uh-uh. Got to drink something, mister. This ain't a—" she began.

"Get me a beer, then. Bring the whole fucking pitcher!"

"Simmer down, Patch," she retorted as she left to fill the angry request. "Usually people don't turn into raging assholes until after they've tasted the brew."

"She'll be back. Here," Doc said, handing Ryan a shot glass with a thin coating of amber fluid on the bottom. "Drink up!"

"Mebbe later," Ryan replied tightly. "Look, Doc. Snap up for a sec. Did Dean or Jak tell you where that vid arcade was supposed to be?"

"No, Ryan. They kept their destination private," Doc declared sadly. "Ah, children. What is one to do with the wee ones? I remember my own pair of imps, how rosy their cheeks would glow whenever they stumbled into some new mischief. Oh, how my dear Emily would shout whenever Rachel and my precious, sweet little Jolyon would get into the kitchen cupboards."

"Doc, we don't have time for the trip down memory lane," Ryan said. "Shake off the booze! We're going to have to go and find Dean and Jak. They'd never be out this late without good reason."

"You and I are both out in the early hours of the morning, Ryan. But I would give anything to be home in my own little wooden bed with the pillows Emily made herself and stuffed with goose feathers, my hand crooked in the hollow of her waist, listening to the soft sounds of her snoring."

As Doc spoke, tears started to fall down his lined cheeks.

"Listen to me, listen to me. I get a few sips of alcohol and I grow unbearably melancholy. How sad. Nobody buys drinks for a sloppy drunk."

"I know, Doc, but I'm trying to deal with the here and now. If you want, I'll leave you behind while I go round up J.B., Mildred and Krysty. If we split up, we should be able to track them down, whether they're still in the vid arcade or not. We can go down to that directory list and find the place on the mall map."

Doc rested his head on the tacky surface of the table as the waitress returned with the requested pitcher of beer and an empty glass mug.

"You want me to pour?" she asked.

"Thanks. No. Sorry I bit your head off earlier," Ryan replied, digging out a wad of the mall currency from when he made the exchange at the Bank of Freedom. He pressed two of the higher-denomination bills into her waiting hand.

The waitress winked. "Mister, you keep tipping this good, and you can bite off whatever you like."

As the woman turned away, Ryan looked out past her and spotted twin men dressed in the forest green of mall security as they stepped into the dimly lit bar.

Ryan couldn't quite make out their faces in the gauze-like texture of the air, which hung heavy with a mix of cheap cigarette and marijuana smoke. The sec men could be off duty, but Ryan doubted it. Something about their demeanor indicated they were alert, on the job and looking for an unlucky mall visitor or resident.

They paused at the head of the long pub bar. The bartender shrugged and pointed at the small table in the rear where Ryan and Doc were sitting. The pair of sec men turned and started making their way back at a deliberately measured pace.

"Fireblast," Ryan hissed.

"What, pray tell, has happened now?" Doc asked, his head still on the sticky tabletop and nestled in the crook of his elbow. Doc's back was to the bar. He couldn't have seen the new arrivals. Ryan was surprised when his drinking companion had spoken. He believed Doc had finally passed out from the limpness of his body and the slowed breathing pattern he entered into after consuming the contents of his final glass of whiskey.

Now Doc's eyes were half-open and staring at him, struggling to raise themselves from the alcoholic mire. Even in the midst of tying one on, Doc had caught the hint of anxiety in Ryan's muttered epithet.

"Company, Doc. Two Freedom sec men," Ryan murmured. "One of them is that Rollins guy we met outside. Keep still—I'll give you a signal in case there's trouble. They won't be expecting anything from an old drunk."

"Hic," Doc whispered, and winked in reply before

closing his eyes and letting his upper body ooze into a pose of slack drunkenness once more.

Once the men got closer, Ryan could see there was a wide age difference between the two. Off his horse, Rollins was as tall as Ryan, with a similar posture and build. That's where the similarities ended. The sec leader was bald, but had compensated for the lack of hair on his scalp by growing a wide mustache. He carried a huge long blaster cradled in his arms, held in a nonthreatening fashion but still within easy reach and use.

The backup was a young punk that looked about twenty, but with a much larger frame than the leader's, and that was saying something since Rollins wasn't exactly tiny. His hair color was hidden under a riot helmet. His eyes were behind a pair of polarized sunglasses. Tough guy. Or a weak, uncertain guy playing at being tough, reveling in the inhuman guise of a walking insect.

"Evening, Cawdor," Rollins said.

Ryan turned to fully face him, while trying to keep his associate framed in his peripheral vision. The younger of the two had apparently received some training, since he was using Ryan's eye patch as a blind side.

"You're up late tonight, Rollins."

"A sec man never sleeps."

"Who's the kid? He hanging out with you for extra credit in sec school or what?"

"It's a young man's world, Cawdor."

"Isn't that the damn truth. Tell your lapdog no insult intended," Ryan replied. "Well, unless you and your sidekick are here to apologize for those clowns who tried to jump me and my friends yesterday out on the road, I'm going to ask you to leave. You owe me a night's peace for my generosity."

"What generosity is that?" the younger man asked, speaking for the first time.

"It talks, too?" Ryan retorted.

"He hasn't heard about Michaelson and Isaac." Rollins said.

"You mean Mike and Ike. Yeah, I was going to chill them both with extreme prejudice, but since you came along and told me ridding the world of their sorry asses might be a problem since I was planning on coming here for a visit, I declined."

"We've got your boy, Cawdor."

On those words, Ryan forgot the pretense of playing it cool. A hot flush of blood ran into his face and brain, feeding the impulse to kill Rollins right on the spot. Ryan was on his feet and over in the black man's face in an instant, his panga drawn up and out of the oiled sheath. As Ryan moved, so did Doc, who spun with his swordstick and placed the shining blade right up against the crotch of the second mall security guard.

"No, son," Doc said to the younger sec man, all pretense of snoozing off a drunk now lost to adrenaline and concern for Dean. "Keep your hands up toward heaven and your blood pressure down toward Hell and maybe, just perhaps, I won't have to flick my wrist and turn you into a eunuch."

"A—a what?" the hapless sec man replied.

"An unfortunate who has faced the blade and had

his scrotum removed, complete with contents," Doc said, twisting the swordstick ever so slightly and increasing the pressure. "Both contents."

"Are you insane, Cawdor?" Rollins rasped, sweat popping out in tiny crystal beads on his forehead.

"When it comes to my boy, you're damn right. I'm a fucking loon," Ryan said. "Now, elaborate. What do you mean by 'got'?"

"Exactly what I said. He's in lockup, along with the albino. They're printing and booking them both into the Wings even as we speak," Rollins replied. "And I suggest you put the blade down before you cut yourself."

"I'd be more worried about me cutting you a new asshole," Ryan hissed. "What are you talking about 'booking him in the Wings'?"

"Cop jargon. Means he's being processed and arrested. For our files. We like tracking repeat offenders. Get into too much trouble and you're no longer welcome in Freedom. He and his pasty white pal nearly blew the vid arcade apart in a knife fight that went bad. One customer is dead, another one wounded and the owner is furious."

The one-eyed man reined himself in and took the knife away, stepping back and keeping his distance from Rollins. "Dean all right?"

The man stared back angrily at Ryan. "He's a damn sight better than the boy he helped chill."

Ryan poked a finger into Rollins's broad chest. "Listen, my boy chills somebody, you can be damn sure they were asking for it, and asking for it on bended knee. He's not a coldheart, and neither is Jak Lauren.''

The big sec man didn't looked impressed. "Whatever. We don't really give a shit about the stiff. He was one of the repeat offenders I was telling you about earlier. Problem child, but his father had the jack to keep buying his way back into Freedom. Now he can use it to bury the boy's worthless ass. Way I look at it, your kid did us a service. One less scumbag cluttering up the mall.''

"I'm glad for you my son's ended a teenage crime wave, really. One of you two guardians of Freedom going to take me to him?" Ryan asked.

Rollins smirked. "All in good time. First tell your drinking buddy to let my sec man keep his nut sac.''

"Ease off, Doc," Ryan said.

"See?" Doc told the young sec man in training as he sheathed the blade into the ebony stick. "Safe to procreate another day.''

"What else, Rollins?''

"You have to make a detour. Morgan wants to see you before you can speak to your boy or Lauren.''

"What's your baron want with me?''

"He's not a baron—told you that before. He just wants to talk, to deal, to offer. Yeah. If you impress Morgan, all this stink might just up and blow over like a bad dream.''

Chapter Nineteen

Ryan sent Doc into the Freedom Center complex to tell Krysty, J.B. and Mildred about Dean and Jak, then walked with the two sec men to a boarded-over mall front. An old sign overhead identified the site as a former Spencer's Gifts. A single door with a sec keypad and a card slot was recessed into the solid front. Rollins slid an ID card into the slot, then punched in a quick seven-digit code.

"Go straight down the hallway until it ends, then go right. You'll pass a few doors on the trip. Don't bother trying them, they're locked. They're just back doors into some of the other mall stores anyway. Keep going until you come into a glassed-in waiting area. A guard will be waiting for you. He's got your description. Tell him you're Cawdor, and he'll send you through."

"You're not coming?" Ryan asked. "Surprised you'll let me in to see Morgan alone."

"Frankly, Cawdor, I've got better things to do. This mall doesn't police itself. Besides, Morgan can take care of himself."

"When do I get to see Dean?" Ryan asked.

Rollins sighed heavily. "Haven't you been paying attention? You can talk with the boy after you've spoken with the boss."

As Rollins turned to walk away, Ryan grabbed him by the upper bicep. The big man whirled and knocked off Ryan's grip with a snarl.

"I'm getting damn tired of you laying hands on me. Do it again and they'll be hosing you up off the floor, pit champion or no pit champion."

Ryan's face was a grim mask. "I just wanted you to know that if anything happens to Dean or to Jak, I'll cut your heart out."

"See the boy comes by chilling honestly. Both of them are fine. Hell, after what they've been up to tonight, I'm glad they're locked away to protect innocent mall citizens from their reign of terror."

"Good. Then I won't be taking you on," Ryan gritted. "At least not yet. I just want to know what kind of man this Morgan is."

"What do you mean?"

"Most places I've been in like this, the man behind the curtain is usually crazy. Power goes to their minds and rots their brain from within, like some kind of rad sickness. They start thinking they're a god or some other higher power, barking out orders to yes men like you, reveling in their twisted fantasies as long as they're backed up by a blaster and their own private army."

"Then you're in luck, Cawdor. Morgan is probably the most rational man I ever met. His private army is busy watching over his domain, not over his own ass. Why he wants to talk with a loser outlander like yourself is beyond me."

"You shooting straight?"

"Why wouldn't I be? After you wrap up with Morgan, get the boss to send you down to the Wings and you can talk to your boy.''

Ryan watched Rollins stride away, talking into one of the portable radios he'd seen hanging from many of the sec men's waists. He wasn't thrilled with having to walk into a discussion with the mall's baron alone, but the way the cards had been dealt so far, he didn't have much of a choice.

The one-eyed man crept down the long hallway, following the directions Rollins had given to him. Just for the hell of it, he tried a few of the doorknobs belonging to the numerous doors he was passing at regular intervals, but all of them were frozen in place. Locked, as Rollins had said they would be. A few bullets from the SIG-Sauer would solve that problem, but the muffled sound would carry and what would be the point anyway?

The glassed-in area outside Morgan's office had a few padded metal chairs, a freestanding ashtray and a low coffee table cluttered with tattered predark magazines. Ryan entered through the swinging glass door and chose a seat where he could get the best view of anyone entering or exiting.

He picked up one of the magazines and flipped through the glossy pages. The mag was called *Premiere*. Ryan glanced at the face on the cover staring back at him. A Candid Talk With Kurt Russell the mag promised. Ryan tossed it back on the table. He had no interest in what someone called Kurt Russell might have to say, candid or not.

A massive wooden desk was near the door, and Ryan imagined Morgan did business behind that door.

Sitting at the desk and frowning at Ryan was another sec guard, with a furrowed brow and a three-day growth of beard. Ryan estimated the guard topped the scales at over three hundred pounds of muscle. The huge sec man also seemed to serve as part-time secretary.

"Cawdor. I'm here to see Morgan," Ryan said.

"I know," the sec man replied.

An obnoxious buzzing sound came out of a yellow box on the edge of the desk. The frowning sec man reached out and punched a button before picking up an attached phone receiver.

"Yeah, he's here," the massive sec guard said, eyeing Ryan suspiciously.

"Good," a voice over the intercom replied. "Send him right in."

"He's packing a blaster," the guard said in a lower tone. "A big one."

This time the voice over the intercom had a hint of irritation. "So am I, Genge. Everyone in Freedom is armed. Part of the 'Welcome to our neighborhood please shop with us again thank you you're welcome bye-bye' kind of charm. Now, do what I said and send the man right in."

Genge stood and gestured toward a door near Ryan's seat. "Mr. Morgan is expecting you, sir."

"So I heard," Ryan said simply.

Ryan passed Genge and stepped into the open doorway, his eye taking in the layout of the colossal yet Spartan office. He heard the door close and click behind him. A single desk of immense size similar to the one in the waiting area was in the middle of the room, flanked by two plush black leather chairs and a matching sofa. A single comp and monitor stood on a smaller table beside the desk, along with a phone-intercom, both within easy reach if seated. The walls were all drab, painted in neutral tones of soft amber.

The rear wall behind the desk was the only exception. It was home to a massive bank of vid screens and security viewing-recording devices. Half of the screens were lit, showing various parts of the interior of Freedom Mall flickering dimly in grainy black and white. There was also a shot or two of the mall exterior, but these images were even harder to make out.

The man seated on the edge of the desk was in his midforties, with dark brown hair graying at the temples and a matching brown beard that was starting to gray in sympathy. The beard tapered down to a point. His hair was too long for the collared shirt he wore and as a result gave him the air of a man in bad need of a haircut.

He was average height, average weight, and the color brown had been visited upon him a third time with his eyes, which would have completely added to the lack of any distinguishing characteristics if not for the vibrancy shining through as he looked Ryan over. The man oozed vitality and intelligence, but not in the usual arrogant way of many smart men who strove to assure their domination over their own pocket kingdoms in Deathlands.

In addition to the white long-sleeved shirt, which was immaculate, appearing to be either new or pressed, the man wore long black trousers and high black boots. A small golden cross could be spotted hanging on a chain from around his neck, flickering now and then as he moved, the metal catching the soft lighting within the office.

He also wore an expensive wrist chron, an old-style one without a digital readout or liquid crystal. A simple wristwatch with an hour and minute hand, and tiny inset window for the date.

"You Freedom's baron, Morgan?" Ryan asked.

The man turned to the left, to the right and then glanced behind himself. "I must be, or else I'm loitering in his office again," he muttered before turning back to face Ryan. "No. Not hardly. Freedom has no baron or boss or lord. I'm merely the administrator."

"Ah, is that what barons are calling themselves now?" Ryan said, keeping his hands out in the open, friendly, nonthreatening. "I've met all kinds, admirals, princes, bosses and commanders—all the same. Barons. Still, you might be telling the truth. You're not overweight enough to be the genuine article, and you don't have any toadies or sluts kissing your ass and falling over your feet."

"I like my privacy. And I've never claimed the title of baron in my life. The name is Beck Morgan. I never got into calling people by their last names," Morgan said easily, sticking out a hand to shake.

Ryan looked at the offered hand as if it was covered in pus.

"No manners where you come from, outlander?" Morgan asked as he slid the offered hand back.

Ryan felt his face flush. The scar running down his left cheek from the injury that had taken his eye darkened. "I've got manners, Morgan. But if I took your hand right now I'm afraid I might try to keep it by ripping your damn arm clean off and beating you to death with it.''

The mall administrator chuckled. "Like you did to the sec droid in the pit? I watched the battle from here. Very impressive, and clever. You fought with courage and wit.''

"And fear—nobody bothered telling me when going in I was supposed to be fighting hand-to-hand with an android,'' Ryan snapped.

"You dealt with the unexpected quite well, Ryan. I hear you're good at that,'' Morgan said. "A talent for survival is a most useful ability.''

"Look, Morgan, you can save yourself some time and cut the diplomatic smile, the first-name calling, the compliments on my fighting abilities and the firm, dry handshake.'' Ryan rubbed his forehead with his right hand. "Do us both a favor and spare me the lecture. I don't plan on being here long enough to get on a first-name basis with you. I'm here for one reason. I want my son.''

The bearded man shook his head wearily. "It's not that simple. Certain parties have been injured. Certain parties demand justice.''

"Don't they always? My guess is, way things work in Deathlands we're looking at Dean's word and Jak's against the man they chilled. Dead men can't talk.''

"Not a man, a boy. And there are living, breathing witnesses. Well, a witness, anyway. No question your son and friend were minding their own business, and once they were provoked, they brought out the scythe and started mowing down the opposition,'' Morgan said. "Are all your people as deadly as you those two and yourself, Ryan?"

"I hope for your future here as boss man of Freedom you never have to find out," Ryan replied. "And don't call me Ryan."

"What should I call you?"

"I don't give a damn," Ryan said dismissively. "I'll say it again. I want my son."

"Fair enough. We're not unfair here in Freedom. You'll have him—soon as you make restitution to the arcade owners and pay his fines. Along with the albino's."

"How much?"

"The fines? Hell, not much. I'll go ahead and waive them to show my good intentions. Consider them paid," Morgan said, tearing up a sheet of paper with a flourish.

Ryan wasn't buying the show. "What about the damages?"

"Nothing I can do to help you there, I'm afraid," Morgan said as he pulled a stack of whisper-thin sheets out of a wire-mesh basket on his desk and flipped through them. Finding the one he wanted, he put down the rest and handed over the single damning piece of paper to Ryan.

"Fireblast!" Ryan spit as he saw the list of figures and the combined total at the bottom of the list. "That's a lot of jack."

"Some of those vid machines are damn near irreplaceable, Cawdor. Any good comp equipment is usually salvaged for something of more value than mere entertainment, and to find full units in working order takes time and lots of money. Lucky for your boy, the arcade owner is a forgiving sort once he feels that proper justice had been meted out."

Ryan gave Morgan a thin smile. "All about greasing the palms, isn't it?"

The bearded man nodded. "Perhaps. To be honest, I like to quote a phrase from an old predark song called 'Hotel California.'"

"Been there. Hot as Hades. Unless you're wanting to build sand castles out of radioactive dirt, I can't advise the trip. Besides, I thought this was the Carolinas."

"The theme still applies. Besides, if you've been there, I'm sure you know most of California fell into the ocean when the bombs hit. Now, the song sort of goes, a person can check in, but he can never check out. During my tenure here as operations manager for the Freedom Mall—"

"Thought you said you were the administrator," Ryan snorted.

"Like you told me earlier. Titles. Words. Barons. Kings. Means the same thing. But during my stay here, I've seen what I've just said come into play hundreds of times. I look at it as providing employment. Running a compound this size takes people, Cawdor."

"'Mr. Cawdor,' to you, Morgan. I want my boy and my friend."

"And I want to be hung with a cock the size of my forearm, but it isn't going to happen," Morgan retorted, his elegant face flashing with anger. "This isn't some little ville on the edge of nowhere, my one-eyed friend. Nor is it a place where you can come swaggering in and do whatever the hell you please.''

''Is that a fact?''

''The fact is this—like it or not, Freedom is a civilized patch that has been carved out of the southeastern hellzone. We've got all the tenants we can handle and a waiting list of thousands who'd like to live here on a regular basis instead of just passing through from one pesthole to the next. Those with the jack give up on permanent residence and just visit here for extended stretches. Any way you want to debate it, people want to stay in here and visit the mall because they can't find what we have to offer anywhere else on the remains of the North American continent.''

''What, high prices? Overcrowding? Sec men with fancy green jackets and a bunker mentality?'' Ryan asked. ''Or that snazzy pit with the broken-down droid used in staging your own gladiator bouts for the unwashed masses? Pretty sad.''

''No, no, no,'' Morgan corrected. ''What we offer to them, besides access to food, clothing and shelter, is safety.''

''That's debatable. What about those stickies on the outside trying to get in that I keep hearing about?''

''Yes, well, no location is perfect. Which is where you come in.''

''I was told the muties want to come in and spend some jack and have a hot meal along with the rest of us,'' Ryan said laconically. ''Seems to me you're missing out on the almighty stickie dollar. Piss-poor thinking for a businessman like yourself.''

Morgan burst out laughing, his amusement coming in a series of mirthful snorts.

"Believe me, Cawdor, if those dumb bastards had the brains to understand the concept of legal tender, they'd be more than welcome to come in and spend, spend, spend. Unfortunately stickies are about as bright as a bag of dirt. Only thing on their mind is burning and killing, not necessarily in that order."

Ryan turned to leave. "Well, thanks for the chat. I guess I've got some selling to do, see if I can come up with the jack to bust Dean and Jak out of your jail."

"There is another way."

"How so?"

"Work for me. Your entire group. Work off the debt. The mall will make good with the vid-game owner, and in exchange you join my sec squad for thirty days. You've got a rep. Let's see how you earned it."

"No."

"Best offer you're going to get tonight, Cawdor. And if you have any ideas about trying to take your son and friend out of the Wings by force, you're sadly mistaken. Even if you could get to the cells, there are booby traps designed to kill if you try opening doors without proper authorization."

"If you're so damn strong and all-powerful, why do you need me?" Ryan finally said, growing fed up with all of the blunt goodwill. He was beginning to wish for the more traditional baron who smirked, pranced and bragged a blue streak. At least those types were men that Ryan could take their measure and figure out where he stood.

Morgan shook his head. "Ease up. I'm getting to that. Let me give you some background first. See, your timing is most fortuitous. There's death in the air of Freedom. Bad enough keeping the peace from within, but now the stickies are becoming stirred up. A group like yours enters, and we take notice. I quizzed that Adrian scavie that came in with you, and he told me a few things. If your son hadn't fucked up in the vid arcade, I would have been coming to you with an offer anyway. Now I can make the offer, and it's one you can't refuse."

"I don't like being pushed," Ryan warned.

"Who does?"

"Why me?"

"I know you're not exactly a teenager. A man lives to be your age, he's got something on the ball. That's why I'm willing to make this deal. Frankly I need your help. Good sec men are impossible to find, much less keep. They tend to have this annoying habit of following the money. I pay a decent wage, but once some dumb-ass baron gets his panties in a wad, off they go to fight yet another private little war."

"I'm not a sec man."

"Now you are. Better still, you're an intelligent sec man. Freedom exchanges information with other villes, other barons. Your face and name aren't unknown in this region. Amusingly enough, since you've never left any of your past adversaries alive, there has been no bounty placed on your head."

"I'm not laughing."

"Well, I found it amusing."

"You seem to know a lot about me."

"I know a lot about anyone who comes into Freedom, or at least I try to."

"You can't know everything. Can't know what I'm thinking about right now."

"I could hazard a guess." Morgan eyeballed Ryan carefully. "What's with you, Cawdor?"

"What do you mean?"

"I mean you look and act the role of a gunslinger, but your vocabulary and carriage belie the brains of an educated man."

Ryan snorted. "Doc Tanner's the one for book learning. Not me."

"That preening fool? Far as I've been told, he wears knowledge like a suit of armor, verbosity aimed at keeping the rest of us poor, slack-jawed yokels out of the loop. No, you're smarter than you let on, Cawdor, otherwise you wouldn't have survived Deathlands as long as you have."

"What do you know about survival? You hide in this back office, away from the mall floors, away from the outside. When's the last time you felt real sunlight, Morgan?"

"Been a few months, but haven't you heard? It's dangerous outside. Skin cancer. Rad sickness. Who needs it? Not me," Morgan replied in a salesman tone. "That's why people come to Freedom to shop, to live, to deal. We're a stronghold, Cawdor, with a movie palace, places to eat, things to buy, places to stay. Safe, wholesome entertainment, minus a few gambling dens, bars and the after-hours gaudies."

"Yeah, men gotta have their drinks, cards and sluts."

"Damn straight!" Morgan said. "All any man could want is in here."

Ryan licked his lips. "Even as big as this place is, you can only stay back here for so long. Outside world will come in soon enough and stomp you flat."

"A year ago I would have told you that was nonsense, Cawdor. Now I'm not so sure. I don't have a problem with outside. I just don't want to deal with it. Why do you think malls were built in the first place, back in the predark days of consumerism?"

"I don't know. Greed, I guess."

Morgan shook his head. "Wrong. Protection. Downtown areas were getting too dangerous. Muggings, rapes, theft. People were afraid to go out on city streets to buy their needed goods. Mail order was fine for some items, sure, but man needs to go out on his own, do his own hunting and gathering, and malls such as Freedom were built in response to his needs. Or her needs. Malls were traditionally a female haven. Sexist, I admit, but I'm just repeating what I've read."

Ryan gestured toward the bank of vid screens. "Looks like you have eyes everywhere."

"Once upon a time, we did," Morgan corrected, standing up and walking over to the wall. He hit a few control keys, switching the screen images, as well as the angles they were showing, as he continued to talk. "I'm being honest with you here, Cawdor. Very few people know the extent of how Freedom has backslid in recent months. Only the key people in my sec squad are aware of this, but all of these screens used to be fully functional.''

''What happened?''

''Most of the exterior cameras are down, and some of the interiors ones are shoddy and in need of replacing or repair. We were using thermal cameras for the outside perimeter—hell, we even had a miniature long-range TV op system on the roof with all the trimmings, laser range finder, tilt pedestal and night vision.''

''Had?''

''Yes, had. All of them gave us good visibility in all ambient light conditions, day, night, smoke or haze. Now we're lucky to even have the two regular cameras up and functioning. Freedom's starting to fall apart at the seams. We have investors, money men from up north, looking to do something to alleviate their boredom. This seemed like a solid plan. Renewal of the past, protection for the future.''

''Sorry, but it still sounds to me like you need techies to fix your problems,'' Ryan said. ''And you'll get your sec men if you're willing to ante up the jack.''

''No. What I need are competent men and women capable of fortifying Freedom. Word is out. I'm hiring qualified mercies. But word travels slow, and now I'm making do with a few good men and a lot of cannon fodder with itchy trigger fingers blowing the heads off visitors who try and steal from merchants instead of arresting them so we can confiscate their possessions and jack. A dead man is of no use to anyone.''

"Have to disagree with you there, Morgan. In fact, the thought has crossed my mind that there's nothing in here to keep me from gutting you like a fish or putting a bullet in your head. By the time your sec man outside could squeeze out from behind the desk, you'd be a dead man. That could solve a lot of problems."

"Oh, really? Chilling me would just result in the deaths of your son and your friend. Understand, I'm trying to be polite here, but if you fuck with me, Freedom is the last place you'll ever see again—alive, at least."

"Didn't say I was going to do it. Just said what was keeping me from doing it? Could take you hostage."

"Enough with the theories, Cawdor! There is a stickie situation to be dealt with, yes! But I'm being honest with you. I need your help in handling them. Your people—"

"They aren't *my* people, Morgan," Ryan countered, cutting the mall administrator off in midsentence. He rose to his feet and began to pace in front of the overblown wooden desk as he continued to speak. "What they are to me are my friends, and my friends do as they please."

"Surely they have loyalty to you?"

"Uh-uh. Stop right there. Big difference between loyalty and ownership. You speak of them like they were my slaves or something. Not even close. We travel together because we care about one another and don't have to worry about waking up with a blade in our backs. I know trust is a double-hard thing to find anymore, but I guess that's what holds us together. We trust one another.''

''Then I 'trust' they'll stand by your request for a favor...for your son's sake, and for the albino's.''

Chapter Twenty

Despite Morgan's lament over a lack of good help, the sec men in the holding pens knew their jobs. Ryan's blaster and panga were both taken at the front desk, and he was carefully patted down in a full-body search, where the thin knife hidden at the base of his back was also revealed and taken until his visit was over.

"For your own safety," the alert sec man said. "Prisoner gets hold of a weapon, might use it on you first. It happens."

Ryan felt naked after being relieved of his weapons before being allowed in to see Dean, but there was no other way to gain access. He was taken to a screened room divided in halves by a thick woven mesh similar to fencing he'd seen around outdoor sec areas. On the other side of the visiting room, a door opened and a pale Dean walked out, alone and unescorted.

Ryan pressed close to the wire and realized he could see and touch Dean, but only though the half-inch hole of the strong metallic material. What was obviously a one-way mirror dominated a side wall. Ryan suspected the sec man who had admitted him into this visitor's center was keeping watch from behind the glass.

"Knew you two were going to get into trouble the minute I laid eyes on you last night," Ryan said gently, his mouth turning upward at the sides as he fought back a relieved smile. "They treating you okay?"

"Extraspecial," Dean said. "Jak, too. Hot food. Clean bunk. No creeps or pervs. Nicest cell I ever been stuck in, far as cells go."

Morgan had been honest about that much of the forced bargain anyway, Ryan thought to himself.

Ryan gestured to the chairs, one per side, and father and son sat down facing each other.

"Quiet in here," Ryan observed.

"Not in the cells. Some drunk keeps singing all about moons hitting eyes and big pizza pies."

"Every place like this has got a drunk, Dean."

"I guess."

"You want to tell me what happened?" Ryan asked. "Take it slow and don't leave anything out."

"Not much to tell," Dean said. "We were in the vid arcade, watching some guys play a game...."

HAVING WATCHED the same two boys play Mortal Kombat for about a half hour, Dean decided to wade in for a try first chance he got. The opportunity came when the game finally became vacant after a particularly enthusiastic Dex had run out of the needed tokens and left with Brack to find more.

"Want to take me on, Jak?" Dean asked as they stepped up to the machine.

"No contest. Hand-to-hand. Beat you good," Jak said confidently.

"Not if you don't know the right moves. Got to punch these button, move these levers. And you don't know shit about comps," Dean bragged.

"Like you do."

"Like I do, yeah."

"Back Florida, pressed wrong button, screwed everything up. Ryan pissed good," Jak retorted, referring to a past mat-trans jump where Dean had decided to apply his magic touch to one of the gateway's operating system's keyboards and had sent the stressed comp banks and hardware into a series of fiery shutdowns. Ryan had been furious, picking Dean up with both hands and slamming him down butt first on a table for a conversation that still made the boy feel guilty.

"I still know enough to beat you at this," Dean said insistently.

"Take best shot," Jak replied.

Each of the boys put their tokens in the twin vid slots and was offered a menu of choices of fighters from which to make a selection.

"There's a girl on here, Jak."

"You pick her," the albino retorted. "I'll try go easy on girl."

Before they could do so, however, the two players who had been dominating the machine for most of the night came over.

"You guys took our vid game," Dex accused.

"Not yours." Jak replied. "Ours."

"See, you newbies, you don't understand," Brack said slowly. "Certain games are off-limits when the arcade champions are in the house, and guess what,

Spooky? I'm here, and that's my vid game you're standing in front of."

The larger of the two moved to push Jak aside. The albino effortlessly sidestepped the attempt, grabbing on to the outstretched arm and tossing the attacker over his shoulder. The teen who had been thrown flew helplessly into the heavy plastic-and-metal side of another of the game consoles, hitting it ass first. His breath exploded out of him with a grunt of pain.

Dex quickly scrambled to his feet, his cap now off, his hair tumbling into his eyes. In his right had he held a knife, four-inch blade with a short bone handle. It wasn't a predark weapon, but one manufactured from the remains. Black electrical tape was wrapped around the handle to help hold the steel of the cutting edge in place.

"Come on, you creepy little shit! You want a piece of me?"

Jak brightened. "Knife fight. Okay. Bored comps."

"Hold up, Jak," Dean said. "This is stupid. If he wants the game, let him have it. Dad will be triple pissed if we get into trouble."

"Your dad, not mine. Too late, Dean," Jak replied. "Watch back."

Jak took off his brown-and-green camouflage jacket and pulled his own sharpened blade, switching it swiftly from the right hand to the left. He kept his luminous red orbs focused on his challenger, watching his foe's eyes. Jak had been in enough hand-to-hand brawls to know to never watch the other's man knife, you always watched the other man's eyes.

Unfortunately, before the brawl could really get under way, Brack decided to stack the odds in his buddy's favor by taking out the small .22-caliber handblaster that Jak had spied earlier. The younger boy had slunk to the back of the gathered group watching the fight and was now aiming the pistol at the back of Jak's skull.

Most of the teen onlookers were viewing Jak and Dex warily circle each other, reacting verbally when's Jak's knife bit first, cutting a red slit across his opponent's stomach. The blustering arcade guard was already on the horn, summoning a mall sec team to break up the fight.

The only one keenly watching Brack's progress was Dean. The other member of the arcade-machine-hogging duo was now boldly preparing to shoot the blaster.

Dean was too far away to prevent the chilling without responding with the same kind of force about to be unleashed on his friend, so he pulled his own blaster and shot first.

The first salvo from the Browning went high, racing like a fleeing man into the screen of a colorful vid game. The bullet shattered the exterior protective shield, going into the true vid screen and entering the very guts of the amusement comp's brain. Sparks flew, from both the point of entry and from the jury-rigged wall socket the arcade game was plugged into. Modified to handle four games on a single outlet, the aperture erupted into flames.

For an instant only the four games on the same circuit were affected. Then every piece of electronic gadgetry in the arcade was shorted out one by one, and the room plunged into near darkness.

Brack fired the .22 blindly at the same instant Dean squeezed off a second shot of his own, catching the boy in the throat. A fine red mist sprayed out from the exit wound. The bullet Brack had shot went wild, hitting the disputed Mortal Kombat game in the coin box.

Seeing in the dimness with eyes like a cat, Jak swung out an open palm and caught the second knife-wielding teen in front of him across the face once, twice. The slaps sounded like the cracks of a ringmaster's whip. Immediately the boy's eyes lost their mock killer sheen and started to glaze over in dismay. He started to cry and Jak pressed his attack, backhanding the boy with his knuckles for a third blow to the face.

"Drop knife," Jak said matter-of-factly. "Or I'll gut from balls to nose."

The boy did so.

"Now, drop your blade, boy, or I drop you," a new voice said.

Dean was no longer serving as Jak's backup. As the albino turned to slowly face the speaker, he found his friend was standing with his hands in the air. A trio of Freedom Mall sec men with long blasters was waiting for Jak's next move.

Jak opened his hand, and the knife fell to the carpeted floor.

He could see Dean being relieved of his Browning Hi-Power.

"Guess this means we lose our memberships, huh?" Dean said.

"LOOKS LIKE we're working for you now," Ryan said to Rollins.

All of Ryan's inner circle, except for Dean, were standing before the seated black sec leader.

"Glad to have you on board," Rollins replied, his face an unreadable mask. "I got the word from Mr. Morgan. I understand you two worked out a deal."

"If you want to call it that."

"You want sec jackets? Armor?" the leader of the security force asked.

"Not really. We're not going to be strolling around busting local problems at gaudies or hassling cart vendors," Ryan told him. "We're here to help you with any stickie attacks and to mebbe assist in the training of your greener men."

"Well, that would probably be two-thirds of my current squad."

"How big a crew are you running, honestly?" the one-eyed man asked.

"That's on a need-to-know basis."

"Don't give me that crap. You want my help, I need to know." Ryan gestured to the others around him. "We all do."

Rollins stood. "Let's talk while we move. I'll show you the armory and the training areas."

As the group followed the big sec man, he picked up where he'd left off in the conversation. "There are twenty full-time sec men and ten reserve. Usually we work active sec details on the exterior of the mall, and the surrounding areas in and around Freedom's perimeter during daylight. Day exterior shifts run twelve hours, from eight in the morning to eight at night.''

"What about inside?'' Krysty asked.

"Different kind of sec man. We're more of a presence in here to remind our guests to behave. Day patrols on the mall interior are on a light duty roster. Most of our hard labor comes after dark, both on the inside after people start drinking and the outside when the muties get restless. More often than not, people on the inside of Freedom have no clue there's a problem outdoors, and that's the way we want to keep it.''

"How does the night shift break down?'' J.B. asked as all of them stepped into former mall loading dock that had been taken over with targets, tumbling mats and exercise equipment. A few sealed wooden cases of weapons could be seen in a corner, locked up in a fenced-in area. Some of Rollins's regular sec squad were working out.

"If you work days, the shift is longer 'cause there's lower stress. Work nights, you can go from eight to four in the morning, or from midnight to eight. There's some overlap. That's on purpose since it falls at the same time we tend to have the most problems. Stickie activity usually hits between midnight and 2:00 a.m., although they've been known to come earlier and try again later.''

Ryan leaned against a rack of barbells. "Okay, here's the way we're going to do this,'' he said. "We'll all stay on the night shift with patrolling and training. I don't give a rip for day duty if the action

always comes after sunset. Give us a few days to get
acclimated, meet your men and we'll try playing
school. J.B. here can talk hardware. I'm on tactics
with J.B. Jak over there might not look like much,
but he's the finest hand-to-hand fighter I've ever
known. All of us have been involved in close-combat
fights with stickies before and survived, so it's not
impossible. Stickies might be scary to some, but
they're also triple stupe. Usually you can outsmart
them.''

"What's standard armament for your sec men?''
J.B. asked.

"M-16 long blasters. M-16 A-2s to be exact.''

"Chambered to take 5.56 mm rounds?''

"Right.''

The M-16 was the traditional weapon of the smart
sec man or hired mercies. The effective range of the
now classic Army blaster was just under 350 yards.
The weapon could be fired in four modes: on single
shot, semiauto, automatic or full cycle. Capable of
firing close to a thousand rounds of ammunition per
minute, keeping an M-16 on full cycle would empty
a full 30-round magazine in under two seconds.

"Got a few extras of the M-16 if you want them,
but there's not much ammo. We're lacking in that
department. Haven't gotten a new supply in months.''

"Which explains why the blaster-and-ammo store
we went to earlier had been closed,'' Ryan said.

"We had to confiscate his stores. The man was
paid, of course.''

"Of course.''

"Been meaning to ask you, Dr. Wyeth—why do

you keep carrying around a target pistol? We could fix you up with an autoblaster with no problem,'' Rollins remarked.

Mildred hefted the ZKR 551 6-shot Czech revolver and sighted an imaginary target as she replied, ''I've always been a believer in staying with what you know, and I know this revolver. Know how it feels, know how it shoots. I can draw, aim and fire without even thinking and hit my target time and time again with this blaster. Switch to something new, even with an increased bullet capacity, and by the time I learn it as well as I know this gun, I'd probably be dead.''

''I see. Very well, the—''

Mildred wasn't finished. ''I like simplicity. The double-action revolver is a self-loading design, allowing the operator to cock the hammer and rotate the cylinder simultaneously, and then release the hammer with one trigger pull. Or if I choose, I can thumb-cock this baby like an old single-action revolver. And I always know how many bullets I have. With an auto, you have to count.''

''Not if you have enough clips.''

''Outside, extra ammo isn't usually an option. A revolver is easy to operate. The ammo in the chamber is clearly visible and never, ever misfires. If a shell jams, you just keep pulling the trigger and rotate the cylinder to the next shell. If you keep trying to blast away with an automatic, you have to stop, eject and remove the dud by hand,'' she said as she replaced the blaster in her holster.

''Give me a good automatic any day,'' Rollins told her.

"To each his own. Like I said, the extra shots don't mean much in that kind of situation. My pistol has a smooth trigger action, again adding to accuracy. And in a pinch, I can fire a variety of bullet loads, even though this one's been chambered to take a Smith & Wesson .38-caliber round. Try doing that with a 5.56 mm auto."

"You make it sound damn near perfect. Although that hand cannon is bulky and takes much longer to reload compared to an automatic. Autoloaders help, but you still lose seconds opening up the chamber, lining up the bullets and closing shop. And we both know the velocity falls short of an autopistol. High muzzle velocity will always provide the maximum penetration."

"Why, Mr. Rollins, perhaps you know more about guns than you're letting on." Mildred said with a smile.

Rollins returned the grin. "Could be."

"What have you got stockpiled?" J.B. interrupted, an uncharacteristic twinge of jealousy making him speak up.

"Not as much as I'd like. We did have more, but a lot of the good stuff has been used previously. Mr. Morgan had more blasters and ammo on order from a baron upstate who was open to trading, but they never arrived."

"Hope the stickies didn't end up attacking a convoy and getting the damn things."

"You and me both."

Chapter Twenty-One

Downtown Winston-Salem, North Carolina, was a morass of skyscrapers and smaller buildings aligned in a boxy grid network. During the boom years, it was known as the city that tobacco built, and locals wore the label with pride...until smoking became a habit less and less tolerated by the general public. Harvested crops went unsold, and advertising avenues continued to dry up, until finally the use of tobacco in the United States became an almost underground movement.

The tobacco companies found their salvation in overseas sales. Asian companies, as well as the former Soviet bloc countries, had always had a lustful gleam in their respective eyes for the various brands of American cigarettes. When the big business of tobacco found their own country was more than willing to cast them out, and the special interests and bought-and-paid-for friendships had evaporated with the prevailing political climate, there was no looking back.

And Winston-Salem was never the same again.

That part of North Carolina hadn't been struck with the explosive force and precision of the mighty earth-shaker bombs during that cold January in the year 2001, nor had nuclear devices been detonated anywhere nearby. Some chem warfare had been launched farther down at the base of the Triad area, but of a form and fashion that only killed off the surviving humans in rapid fashion while leaving the buildings and machinery and other nonliving constructs intact.

The primary stickie base in that part of Carolina was located way downtown in a ramshackle old tobacco warehouse on Liberty Street. The large double doors were padlocked shut, but there was a private back entrance that allowed full access to open space within, a wide-open space that housed an entire community of the freakish mutants.

Many of the muties were quiet, half-sleeping from inactivity and boredom, loath to step outside into the sunlight. A more active splinter group was seated in a semicircle made of old recliner chairs and sofas.

"Norms," one of the stickies said in a thick, halting voice.

A period of time passed while damaged, rad-altered and inbred brain cells tried to shake themselves into providing enough energy to fire the necessary pinprick burst of electricity for another coherent thought.

Five minutes passed, maybe six. There were no complaints. Many stickies had no concept of time. Sunup and sundown was the extent of how their own internal biological clocks ticked. Stickies needed very little sleep due to their higher body metabolisms. The only thing fast about them were the killing rages they could be induced into by high stress and fireworks and explosions.

The same stickie spoke again. "Norms...suck," he declared.

"Yeah, Howie," a second mutant agreed, his

words articulated with more care and speed . "You said it. Took you long enough, but you said it for all of us."

Other stickies now began to speak, their comments overlapping and interrupting.

"Drove the norms out of the city, but they still want to stay in the mall."

"I hear the mall's nice."

"Norms like it. Norms like nice things. Nice soft things."

"Mmm. Norms are soft."

"Norms are pussies."

"Could go for some norm pussy."

Stickie laughter rang out in the warehouse. Rough sex with a norm was always a treat, and they knew the mall was full of succulent norm flesh. More discussion created a sexually charged atmosphere, and one or two of the slower stickies were aroused and turned their attention to more immediate fulfillment.

"Yeah. Yeah," one of the pair breathed as his right arm worked. He looked at himself with approval as he tugged and pulled to create the enjoyable feelings.

The second stickie involved in self-gratification wasn't paying heed. He was involved with his own pleasure, preferring a softer, gentler touch that left him unaware of his surroundings.

"I don't believe this," a new voice said. Unlike the others in the room, this voice was hurried, with the words almost rushing out and stepping on top of one another to get what was needed said as quickly as possible. "Playing with yourselves again? If you're horny, go find a mutie slut. Just spare me the sight of you guys flogging your logs for the amusement of your fellow muties.''

Norm and Budd came out of the small office near the semicircle of furniture. Once the office had been used for the dispatcher to check in and send out truckloads of tobacco, but now it was a base of operations for the new leaders of the stickie horde.

The pair had been living in Winston for many weeks now, and as the scarred human had predicted, the two had managed to align the stickie population into more of a coherent fighting force than ever before, even raiding convoys for weapons. Any qualms about Norm's ancestry had been dismissed by his sheer ugliness and by the long-haired Budd's willingness to back his friend up to the table.

Politics weren't a stickie pastime. As long as they got to spend time burning and chilling, they were content to take Norm's lead.

''See, Budd?'' Norm said, his voice dripping with disgust. ''This is why stickies are the joke of Deathlands. When you could be plotting to take over, you're too damn busy holding jack-off contests.''

''Got someone for you to talk with,'' one of the members of the half circle said slowly as he zipped up his pants. ''Show you.''

Norm and Budd followed the stickie to a corner room in the warehouse.

''Who is it?'' Norm asked.

''A scavie. Has information to sell.''

''Never heard tell of that, a man willing to rat out his kind to a mutie,'' Norm said. ''Could be a trick.''

''Perhaps…he wants to live.'' Budd said. ''Man

wants to live…might do anything. You should know."

Norm's lidless eye glared at the stickie. "He should *still* know better."

Budd stopped before exiting the room. "What about you, Norm? How do you fit in?"

Norm's face became even uglier. "Shut your hole, Budd, before I shut it for you."

The disfigured man walked into the dimly lit room, where Alton Adrian was tied to a rickety kitchen chair. The man had been stripped naked, his long hair and beard the only covering on his entire body. A dirty gag was wadded into his mouth. The areas of exposed skin showed evidence of the loving touches laid upon him by his stickie captors.

Norm began walking around the terrified bound man in a slow, lazy circle. "Most of the problems I've ever had to deal with in Deathlands come from people trespassing," he said. "Going where they don't belong. There's ways of making jack doing this—if you find them on your land or using your stuff, you charge them a fee. Make them pay. Used to get my joint sucked two or three times a week when I was a mercie running a toll road. See, if they didn't have the jack, well, I made those going on through pay in different ways."

"Who are you?" the scavie asked in a weak voice muffled by the gag.

From behind Adrian, his captor spoke softly, in a near whisper: "No questions. I'm talking now. You were over at the old hospital, my friend. Round in the same area where six of my men disappeared a few days back. Now, I'm sure you'll agree that stickies are not the most brilliant of the many noble creatures roaming Deathlands, and perhaps they got lost or ran off or even found a room and ended up locking themselves in. I don't know. All I have is the evidence in front of me, and that's you.''

Norm reached down and cupped Adrian's chin with a hand covered in scars. His fingernails were long and sharp, jagged and uneven. He moved his hand up and ripped the gag out of his prisoner's mouth.

Adrian inhaled deeply, the smell of rotting flesh flowing into his lungs as he breathed. He gagged, but kept his composure as best he could.

"One of my friends says you have information to barter for your own miserable life," Norm said.

"Y-yeah."

"What is that information?"

The scavenger paused, wondering if he could talk his way through being chilled on the spot. "I know what happened to those six stickies."

Norm's one bulging eye seemed to grow larger in the broken socket of his face. "Do you, now?"

"They're chilled. All of them."

"How?

"They were chilled by a man named Ryan Cawdor."

The utterance of the name had a most curious and unexpected effect on the scarred man standing before the helpless Alton Adrian. The mention of Cawdor caused Norm to twist his once burned fingers into a bony fist and strike out, catching Adrian full in the mouth. The skin on his knuckles peeled back from the gap where the scavenger's front teeth were missing, making Norm bleed freely. The force from the surprise blow caused the chair to tip over on one side.

"You stinkin' liar!" Norm cried, kicking Adrian in the ribs. "No fucking way is One-eye here! No fucking way!"

All of the control, all of the posing, all of the attempts to pass himself off as something more than man or mutie had been erased the moment Ryan's name came into the picture. Norm was gone, and in his place was Johnson Lester, the cowardly sec man who'd encountered Ryan twice before.

Lester, who blamed Ryan for the downfall of Willie ville, and for his own miserable luck in being forced to work the wheel, and being caught when the ville was blown apart.

Lester, who'd been saved by a stickie and traveled to Winston in hopes to staking his own claim to power.

Lester, who was now undeniably insane.

"Sure," Adrian replied, speaking through his split upper lip. "Sure, he's here. Ryan Cawdor, or One-eye, with the eye patch, and J. B. Dix, and the albino, and the old fart they call Doc, and the woman with red hair—"

"Mutie!" Lester screamed, cutting Adrian off. "She's a mutie bitch whore!"

"All of them killed those stickies," the scavie said. "Now they're in Freedom. Working sec. Mall's been getting ripped by stickie attacks. Got them to help. Heard about that right before leaving Freedom yesterday."

Adrian was talking faster now, hoping he'd be freed. He spoke of frozen heads and hidden loot, but quickly went back to Ryan when his captor demanded to know more. He'd switched the man's attention to another object of hate. He'd given him information. Perhaps he'd managed to talk his way clear, and if so, he was getting the hell out of North Carolina as fast as he could run, and going all the way back to Georgia, and to his family, and his home.

And when Adrian finally fell silent, his throat raw and aching, Lester had crawled back into whatever mental cubby hole the scarred man kept his former persona tucked away in and the much cooler Norm had come back out and was driving the wag.

"You were correct, Mr. Adrian," Norm said, cool, calm, collected. "Your information has proved most valuable."

Alton dared another question. "Can I have my clothes?"

"Why? Of what use are they to you now?"

Adrian's stomach turned to ice, as cold and hard as any of the men frozen solid in the cryo laboratory he'd seen before.

"Need my clothes to leave," he stammered. "I— I'm leaving this hole and never coming back."

"Well, you're right about one thing. I do indeed doubt you are ever coming back," Norm said, smiling cruelly as he opened the door to the earthen cell and waved in the two waiting stickies. The muties effortlessly lifted the scavenger and the chair he was bound to between them and followed Norm out of the door.

And then it was Adrian's turn to scream, cry and

curse as his own inner demons and fears came scuttling out, unleashed and gibbering as he was carried into the center of the cavernous tobacco warehouse and dropped painfully to the floor. The wooden chair splintered and broke, and he was free, his arms and legs tangled in strands of wire. He rolled in the dust, struggling in the dimly lit area to stand erect.

How could his big score have gone so badly? He'd only wanted a second look at the cryo chambers for himself and now he'd succeeded in chilling himself.

He got to his feet and saw the circle of the stickies closing around him.

"Please," he begged, weeping, tears running down his cheeks and into his beard. His cut lips started to bleed from Norm's sucker punch once more. "Please!"

The smell of the blood from the injured human made the circle of stickies anxious. Norm stepped forward from the circle, carrying a small metal canister painted in deep green.

"Do you know what is inside this container?" he asked to a chorus of oohs and aahs.

Two stickies hesitantly raised their hands, like obedient pupils in a classroom.

"Not you, dammit," Norm growled. "I was talking to our guest."

Adrian didn't answer.

"Come now, you're a scavie!" Norm needled him, holding out the canister like the eager host of a pre-dark game show. "You've seen this before! Inform us!"

The naked man continued to cry.

"I take it back," Norm snorted, raking his gaze over his brethren. "As bad as you stickies get, at least you don't shit yourself and start sniveling when your number is up."

Norm stepped up to the weeping Adrian and grabbed him by the hair, pulling hard, making the man crane his neck and fall back as he looked up into the horribly disfigured man's eyes, which seemed to be glowing with a malevolent evil. Adrian looked up and knew in his heart he was viewing the devil himself.

"This, friend Alton, is a container filled with black powder. As I'm sure you've heard, what with your thriving career in information exchange, that stickies have developed most unusual ways of using this substance for their own amusement. A cut here, a stab there, and fill the hole with powder. Or if one doesn't want to make a hole, one can use some of the other orifices of the human body. Eye sockets, ears, the nose, mouth. A particular favorite is ramming a heaping helping of powder up a man's ass and lighting a fuse. Boom! Blows his cock clear across the room!"

The gathered stickies began to gibber and talk among themselves, waiting for the word. Norm turned to them to grin and wallow in the sensation of power, still keeping his grip on the scavie's hair.

"If the powder disturbs you, we can try some other stickie game. Perhaps tie you down spread-eagle, and push thumbtacks in your eyes. Push straight pins under your fingernails, into your balls. Take a knife and cut you to pieces, a bit at a time. There are always alternatives."

Adrian was listening and decided Norm was right. He reached up, grabbing the scarred man's hand that gripped his hair. He grabbed the hand with both of his own, and pulled with all of his fading strength. Norm fell flat, dropping the powder and losing his hold on his prisoner's hair. Adrian rolled over on his captor and began to throttle him with both hands.

"If I die, you're going with me!" he screamed as he squeezed as hard as he could, willing all of his own hate and fear into the man below him.

His last, desperate ploy never stood a chance.

The stickies fell upon him from all sides, their terrible clinging hands adhering and lifting, tearing his body and flesh in all directions in a massive display of carnage. Red blood and white bone; tan skin shredded and burst purple internal organs, all on display as the man was disemboweled and eviscerated like a fleshy piñata by the mutie pack's horrible abilities.

Budd helped Norm to his feet as the other stickies paraded the various body parts of Alton Adrian around the warehouse.

"Tonight," Norm stated. "We go tonight."

"Not ready," Budd tried to protest. "We need time."

"Cawdor is in there, laughing at me. We go tonight. I'm chilling him personally! We go tonight!"

Chapter Twenty-Two

After two days of their assigned duties, everyone in Ryan's group was bored with the riches offered by Freedom Mall. Even with their newly enhanced positions as sec men, there was nothing free in the way of entertainment. Sleeping, eating, relaxing—it all came with a price, and the price wasn't cheap.

Still, there were distractions.

"Haven't been down this part of the mall before," Mildred said to her two companions. "What's the map say?"

J.B. took out a folded pocket guide to Freedom and consulted the layout. "Multiplex."

"You mean movies?" Mildred asked.

"Yeah. Reckon so."

"A theater! Splendid! Perhaps we can hope for a classic from days gone by? A brightly colored musical with the likes of Kelly or Astaire? A moody film noir with Bogart or Cagney, or even that femme fatale Barbara Stanwick, leading poor, baffled Fred Mac-Murray to his own lust-caused doom?"

J.B. turned to Doc with a look of mock surprise. "Didn't know you gave a damn for movies, Doc. Thought you hated them."

Doc shook his head vigorously. "Incorrect! False! Not true! What I hate, John Barrymore, is television.

Puerile dribble to sell boxes of soap! But this, this is a movie palace, and for once I shall view a motion picture at the scale the makers intended instead of viewing them via a vid player on snow-enhanced tape."

"I doubt that, Doc," Mildred said as they approached the front of the theater. There were slots out front for movie posters and announcements, but all hung empty or blank. A single tube-shaped box office could be spotted on a slight incline, and behind the office was the door into the concession stand and lobby. Very efficient and very bland.

"This is one of those concrete-bunker affairs. Small screen, small seats, small portions at the concession stand. The only thing big about a mall cinema is the prices."

"Small screen?" Doc said, his expression one of disbelief. "Why on earth would a theater proprietor want to vex his patrons with a small screen?"

"Economics," Mildred replied. "Smaller the setup, the more screens you can cram into a space. Smaller seats means more warm bodies. Why run one show when you can run six, then sell six times the amount of overpriced concessions at the same time?"

"Disgraceful," Doc said. "I'd always been under the impression there was something romantic about the movies in their natural habitat."

"There is," Mildred mused. "There's nothing like seeing a movie on a big screen."

"I wouldn't know," Doc sniffed.

"Me, neither," J.B. added. "Seen some in villes on old 16 mm projectors. Hard to see and hear."

"Next show's at nine o'clock. What time is it?" Mildred asked.

J.B. checked his wrist chron. "About ten minutes to. We got the time and the extra mall creds to see a picture, if you want. We don't go on sec patrol until we meet up with Ryan and the others at midnight."

"I wonder if they have popcorn?" Mildred asked.

"From my understanding, it wouldn't be a proper motion-picture palace if it didn't," Doc said as they approached the glassed-in area marked Box Office.

"What movie is playing?" Mildred asked the man sitting behind the glass through a small metal grid. He was dressed in a crushed-velvet vest and matching bow tie. An employee tag identifying him as Boston hung from the breast pocket of his vest.

"You'll love it, lady," Boston replied. "Ripping good horror show. Zombies come back from the dead to feast on the human flesh of the living. Great gore with some hilarious comedy. Splatstick, is what I've heard it called. Sells out every time we screen it."

Doc's hopes of a musical comedy were swiftly being dashed upon the unyielding rocks of commerce.

"Most disturbing. When was this film made?" the old man asked.

The ticket salesman paused for a moment and closed his eyes, as if accessing a bank of data files stored on the hard drive of his brain.

"*Dawn of the Dead.* 1979 predark calendar. A Laurel production. A United Film Distribution release. Full color. Running time of 126 minutes uncut, or significantly shorter in the cable edit, and who the fuck wants to see the censored version anyway, so it doesn't count.''

''A full two hours plus,'' J.B. said approvingly as a man who loved a bargain. ''Not bad.''

The ticket seller continued to speak, unaware or uncaring of J.B.'s approval. ''Written, directed and edited by the great George A. Romero, who also gave us *Stephen King's Creepshow, Martin, Day of the Dead* and many other fine horror pictures. Cinematography by Michael Gornick. Music by the Goblins with Dario Argento. Sequel to the classic *Night of the Living Dead,* which is pretty good, but it's in black and white, and the only version I've seen was fuzzy as hell, so the blood and guts look all fake.''

''For Christ's sake,'' Mildred said to her two companions, ''I can see this kind of crap on an all-too-regular basis in Deathlands. Why would I want to go to a movie and pay good money to experience it?''

''Nothing else better to do,'' J.B. replied.

''Aren't you showing anything else?'' she asked Boston.

The man shook his head. ''Lady, at this moment we only have four movies in complete enough condition to screen—*Dawn of the Dead, Mannequin 2: on the Move, Spy Hard* and *Escape from New York.* This theater rotates them on a monthly basis. Every once in a while, I'll pull out chunks of other flicks I've spliced together from stray film cans just so we can offer something different, but most of our customers want a complete show, and I can't blame them. Plenty enough vids with a beginning, middle and end to keep their interest at home. We have to try and make coming to a movie theater a special experience.''

"Ironic, isn't it, Doc?" Mildred said.

"What?"

"Back in the fifties, television nearly ran movie theaters out of business. Producers had to come up with all kinds of gimmicks and sensationalism to keep attendance levels high. Wide screens. Quad sound. Fake insurance policies sold at the door in case you or a loved one dropped dead of fright while watching the film.''

"Sounds like a sideshow to me," Doc said.

"Show business is show business," Mildred replied. "Until the advent of home video in the late seventies, the movie industry had become a mere ghost of what it once had been. Once home vid players come into vogue, there was money all around. Financially a profit could be made not only on tickets sold, but also on vid rights, cable, network-television rights and so on.''

"I think I understand. Here we are, one-hundred-plus years later, and most physical films capable of being viewed on the big screen have been destroyed—''

"But videotapes of the movies survive. Exactly," Mildred finished.

"So, we going or not?" J.B. asked.

Mildred looked at the fellow manning the ticket booth. "This place sell popcorn?" she asked.

WHILE MILDRED, Doc and J.B. were preparing to enjoy a movie, Ryan, Jak and Krysty were on duty in the small sec headquarters in the back of the mall. The monitor board in the sec room burst into vibrant color, with an incessant warning alarm.

"What the fuck is that?" Ryan asked, instantly alert as he leaped to his feet.

"Motion sensors," a techie in a blue jumpsuit replied. "We've got intruders up on the roof."

"Show me."

When he tapped into the same vid system Ryan had seen earlier in Morgan's administrative office, two screens lit up, and what they revealed was smoke and flame.

"Roof's on fire," Ryan said. "Think the stickies are using another catapult?"

"Don't see how. There has been nothing on the group level outside within the sec circle."

"Muties must be behind this somehow," Ryan murmured, standing behind the techie and gazing at the scene.

"Probably so. Both ends of the mall roof are showing movement," the techie said. "How they got on the roof is anybody's guess. We've only got cameras for this side. I don't know if the other section has been lit up or not."

"What's with the alarm?" Rollins said as he clomped into the room.

"We've got company," Ryan replied tightly, gesturing toward the screens. "Look for yourself."

"Shit. Fire. I hate fires," the sec man said.

"Has to be stickies."

Rollins nodded in agreement. "Let's take a look. You get the two of yours, and I'll alert two of mine.

We'll go up and recce on this side. I'll alert a team on the other side of Freedom to check their end, as well.''

"Got it."

Rollins's men were already waiting when he and Ryan exited the monitor room. The four men raced down the access hallway, picking up Krysty and Jak on the way. Like Ryan, both of his friends already had their hardware in hand, with Krysty holding her .38-caliber Smith & Wesson and Jak his huge .357 Colt Python with the six-inch barrel.

"What's with the parade, lover?" Krysty asked.

"Visitors. Set off the motion sensors on the roof. If we're lucky, it's just a flying squirrel or a bunch of birds or something," Ryan told her.

"In the middle of the night?" Rollins said. "I doubt it's birds. Squirrels, either, unless you've ever seen one that weighs a hundred pounds."

Ryan laughed. "Brother, I've seen things in Deathlands that make a hundred-pound squirrel look like a stuffed cuddly toy."

Rollins cocked his blaster. "Don't matter to me none. A hundred pounds or a thousand, a few rounds to the head will take care of the son of a bitch. I just don't want to be the one stuck with the shovel having to bury his big fuzzy ass."

The narrow workmen's stairwell to the roof was dimly lit with red bulbs, giving the group the sensation of walking up through the intestines of a volcano. There were no sounds here. The alarms that had been tripped on the rooftop were silent this close to the scene.

When they came out of the elevated trapdoor entrance onto the rooftop, the group of six split into two parties. Ryan kept Krysty and Jak. Rollins took his own pair of trained men. This decision was made wordlessly and without conscious thought. Each man wanted his own crew backing him up. Ryan could respect that.

Rollins swung open the door and carefully leaned his head out, letting his eyes adjust to the scene.

As far as the eye could see from the protection of the small freestanding doorway of the roof level stairs access, fires were burning in patches.

"Smell it?" Ryan asked.

"Some fuel," Jak replied.

"Flammable liquids. They've sprayed the roof and lit it up somehow," Rollins said. "How in the hell did they do that?"

"Must have a really long hose."

"Well, the fires I can see. Let's try finding them. Maxwell, you got the hardware?" Rollins asked.

"Yes, sir," one of the two sec men who had accompanied Rollins replied.

Ryan looked at the device the younger man was holding. "It's an image intensifier," Maxwell explained.

"Thought we could use it to see what was on the ground," Rollins said.

"I'm getting some ground movement," Maxwell replied. "They look too damn far away to have done this, though."

Those were the last words the young sec man ever said before a loud shot rang out above the soft crackling of the flames. The oversize image intensifier he was holding to his eyes disintegrated into a cloud of plastic shards, and his face immediately followed, the upper half of his head breaking open from the slug that killed him.

"From above!" Jak cried, raising the big Colt and firing into the darkness overhead.

"How?" Krysty asked, and then she saw what Jak was aiming at. A stickie was indeed overhead, hanging from the tubing of a makeshift glider like an evil, diseased bat. She could see the mutie's pale face as the craft swooped around, diving again for another pass. More of the flammable liquid was dropped, sprayed from an oversize plastic-bag apparatus to cause a new burst of flame to shoot into the air.

A side effect of this action was to bring the glider and the mutie into fully lit focus.

A series of shots rang out, and the stickie went limp in the harness of the flying machine. Without the creature's guidance, the glider began to swoop and spiral, finally landing in the midst of an already burning patch of roof in a more explosive show of vigorous flame.

"Never thought I'd see a stickie smart enough to try that," Krysty remarked. Her words reminded Ryan of the comment Morgan had made about the stickies seeming to act smarter in their more recent forays against Freedom.

"Not that much to gliding, as I understand it," Rollins said. "And the crafts are certainly portable enough. They break down—nothing but plastic, canvas and some metal tubing. Fold them up and put them in a bag after you're done.''

Jak wasn't so admiring of the tactics. "Dead. Stupe.''

"Mebbe not," Ryan said. "Whoever sent that mutie up there hovering around knew his card would get slotted quick enough. Those gliders have some maneuverability, but they're not very fast. The mutie was able to get some good fires going while up there, but that could've been handled in a number of different ways.''

"You saying we were supposed to see that stickie?''

"Diversion," Jak said.

"Need to get around the fires, closer to the edge of the roof. If I was planning on attacking from the top, I'd try and come up where the visibility was poorest. Like way over there behind those old air con units," Ryan said.

"So...?''

"So hold on while I check it out.''

Ryan moved quickly, running as quietly as possible along the back of the front line of the rooftop's massive array of ancient and rusted air-conditioning circulation pods, using their bulk to hide and protect his progress. The stickies near the edge of the rooftop were waving flaming torches and yelling and whooping, and already more of the small fires were starting to burn.

They also had weapons. The stickies were now armed with high-powered blasters, such as the one that had chilled Maxwell. Ryan heard the occasional crack of blaster, and once or twice stray rounds had whined past and ricocheted off the thick metal units protecting him, causing them to boom hollowly and flaking the thick rusty covering. The stickies weren't aiming at him. They didn't even know Ryan was there. They were wasting rounds, showing off and enjoying the fires.

Ryan knew his friends would also have heard the shots. His SIG-Sauer was cocked in his right hand, and he ran in a crouch, stopping only to peer between individual units to make certain he wasn't seen.

He crawled on top of the last unit, keeping himself as flat as a sheet of paper as he wiggled across silently, inch by inch.

"Hey, you. You're trespassing," Ryan called out, pausing a second to line and sight before shooting the stickie through the top of the head. The baffle-silenced slug drove through the mutie's lopsided cranium, pureeing the rotten brain inside and causing a twin jet of blood to spurt like a backwash out of the stickie's nose. Ryan's shot had landed neatly dead center, and the bullet kept crashing down like a runaway freight elevator, leaving behind a wet trail of destruction inside the mutie's thrashing body.

The stickie's corpse collapsed onto the roof, into a burning pyre. The smell of burning flesh was instantly recognizable in the night air.

Ryan, however, wasn't waiting around to admire his handiwork. He was already rolling, firing his blaster as he moved. The element of surprise was still with him. When the first stickie died, all eyes fell upon its death throes, but no one thought to look up.

Gripping his right wrist with his left hand, Ryan braced himself against the kick of the powerful pistol as it spit death again and again. His aim no longer needed to be as precise as the first kill, so he took chest shots, the safest option against his now moving targets.

A chest shot was never as elegant, clean or final as a head shot, but it had the advantage of not mattering much whether you were a couple of inches high or low or to either side. If your aim was high, you still took out the throat or heart or one of the lungs. Shoot a man—even a stickie—in the rib cage and watch him fall down gasping for air.

Go low, and you had an old-fashioned, hurt-like-hell gut shot, which was more than likely going to end up being a killing hit when delivered with a 9 mm round from a P-226 blaster. As J.B. had said more than once, "You hit when you miss with a chest shot. Nothing fancy about a shooting like that, but it gets the job done."

Ryan's backup was close behind him, closer still when the first shot exploded in the burning night.

The big sec man slowed as he approached the scene. "Christ, Cawdor, you chilled them all," he said.

"Don't fall all over yourself thanking me, Rollins."

"I've never seen anything like it," the younger man in the mall sec colors said. "Five stickies downed by a single man."

"Friend of mine once told me a running man with

a sharp knife can slit a thousand throats in a single night,'' Ryan said. "As long as he's quiet about it."

The lead sec man waved over his single living follower. "Use the tank extinguisher. It should have a full charge. Put those fires out as fast as you can."

"Yes, sir!"

"Still wish you would have left one alive for questioning,'' Rollins griped. "Dead muties can't talk."

"Since when have you ever known a stickie to volunteer any information? Even if they knew anything, half the time the stupe…" Ryan's voice trailed off, the sight of Krysty's face tight with pain taking his earlier thought away.

"I'm okay, lover," she said softly, catching his eye peering intently at her. "But we got major trouble."

"What?"

"Bad. Very bad. I've got a mental picture of the roof of this mall, and it's bright red, all red."

"What the fuck is she talking about?" the sec leader said angrily. Ryan could see confusion and fear in the big man's face. He'd gone about his life expecting stickies to perform and act a certain way. Now that the patterns had changed, he was losing his grip. Ryan wasn't surprised. Most men would have done likewise when confronted with the abnormal, and there was nothing normal about the ways these stickies were behaving.

"Told you before, Rollins, she's a seer," Ryan said. "Senses danger. Bad things to come."

"As red as blood, as red as fire," Krysty whispered, every hair on her head moving gently back and forth like wheat in a strong breeze.

"Shut her up, Cawdor," Rollins ordered, his eyes wide.

"Why? She scaring you? Good."

Rollins shook his head. "We don't have time for crazy mutie talk."

"We'd better make time," Ryan insisted. "Shit's about to hit the fan."

The small radio on Rollins's gun belt squawked, the shrill tone adding to the mounting tension between the two men.

"Go ahead, answer," Ryan said. "I don't think either one of us is going to like what we hear."

Rollins snatched the black-and-silver portable comm radio off his belt and thumbed the Send button. "What?" he half yelled into the tiny voice grid.

"This is Jameson, sir. From the west wing," an excited voice said.

"I've got problems of my own, Jameson. Make it quick."

"The stickies, sir. They're over here. The bastards are coming in from all sides. We shot down one in a hang glider, but not before he dropped a shitload of rope ladders and some kind of flaming napalm. We're boxed in, and more of them are crawling up the sides. What are we going to do?"

Chapter Twenty-Three

The interior of Freedom Mall was a scene of mass chaos. Word about the mutie attack from all quarters had spread effortlessly through the storefronts and common areas of the mall, creating a panic where panic was the only foe to fight. And as the word spread and the fear grew, a planning flaw in the reconfiguration of the mall's sec setup was becoming painfully evident.

The main entrance into the massive two-story construction was also the site of the primary exit, since all fire doors, loading docks and the nearly forty other former exit-entrances into Freedom had been long since barricaded shut with concrete and stone, and chain and metal.

As the masses tried to flee from terrors both real and imagined, the greed in men's hearts came bubbling up to the surface. Realizing that all of the available members of the Freedom Mall sec staff were busy with the stickie onslaught, looters appeared in all of the stores and shops. Some of the establishments were closed for the night, others abandoned by their owners, who had fled into the mob attempting to escape. These were loudly ransacked.

However, other store owners had no interest in leaving their staked territory. Any thieves entering these stores with stealing on their minds found proprietors hidden inside armed and waiting for whatever threat might come bursting through their doors. Crazed human or crazier mutie, they didn't care. Try to infringe on what was theirs, and a person would be cut down in a hail of blasterfire.

At the multiplex, Doc, J.B. and Mildred had learned of the crisis when the movie had been stopped in midreel. Mildred hadn't minded the interruption in the least. The humor of *Dawn of the Dead* was being totally lost on her, as well as on Doc, although J.B. seemed to be greatly enjoying himself.

The angry audience had taken offense and was ready to lynch the projectionist until Boston from the box office came out with news of what was happening outside.

Now the three friends were struggling to make their way through the teeming, panicked masses. The looting of the many mall business establishments had already begun, an unstoppable wave of shrieking lust for food, clothing and, best of all, material possessions.

"By the Three Kennedys!" Doc bellowed, raising his voice to be heard over of the cacophony of the mob. "These ignorant fools are raiding their own henhouses! Can they not see they are assisting in the destruction of their own sanctuary?"

"They don't give a damn, Doc," Mildred replied sadly. "They just don't care. I haven't seen the likes of this since the 1992 L.A. riots. Tomorrow there might be some remorse mixed in with twinges of guilt, but tonight is wilding time. The time of the unleashed collective id.''

"Don't quote Freud to me, Doctor. Sometimes a cigar is a cigar, and sometimes a pack of wolves is a pack of wolves," Doc retorted, using his sheathed swordstick to beat and jab a clear path through the milling mass of people.

"Watch it," one unruly mass of muscle and leather spun and bellowed at Doc. "Poke me again, and I'll jam that toothpick up your skinny ass."

"Better men than you have tried, sir," Doc bellowed back.

J.B raised his M-4000 scattergun. "Keep moving, friend, or I'll clear a path the old-fashioned way," the Armorer intoned. "Right though your gut."

The talking mass of muscle looked at the twin barrels, snorted and continued on, allowing the trio to pass unmolested down the annex area to the entrance of the satellite mall-sec headquarters. As official members of the sec team, each knew the entry code. Doc took the honors, beeping in the series of numbers to command the door to unlock.

No sliding pneumatic doorways here. After the door popped open and swung inward on the hinges, it remained that way until pulled tightly closed and left sealed for the next visitor who needed access to the sec area.

What the friends found inside were two faces belonging to their fellow sec men, two men armed with M-16 autoblasters leveled right at them as they entered.

"Come on in," Ike said, a turbanlike white bandage wound around his head.

"Always good to see friends," Mike echoed.

"REPORT, AND KEEP IT SHORT," Rollins hissed into the hand comm unit. Around him his remaining backup man and Ryan and the others cast nervous eyes into the darkness around the roof of Freedom Mall.

"The roof's on fire over here. Going up fast," the frightened voice replied through the unit. "And we're pinned down by high-powered blasterfire. Can't get through the access hatch. Where'd they get the blasters, sir?"

"Where doesn't matter. Dealing with it is. Regroup your party. You'll have to move over and above to get to where we are. We've secured this end. In fact we'll try and meet you halfway if possible. Rollins out." The big man terminated the communication and returned the radio to his belt.

"They need backup," Ryan said.

"I know."

"Is it possible to go from one end to the other by roof?" Krysty asked.

Rollins leaned down to tighten a lace on his combat boots. "That's the idea. We'll use the stickie fires to guide us."

Ryan took off at a measured sprint, Jak and Krysty both at his heels.

STILL IN A CROUCH, Rollins followed Ryan's lead. Both men stayed low until reaching the outcropping of the built-up skylight area used to provide natural lighting to Freedom during daylight hours. Ryan continued to squat, his knees protesting from being forced to support his full body weight for so long.

Each of them held their breath, waiting, listening for any type of noise to come.

Rollins had attempted another communication with Jameson's sec team, but had gotten nothing back in the way of an answer but static.

Ryan eased out of the crouched position and turned to look beyond the elevated skylight edge. The air was still. He looked down through the skylight and saw even more fires burning within Freedom, along with looting and destruction from a panicked populace. The unmistakable smell of smoldering embers and burned bodies hung in the dead air.

"No sign of anything out there. Inside is another story," Ryan whispered.

He turned to Rollins, who was also standing. The man had removed the radio from his belt once more. He turned down the sound of the device before thumbing the Send button.

"This is Rollins. Anyone else on this frequency?" Silence.

"Dammit, Jameson, answer me!"

"You didn't say 'please,' Mr. Rollins," a new voice said, distorted by a poor connection linking the two units.

"Who the fuck is this?" Rollins demanded.

"Does it matter? No, wait, stop. Don't answer that. I'm sure you'll make a point of yammering on and telling me it does. I'll make it quick since I've got a mall to take over. All of your sec boys on the roof of the south side of Freedom are dead. We used their heads for some extra burning fun. My new friends have been showing me all sorts of clever ways to kill a norm. Hair burns quick if you pour on some black powder or charcoal fluid.''

"Jameson! Where are you?'' Rollins demanded, talking over the bragging voice.

"Can't help you there, buck. I don't know which one of those crummy excuses for a norm was the late Mr. Jameson.''

Ryan took the radio from Rollins and asked a question of his own. "Like the man said, who is this?''

"I know that voice! How's it hanging, One-eye?''

"Why don't you meet me and find out?'' Ryan replied, surprised at hearing the old nickname.

"Sorry. Can't do that. I'm not on the roof anymore. None of my stickies are on the roof. Like me, they're already down and inside the mall.''

Ryan listened closely. The voice sounded oddly familiar somehow, but he couldn't place it.

"See you there!''

RYAN HEFTED his SIG-Sauer in a two-handed grip as they came upon the rooftop massacre. The sec squad on this end of Freedom hadn't been able to repel the invaders nearly as effectively as Ryan's team. Five men and one woman were effectively scattered around, their corpses ripped into gory pieces or burned beyond recognition.

The killing muties appeared to be long gone, except to Krysty's advanced means of perception.

Everyone else felt it, too, a feeling of unease.

"Not right," Jak observed.

"I know," Ryan replied, and then the stickies were on them, giggling like demented children as they leaped from their hiding places, coming out from the stairwell access or hanging down the walls of the front of the mall and using their fingertips to adhere to the edge of the roof.

Ryan was impressed, and slightly surprised. These were tactics he would have bet a stack of jack with a clip of ammo chaser to be beyond a stickie's mental capacities.

Muties. Who could predict them, really? He'd met stickies like Charlie back in Colorado who were so intelligent and crafty, they could give Trader a run for the proverbial money. Or mutants with charisma such as Lord Kaa and his hypnotic third eye, or even their most recent tussle with the formidable self-styled Pharaoh Akhnaton in the Barrens. All of them were crazy, dangerous and gifted with mental abilities and insights that made them more of a threat than the traditional human foes he was so frequently thrown up against.

Now here was another batch of stickies showing off, using hide-in-plain-sight tactics of combat. It was as strange as hell, not to mention disturbing, since while their tactics were something to behold, their hand-to-hand combat skills were as poor as ever. A few were holding long blasters, but instead of firing them, the stickies were using them as clubs to swing and bash.

Ryan's internal musing was interrupted when a

short stickie slithered out from beneath an air-duct vent's bottom slat and grabbed him bodily by the legs, the long thin fingers adhering instantly to the leather of his thigh-high combat boots.

The one-eyed man toppled over like a empty bottle, dropping his blaster to the roof's pebbled surface. The SIG-Sauer skipped away, landing out of reach near a burning patch of tar as he struggled to free himself from the mutie's deadly embrace.

Its hands slid higher, feeling his legs and crotch, oozing the secretions that allowed their sucker-covered fingers to stick to almost any known surface.

"Stop moving or I'll rip it off, norm," the stickie grated.

Ryan decided he'd take that chance. Twisting onto one side, he drew his panga from its sheath, the keen blade sliding out with practiced ease. Swinging the razor-sharp edge from the elevation of a high arc, Ryan brought it down on the unprotected back of the stickie's neck. There wasn't enough leverage of weight behind the blow to totally decapitate the mutant, but the blade still sunk down into flaky, yellowing skin with a satisfying thunk.

Hot blood sprayed out from the bite of the blade as the attacked mutie yowled in shock and pain, reaching back with one hand at the injured area. Feeling the sucker-enhanced grip loosen around his lower legs, Ryan pulled himself and the panga free, rolling on his back now and kicking out explosively, shutting up the mutie's cries of agony with the heel of his boot.

The creature's head snapped back like a sprung trap, breaking its neck. A sharp crack was the only sound heard as the shrieks from its throat were cut off sudden and quick by the killing force of Ryan's blow.

Behind Ryan, Jak danced lightly off to the right, hurling out a series of leaf-bladed throwing knives. The starlike blades zipped forward, one after the other in a rapid succession as quick as shots fired from an automatic weapon. The albino's keen, ruby-red eyes were designed for this sort of fighting—in near darkness with the only light for illumination coming from the crackling fires.

Like a feral creature, he was obviously delighting in regressing to a near animal state as he threw the blades. Like an arcane form of magic, a blade would appear in his hand, only to disappear with the flick of a wrist, then instantly reappear in the face or throat of one of the marauding stickies.

Still, more of the muties were coming, this time by rope ladder as far as Ryan could tell. Another smart move on the part of whoever had planned this attack.

And some of the muties seemed to have a brain between them since they were actually starting to lay down a covering of automatic-weapons fire, chilling Rollins's last sec man quickly and effectively.

"Shit," Jak spit from between clenched teeth, his Colt empty. "All out."

"We're getting outnumbered and outgunned," Ryan bellowed. "We've got to retreat. There's not enough cover to try and save the roof."

A shot rang out, explosive and loud, a single burst of man-made thunder that broke into the stillness. Krysty was taking time to aim and shoot, conserving the ammunition for her hand cannon as she chose her targets.

Off to one side, Rollins had one of the stickies by the neck. The mutie had used its uncanny adhesive-tipped fingers to return the murderous caress as both of them screamed into each other's face.

"Rollins, watch it!" Krysty screamed just as the two of them fell over the raised edge of the mall's roof, struggling all the way down into the darkness.

"NICE BLASTERS," Mike said.

"Thanks," Mildred replied.

"They for sale?" Ike asked.

"Nope," J.B. retorted.

"I didn't ask you, four-eyes. Besides, I owe you anyway for bashing me over the head."

"You deserved it. Just wish I'd hit you harder."

"Seems to me, I'm the one with the bargaining power here." Mike said, gesturing with his blaster.

"Seems to me, the two of you can't come up with half a brain between you. So what?" J.B. replied, giving as good as he got.

"So mebbe I'll take your blasters and chill the three of you."

"Not too bright, even for you clowns," Mildred replied, shaking her head, the beaded plaits of her hair swaying back and forth with the movement. "Have you been out in the mall? Triple-bad scene."

Ike smiled in agreement. "I know. Things have gotten pretty hot up on the roof, as well. Muties popping up like fucking rats. Falling around up there like rain."

"Ohh..." Doc moaned.

"Doc! What's wrong?" Mildred asked, turning to the older man.

"My blessed heart, my heart," Doc said, clutching at his chest with both hands and staggering forward a single step before entering an unsupported free fall with a one-way plummet down flat on his hawklike face.

A close listener would have heard an additional sound. As Doc fell forward in a very convincing collapse, there was the light, deadly snick of the steel blade hidden within the ebony sheath of his lion's-head swordstick hissing free. The sharp weapon came sliding out, and the old man slashed fast and hard with the revealed blade of the rapier as he allowed himself to continue his fall facedown and out of harm's way.

Doc wasn't worried about fair play. He used the blade and aimed for the two men's faces and eyes, carving out red rivulets as he fell like the strike of a plummeting eagle.

Backing his distraction, Mildred and J.B. each chose a target.

Mildred's face was set like a carved piece of onyx, her dark eyes narrowed and bright as she took aim along the barrel of the Czech target pistol.

J.B. peered impassively from behind his new specs

as he flipped the scattergun into position in a fluid movement of death.

The resulting sounds of the twin triggers being pulled in the corridor were like the release of tightly bottled nitro.

Later, after all was said and done, Doc was very grateful the resulting splash of crimson blood and entrails had found its way out of the backs of the traitorous sec men and onto the floor. Not a drop landed on his long white hair or faded black frock coat.

"I didn't like those bastards the first go 'round," J.B. said. "Told Ryan we should've chilled them then."

"You okay, Doc?" Mildred asked, lifting him up carefully and bringing the spindly man first to his knees, then to his feet.

Doc took a step and winced. "Other than my poor bruised knees, I shall live."

"Crazy move." J.B. grinned. "Crazy, suicidal move."

"I am afraid you are the worst of influences, John Barrymore."

"You two can compare notes on being heroes later. We've got to find Ryan," Mildred said, swinging open the heavy sec door that allowed access to the rooftop.

"No need," Ryan said as he, Krysty and Jak came in.

"Where are the other Freedom sec men?" J.B asked in surprise.

"The ones worth a damn are probably dead. Rollins bought the casket upstairs. His backups did the same."

The friends quickly greeted one another with exhilaration that all were still alive and relatively safe, as safe as could be inside the rapidly deteriorating conditions inside the mall.

"What next?"

"First we get Dean," Ryan said.

Chapter Twenty-Four

The cell block attached to the Freedom Mall sec force was known as the Wings. Why was a mystery, although Doc suspected the slang term might have origins in either the prevention of the prisoners from being "as free as birds" or that it was more theatrical in nature, keeping troublemakers in Freedom offstage and out of the public eye by being locked away in the wings, the wings being a reference to the areas off the main stage to the right and the left.

Either way, the reunited group of friends were lacking one of their own, and that was Dean Cawdor, who had been shut away, awaiting release when their terms as hired guns had paid his freight—and Jak's—for the damage to the vid arcade.

Retracing his steps of the daily visit he paid Dean, Ryan walked past the deserted admittance desk, through a half door, into a back-hallway annex. He looked in the empty visitor's center and waved his friends along to the rear section, where a heavy steel door with a U-shaped handle was closed.

"This must lead to the cells," Ryan said.

"Yeah," Jak confirmed.

Mildred drew her pistol. "We going in?"

"Might have to blast if the door is locked," J.B. said.

"Try it and see, Ryan. Open the portal and let us see what awaits," Doc added.

Ryan took the handle and pulled. Then he pulled harder, feeling the veins in his arms start to pop out against his tan skin.

"Try pushing, lover," Krysty suggested.

"Getting to that." Ryan pushed, and the steel door swung inward.

"Not used to the old-fashioned doors with hinges." He chuckled, annoyed and amused at the same time. "Spending too much time in redoubts, where you press a few buttons, and the sec doors slide away."

Ryan's good cheer was interrupted by a sudden cacophony of a clanging alarm bell.

"Shit!" he cursed. "Where'd that come from?"

"No idea," Krysty said. "You must've missed some sec turnoff switch."

"You're the one who told me to push," Ryan retorted.

"Well, other than being annoying as all hell, I don't think it's going to bring sec men running this way," J.B. drawled. "They've got more important things to deal with now than a child's jailbreak."

Ryan turned to the Armorer. "I agree."

Doc spoke up. "Still, I shall remain back here, in case we do have visitors."

"Good idea, Doc," Ryan said, speaking loudly to be heard. "Hate to see all of us trapped or locked up alongside Dean. That'll be some poor bastard rescue. Krysty, you want to hang with Doc, too?"

The redhead nodded. "All right. Be careful."

"Always."

"I'll close the door. It might cut down on the racket back here," Mildred said. "That alarm bell is somewhere out front."

Ryan led the way inside, his own blaster drawn and ready. To his left was a blank wall with a wooden desk and metal rolling chair. On the desk were papers, a book of mug shots and an ashtray filled with the remains of a score of hand-rolled cigarettes. To his right was the cell block proper. Six cells, three per side, separated by a narrow walkway painted a chocolate brown. All of the cells appeared empty.

As promised, Mildred pushed the door shut and the clanging sound became much softer and bearable. The alarm was apparently meant to alert those outside of the cell block in case of a break.

"Dean?" Ryan yelled over the now muffled clanging. "You in here?"

"Dad!" Dean yelled back, rolling out from beneath the bunk of the last cell.

As Ryan jogged down to the last cell in the long block, J.B. examined the other, empty cells, eyeballing their sparse furnishings in case another inmate had taken Dean's lead and decided to hide in plain sight.

"You're supposed to sleep on those beds, Dean, not under them," Ryan said as he looked down fondly upon his son.

"I know. Things been going triple strange. Once that alarm kicked off, I figured I'd hide until I knew the score."

"Funny," J.B. mused. "All the other cells are unoccupied."

"Another batch of jails on lower level," Jak said.

"Heard talk when I locked up earlier. Almost separated me and Dean. Didn't."

"Morgan promised me Dean wouldn't be hurt. I made it clear I didn't want my son having to deal with horny pervs wanting to get at his ass. Guess Morgan listened. Kept this group of cells clear," Ryan said as he stared down at the locked cell door.

The cell was primitive, the metal bars obviously brought in from an old police station and welded into place. The back wall was solid concrete stone, and so was the windowless left, the front and right sections being made of the bars, which were painted black.

"Been nobody here but me for days," Dean confirmed. "Boring as hell. Three meals and no conversation. What's going on? Where are the guards?"

"They've got bigger problems on their hands besides keeping watch over a kid. Freedom's under attack by some angry stickies. Guess they wanted to participate in a blue-light special with the rest of us," Ryan said with a wicked smile.

"Never did find out what those specials were supposed to be about," J.B. groused.

"Probably for the best. Want to see if you and Jak can find some keys around this dump?"

"On it." The two men went back and began looking through the drawers of the desk at the back of the cell block.

"You okay, Mildred? You look kind of sick," Dean said, peering at the black woman through the bars of the cell.

"Stickies are enough to make all of us feel queasy," Ryan said.

"Stickies don't scare me, it's the people," Mildred replied, running a free hand down her jacketed arm. She suddenly felt cold. "I know you've already been face-to-face with those chilly-crazy bastards, Ryan, but all I've seen running rampant so far is a horde of rioters and looters. It's almost like they were waiting for an opportunity like this to tear the mall down from the rafters."

"Yeah, well, you know how it is, Mildred. The more people you cram together, the more trouble you invite."

"We keep crawling back up, and knocking ourselves down again and again."

"No keys in desk," Jak reported.

"Not surprised. Guard usually has them on a ring on his belt," Dean said.

"Why not tell us?" Jak demanded, slinging out a pale hand and slapping the cell bars next to Dean's face.

"I was hoping for a spare set, stupe," Dean said. "Got to be a second set of keys somewhere in case the first set gets lost."

"Well, guess we'll have to blast," Ryan said. "We sure as shit don't have time to wait for the sec man on duty to come back with the keys."

While the rest of the group had been talking, J.B. had also returned from the desk search. He bent down for a closer look at the sec lock on the cell door.

"Oh-oh," J.B. said.

"What's 'oh-oh'? That's a phrase I'm not used to hearing out of you, J.B.," Ryan demanded.

"We got a problem. This isn't your ordinary cell-door lock. Been modified.'' The Armorer pointed a finger up to a box in the corner of Dean's cell that appeared to be some kind of ob unit. ''There's a charge in the lock mechanism,'' he explained. ''Don't use the key and you break a circuit. My guess is, there's enough high ex in that box back there to envelop the entire cell and whoever is dumb enough to be standing in front of it.''

''Meaning what?'' Mildred asked.

''Like I said. Oh-oh.''

''Can't you bypass the lock?'' Ryan asked.

''Mebbe,'' J.B. replied, taking off his fedora and running his fingers through his closely cropped hair. ''I know how to, anyway—''

''Good!''

''Just never done it before on a deal like this.''

''J.B., there's a first time for everything.''

The radio at Ryan's waist crackled, and then an annoying squawk came out.

''Your radio's on?'' J.B. asked. ''Had to turn our sets off. Sec men screaming, yelling. Couldn't understand a damn thing.''

''Mine's on another channel. So's Krysty's. Did that to escape the other racket. Jak didn't have a unit,'' Ryan replied as he took the compact box off his belt.

''Not want one,'' the albino noted.

''Ryan here,'' the tall man said, speaking into the comm unit.

''What's the holdup, lover?'' Krysty replied, the alarm bell ringing under her words. ''Doc and I just had to shoo away an angry mall tenant who came rampaging in here. Seems his vintage-clothing depot was ransacked and he's mad, threatening to pull his shop out and report us to the mall managers.''

"How'd you get rid of him?"

"Told him to go tell somebody who cared."

"Good girl. We've hit a snag.'' Ryan went on to explain the problem.

"Gaia! If it's not one thing, it's another,'' Krysty said, her voice still clear despite the static.

"J.B.'s going to crack the door. Rest of us are coming back up front with you. No sense in all of us getting caught in the middle in case something goes wrong.''

"Right. Krysty, out.''

Ryan reached in through the iron bars with his hands and arms, drawing his son close for a brief, tight hug.

"Hang tight, Dean. J.B.'s the best in Deathlands with this kind of rig. You'll be out before you know it.''

As Ryan broke the hug and stepped back, J.B. was already sitting on the floor, his legs crossed under his body. From his leather coat he'd taken a small metal box and a stained cloth. In the cloth was a series of shiny metal tools resembling surgical weapons. The box held his lock picks.

"Here, J.B., take my comm unit,'' Ryan said. "We'll keep in touch with you by using Krysty's radio.''

Goodbyes were exchanged, then the boy and the Armorer were alone, seated on the cold floor and facing each other through the iron bars of the cell.

"You really know how to deactivate this thing?" Dean asked, nodding toward the lock.

"Of course."

"So, let's do it."

OUT IN THE ADMITTANCE AREA of the Wings, long minutes had passed. J.B. hadn't checked in via the comm. There was no real reason for constant chatter. If he failed at his task, the others would know immediately from the explosion.

"How do you think it's going out in the mall proper?" Mildred mused.

"From what I saw coming in, lousy," Ryan replied.

"Just human nature," Doc said, twirling his swordstick between his fingers. "With all of the good, you get more of the bad. This proud beacon named Freedom was an ambitious experiment. In a smaller configuration, it might have continued to thrive. Alas, the body outgrew the head, and now it falls."

"Damn stickies," Jak said.

"Stickies didn't help, but Doc's got a point," Krysty added. "Freedom didn't have near the amount of sec men needed to properly protect the place, either from the outside or from itself."

Ryan glanced at his wrist chron for the fiftieth time since he'd come out of the cell block. "Taking too long," he said, and activated the radio.

"J.B.?"

Silence.

"J.B., answer me."

Silence. Static.

"J.B., goddammit! Answer me before I come in after you!"

"What?" the Armorer's voice came back. "I'm kind of busy here."

"Been twenty minutes. Taking too long."

"Working as fast as I can, Ryan."

"Well, work even faster!" Ryan said, his frustration mounting. "Last thing we need is to have all our asses locked up or to be backed against the wall by a group of pissed-off mall customers running from a gang of stickies."

"You want to get down here and do this?" J.B. retorted, his angry voice crackling back over the small hand comm.

"If you think it would help, yeah!" Ryan spit at the radio unit.

"You don't have the patience," the Armorer countered, even as his nimble fingers seemed to increase their speed on the cell door's locking mechanism. "You never did."

"Bullshit."

"Get off it, Ryan. You used to drive Trader crazy back in the old days, always wanting to go in with blasters blazing, and Trader wasn't exactly what I'd call a patient man, either, if you know what I mean."

Ryan's face darkened. "What I know is that those alarms are going to draw some attention, stickie attack or not."

"Look, if I could blast the bastard lock, I would," J.B. replied tiredly. "But we don't have that particular time-saving option available. This is delicate work. I

can rush it if you want Dean back without a head.
That I can do for you.''

"That isn't an option, J.B.''

"Okay. So, unless you want to start leading your
son around by the hand to keep him from bumping
into the furniture, I can't afford to rush this. If that's
not the case, I suggest you back the hell off and stop
pushing. When he's free, you'll be the first to know.
Dix, out.''

"Fine,'' Ryan said in a cold tone as he flipped the
comm's voice toggle to Off. He knew J.B. was right,
but that didn't make waiting any easier, nor the did
remote chance that his friend might indeed make an
error and cause injury to the imprisoned Dean.

Krysty started to say something, but Ryan held up
a hand.

"Don't,'' he said. "Don't want to hear it.''

AT THE DOOR of the sec cell, J.B. was sweating pro-
fusely. Trickles of perspiration were running down his
forehead and onto the bridge of his nose and on his
cheeks. His glasses were slightly fogged from the
body heat, but he didn't dare try to take the time to
keep wiping them when he was so close to succeed-
ing.

Still, the film over the lenses was becoming quite
annoying.

"Can't see worth a shit. These new glasses fog up
a lot quicker than my old ones,'' he griped.

"Try the other pair,'' Dean suggested.

J.B. snorted. "I'd rather take my chances with
these.''

"I'm serious. Right now I'm not going to be laughing at how they might look, that's for sure."

Taking his hands away from the locking mechanism, J.B. quickly took out the case with the wide-framed lenses and placed the pair of backup glasses on his nose.

Dean couldn't help himself; he giggled.

"Nerves," the boy explained.

"Right."

J.B. went back to his task, making another quick adjustment.

"Okay. Dean?"

"Yeah, J.B.?" the boy replied.

"Oh, never mind."

"What?"

"I was going to tell you to step back to the rear of the cell, but if this thing goes off, it's not going to matter where you're standing."

"Oh," Dean said, debating this. "Thanks for thinking of me."

"I've got one wire left to cut on this sec lock. Cutting it should short the current and allow the door to be slid open without activating the charge."

"Guess the key word here is 'should,' right?"

"Yeah."

"You think I should crawl under my bunk?"

"Only if it would make you feel better."

"Nah. Guess I'll stand here and face it with you."

J.B. reached out with the miniature pair of pliers. "There is one thing you could do for me, Dean."

"What?"

"Stick your fingers in your ears. That way, you won't have to hear the blast in case I did screw up."

Before the boy could offer a reply, J.B. squeezed the pliers shut and cut the connecting wire.

Chapter Twenty-Five

Beck Morgan, puppet master of Freedom, had chosen his stand near a former Royal Thomasville Furniture Store that had been remodeled into a tattoo parlor. The wooden chair hanging over the doorway and marking the store's entrance hadn't been removed when the new tenants came in. All they had done was add a posed mannequin covered in a patchwork of ornate body art showing off the proprietor's wares.

Morgan had gotten out his private arsenal and was battling a bottom-floor stickie horde almost single-handedly. The leader of Freedom Mall was bleeding from several superficial wounds, most of which appeared to have been caused by shrapnel from the blown wall or from the pieces of brick and concrete the stickies were lobbing at him instead of bullets.

The mastermind behind the stickies' attack on Freedom had chosen their lower point of entry and advancement well, blasting in through a former side entrance into the predark mall that had once been nothing but tinted glass and metal framing. The wall had been bricked shut and reinforced during the Freedom renovation to make the former retail pleasure palace a virtual fortress, but this was still a potential weak point that had been allowed to exist without worry or fear.

Until now.

"Come on, you stupe bastards! I've got a lead tattoo for your sorry asses!" Morgan boomed before launching into another steel-jacketed salvo. He knew his supplies of ammo were running low, but he couldn't afford the luxury of taking the Uzi in his hands down to single shot.

A huge mutie came rushing around the temporary barricade of rubble and debris Morgan had chosen for his safe haven. The man-beast's arms were flailing, and its eyes rolled in their huge sockets like pinwheels as the creature ran, bare feet slapping hard on the tile floor. Before Morgan could squeeze off a round, the mutie had eagerly jumped the barricade.

"Budd will get you," the mutie proclaimed.

"Death at close range or far off, it doesn't matter much to me, asshole!" Morgan cried as he snapped the clip of his blaster and fired at the stickie, causing the brute's wide torso to churn up in a frothy, bloody mess. The shots didn't even slow the big mutant as it continued to lumber forward, grabbing the shocked leader of Freedom by the shirt with both hands and boldly lifting him up into the air.

Blood continued to pour from the wide furrows Morgan's weapon had made into the stickie's chest, and still the creature lifted the man even higher. The mall administrator kicked his feet weakly as he struggled in the crushing grip, trying to shut out the unearthly shrieking the mutie was making in a language only others of its kind could hope to understand.

Ryan, in the lead of his own group of friends, saw the situation, took in the risks and made his choice, launching his lean body like a missile and hitting the big mutant at knee level. Knocked off balance, the already injured stickie buckled beneath Morgan's weight, and both of them crashed to the floor as Ryan rolled frantically away to avoid joining the pile.

The one-eyed man whipped out his panga as he got back to his feet and buried it into the back of the stickie's exposed head even as Morgan pressed the advantage Ryan had given him, managing to pull a .38-caliber pistol from an ankle holster. He squeezed the trigger once, then twice, sending a twin barrage of bullets at another stickie who had chosen that moment to also try to come over the barricade.

By this time, Jak, J.B., Mildred, Krysty, Doc and Dean had pulled their own various pieces of steel hardware and readied them for battle.

"Cawdor," Morgan said. "See you fetched your boy."

"No thanks to the lock on the cell door."

"Never dreamed they'd launch this kind of assault so suddenly. One of the mutie bastards has some mercie training, that's for damn sure," Morgan said.

"We help wrap this up and get you out, we're done, Morgan," Ryan told him.

"Fine," the mall leader replied.

Doc clawed out his massive Le Mat revolver, thumbing back on the hammer. Steadying the heavy blaster as best he could, he aimed the portable cannon at the midst of another advancing swarm of stickies and fired. The thunderous boom of the weapon came hurtling out with a sound that managed to still the battle cries of the living and the dying.

More slugs whizzed over the group's heads, many of the lead-alloy-core bullets coming dangerous close to finding a target. One near-fatal bullet cut into the upper notch of J.B.'s battered fedora, pulling it back off his head where it landed softly on the ground. The Armorer reached down with a curse and snatched up the beloved hat, searching for the possible hole the weapon's firing might have made.

"Clean," he said after a brief perusal. "No holes."

"Glad the lid meets your approval, J.B.," Ryan said loudly over the tumult. "How about admiring it later when the chilling's finished?"

"That you, One-eye?" The question came from the stickies' side of battle.

"Who wants to know?"

Ryan's query was ignored. "You and your group are dead, One-eye! Chilled and buried! We'll put your head in the fire, let it cook for an hour or so, see if that mutie slut of yours wants to ride you then!" a disfigured man said in a near scream of a voice that came from the ruined slash of a mouth. It was a voice that Ryan had heard before, along with the name "One-eye," a voice of a man he had to have met before to be aware that Krysty possessed mutant abilities.

"Another Freedom burned to the ground, One-eye! What do you think about that?" Norm jeered, and when the man with the half-melted visage said those words, Ryan knew who he was now facing.

"Lester?" Ryan asked in a disbelieving manner. "Lester, is that you?"

"Who?" Dean replied.

"Quiet," Krysty whispered, cutting the boy off.

She didn't want to think about Lester, or Baron Willie Elijah or, most of all, Lord Kaa, who had chosen her to be his bride and to mother his successor, his child and future mutant ruler of the Deathlands.

That had been months earlier.

"Can't be," J.B. said softly. "Can't be. That elevator slaver wheel chilled everyone that was chained to it. No way our boy Lester could've survived."

"Wrong, J.B.," Mildred replied. "As you might recall, none of us bothered going back to sift through the ashes for a body count."

"All your fault, One-eye!" Lester-Norm cried out. "Your fault I'm a freak! You brought death to Willie ville! Death and fire! Now I've brought it back to you!"

"Aw, come on, Lester," Ryan replied. "You were a freak before I even met you."

The infuriated man once known as Johnson Lester shrieked as he lunged for Ryan. The newly christened mutant—the former human being—both combined in a single chilling package with one goal in mind—the death of Ryan Cawdor.

Norm was on top of the one-eyed warrior before he even had time to pull up his SIG-Sauer and end the madness in human form, on him all hot and bothered and quick, faster than any mutie or man could be. The angry killer wrapped his arms around Ryan's lower body and legs and shoved forward, shoved as hard as he could.

Ryan's hand was slick with sweat and blood, and before he could bring his panga up for a killing blow, he lost his grip on the blade's handle, and the long knife went skittering away across the pebble-strewed tile of Freedom's flooring.

"Fuck this. Time to end it," J.B. said, unlimbering his shotgun.

"Hold up. The way that freak is twisting around, you might hit Ryan," Krysty replied. "Especially with a scattergun."

"Give me your pistol, then."

Krysty shook her head. "Just hold off, J.B. until they're farther apart. Stupe isn't even armed."

Ryan stumbled back, still trying to stay on his feet. He put his hands together, feeling the fingers interlace and lock together, then he brought them down hard as a unified whole on his adversary's back. He did this once, twice, breaking the man's grip on his legs. Ryan went back a step, waiting and watching intently as his foe reached down for one of his own pants-covered ankles.

Ryan guessed the scarred man was going for a hidden blade or small-caliber pistol, so he lashed out with a booted foot and caught Lester in the exposed side of the throat.

The force of the kick sent the air wheezing out of the smaller man, and Ryan could only guess at the sensation of multicolored explosion of agony, but he didn't know his enemy's ability to take pain. The disfigured man channeled the suffering, used it to make his perceptions bright and clear. For a man whose entire head was once ablaze, a kick to the throat was like a lover's kiss.

Ryan was ready for Lester as he came lunging back up, his shoulder slamming the one-eyed man in the chest, making his ribs throb and ache. Lester's arms were slithering around him, locking behind his back as the force of the charge sent the two of them falling backward.

The one-eyed man's first impulse was to slam his hands against the unprotected sides of Lester's scabbed head, boxing his ears, until it dawned on Ryan the man had no ears. Second choice in a close fight such as this was to go for the eyes.

Ryan locked his thumbs into the man's eye sockets and pressed. Ability to absorb pain or not, this move brought forth a keening wail of agony. Lester tried to bite off the sensations of having his already damaged eyes gouged out and instead sunk his teeth into his enemy's right wrist, breaking the skin and causing streamers of coppery-tasting blood to spurt out. However, fear of being blinded outweighed his ability to throw away the pain and caused him to release his grip on Ryan and go reeling backward.

Krysty's blaster fired four times, each bullet finding a secure home in Lester's chest cavity. The self-styled leader of the Winston stickies tumbled backward and moved no more.

"Nice shooting," Morgan remarked.

The other stickies, seeing their leader fall, eased up on their attack, choosing instead to follow their own whims.

"They're easing off," Morgan stated. "Time for us to ease off, too, I think."

"Where the hell are you going?" Ryan asked.

Morgan shook his head in disbelief. "Freedom's lost, Cawdor, but I'm still in debt for your assist in saving my hide. Lay down some covering fire and tell your group to follow me. There's a way out that should lead you away from any stickies until you're safe on the other end of the back parking lot.''

Ryan didn't argue. "Dean, follow Morgan! Rest of you pick up after Dean, one by one. Me and J.B. will lay down covering fire and bring up the rear.''

Most of the remaining stickies weren't interested in fighting against Ryan and J.B.'s marksmanship, and chose either to stagger back outside or turn and go down the main aisle of the devastated mall interior.

"Come on," Ryan said to his friend as the two men raced hurriedly away. "I think we've done enough shopping on this trip.''

Chapter Twenty-Six

Morgan had taken the group back into the catacombs that lined the far interiors of Freedom Mall, bringing them past unfinished walls and ancient pipes kept behind heavy wire fencing. The padlock holding a chain around the front of a solid sec door was unlocked with a key on a ring hanging from the former mall leader's waist. He led the way down a flight of flimsy metal stairs, which vibrated from all of their combined weight.

At the bottom was a bank of equipment lockers with a padlock and chain identical to the one that had kept the door to the small chamber closed, a folding card table weighed down with a toolbox and some scattered papers and files, a relatively clean portable gasoline generator and a half-bubble-shaped hatch sticking up like a boil in the center of the floor.

"Open the floor hatch," Morgan said as he pulled on the cord and caused the gen to chug into a steady heartbeat of sounds. "Probably take two of you. Damn thing sticks."

Ryan and Jak turned the floor-level locking wheel, straining until it broke free with a wrenching of metal and allowed them to lift up the half-egg-shaped hatch. The second the seal between floor and hatch had been pried loose with a soft sucking sound, Jak went skittering back with a crazed look on his pale face.

"Gaia!" Krysty gasped, her green eyes popping open in shock.

"By the Three Kennedys!" Doc wheezed as he turned and staggered away from his earlier position of wanting to see what the opening of the hatch might unveil.

Mildred, who had autopsied the dead and cut into the living, involuntarily gagged.

Dean's chest heaved as he struggled not to vomit. The boy was afraid to even try to speak until he regained control of his senses.

Only J.B. appeared not to have been struck totally by surprise over the odor that had been unleashed, and that was because of his long-practiced poker face. Behind the lenses of his glasses however, even his pale eyes were involuntarily watering.

"Fireblast, Morgan, what the hell is that smell?" Ryan asked, his own eye tearing as the ghastly odor wafted up.

"Human waste, I imagine," the former leader of Freedom Mall said succinctly as he searched his ring for yet another key to unlock the equipment lockers. "Stinks, doesn't it?"

"'Stink' is entirely too polite a word," Doc quipped.

"You mean the way out of here is through the bastard sewer?" Ryan demanded.

Morgan shrugged. "What better place to have a secret tunnel?"

"Only secret is how something can stink so bad,"

Dean said, his voice pitched deeper since he was using a hand to pinch his nostrils closed.

"Waste has to go somewhere. We modified the original plumbing as best we could, but despite its immense size, Freedom was never designed for twenty-four-hour inhabitation," Morgan explained as he inserted yet another key in hopes it would be the right one for the lockers' padlock. "Bringing in fresh water and disposing of waste was starting to be a logistical nightmare for which I had no real solution. Guess I can thank the stickies for ridding me of the problem of having to deal with yet another crisis."

"Smells like shit," Jak said bluntly.

"That's because it is shit," Morgan said in reply as he finally found the right key, and the chain around the bank of lockers fell with a clank to the hard ground. "And piss. And gallons upon gallons of shower water, sink water, tub water, any liquid that goes down a drain. Been a while since I made the trip. All I can say is hold your nose and walk fast. You'll get used to it."

"How are we going to see?" Krysty asked as she bent and tried to see down the odorous crawlway.

"There's some lighting courtesy of the generator," Morgan replied, gesturing to the small engine that was chugging in place near the entrance down into the tunnel. "However, I would advise against lighting any matches or firing your weapons down there. It might ignite stray gases and toast all of your asses."

The man turned away from the generator and opened one of the wall lockers. He took out the subgun and long blaster that had been stored away days before when Ryan and his group first entered Freedom Mall. He quickly handed over the Uzi and the Steyr.

"Thought you might need these. I'd planned on getting them to you earlier, when you first joined the Freedom sec squad, but circumstances prevented their delivery."

"Thanks," Ryan said as he and his friends eagerly took back their weapons.

Morgan unlimbered a large 9 mm Weaver PKS-9 Ultralite submachine gun and a double handful of clips from the locker for himself.

"You taking us down?"

"No. I've got my own problems to deal with here before departing."

"All right. Jak, you're in first."

The albino stepped down, followed one by one by the rest of the group. Finally only J.B. and Ryan were left. Morgan was waiting for them to vanish before closing the hatch back up.

"Welcome to come with us," Ryan said.

J.B. gave him a warning glance, his sallow face darkening with a deep scowl.

Ryan returned an icy cold stare. "Dammit, J.B. The offer's sincere."

"Turning this into a damn parade," Dix muttered. "Only need drums and balloons."

Morgan laughed. "Blunt as stone, but your Armorer is right. Thanks for the invite, Cawdor, but no. There's already seven of you, and that's about six too many in my learned opinion. I work better alone. I find a single moving target to draw less attention than an entire flock.''

''Your choice.'' Ryan stuck out his hand. Morgan extended his own and met Ryan's palm for a quick, firm handshake.

''I've still got a few items I want to salvage—and a few scores to settle—before I make my own great escape from this cavernous hellpit,'' Morgan said, his voice dropping down a bit in fond memory of Freedom. ''Pity about that, really. I rather liked being in mall management.''

''Yeah, well, it's harder than dick to find a career with any sort of longevity these days,'' Ryan agreed. ''You ought to look into farming.''

Morgan cackled. ''See you on the other side, Cawdor.''

Ryan waited until J.B. clambered down into the floor hatch before lowering himself into the narrow access.

RYAN STEPPED OFF the last rung of the rusty metal ladder into thigh-deep water and nearly stumbled when the soles of his heavy combat boots tried to find a secure purchase on the slippery tunnel floor.

''Fireblast,'' he snarled, grabbing the ladder with one hand as securely as possible while halting his fall. He had no desire to fall into the foul-smelling sewer water. He closed his eye for a few seconds, willing himself to get used to the faint lighting. Bare bulbs glowed from sockets set into the ceiling at ten-foot intervals, but only every third light was still working, and if the generator above happened to lock up or run out of fuel, even those feeble signposts would be extinguished.

"Good show," Doc said to Ryan after the big man had arrested his fall and stepped off the ladder into the water. "I can only wish for my long lost days of yore when I, too, possessed such agility."

Even in the gloom, Ryan could still notice that Doc's white hair was dripping, and the greenish black of his frock coat had taken on a much darker hue. Doc's trousers were also soaking wet, accenting his bony frame.

"Doc took tumble," Jak volunteered. "Went splash."

"This accursed floor is as slick as shit through a goose," Doc groused. "It is a wonder all of us haven't gone down in a tangle."

The albino snorted, his red eyes glowing merrily in the semidarkness. "No one else fell. 'Cept for you," he said.

"Carry on Krysty," Ryan said. "Head count."

"Seven. Everyone's here and accounted for," Krysty said. "What next?"

"I'm fresh out of elaborate or idealistic ideas. I say we get the hell out of here and forget we ever heard about Freedom Mall," Ryan replied.

"At least we don't have to worry about choosing a wrong direction," Mildred said. "For the time being, this tunnel appears to run only two ways, forward and back."

"Then let's make a run for the future," Ryan answered. "Walk fast, but don't run. Floor's too dangerous, and we don't know what we might encounter while we're moving. Follow me close, we won't have much time.''

Ryan set the pace, which alternated between a quick jog and a brisk walk. He kept Jak close behind him in hopes the younger man's superior night vision might help to avoid any pitfalls.

"Getting hot," Dean said. "Starting to sweat."

"Boy's right." J.B. called out from the rear of the convoy.

The albino tensed. "Don't call me boy."

"Not you—the other kid."

"Blast you, J.B." Dean snarled under his breath.

"Save your breath for running," Ryan barked. "We're going to need all our energy to make it out of here in one piece."

"Feels like rain," Krysty said, feeling her hair tightening on her head.

On those words, a lengthy overhead pipe that stretched endlessly forward and back began to release a fine misting of water at any and all stress points. Rancid-smelling water fell down on them like a curtain, adding to the decreased visibility in the tunnel.

"This shit will soak us all to the skin soon enough," Ryan said.

"Least water not cold," Jak answered.

The pipe continued its downpour as the group raced down the narrow and winding passage. The trip was taking on a definite air of unreality. Instead of minutes, it felt as though they had been slogging through the darkness for hours, day upon night in the confines of the tunnel, and all of it had been dank, dark and wet.

"Is it my imagination, or is this water getting higher?" J.B. asked.

"To waist level now," Jak said.

"Not a problem. Got to be near the exit soon," Ryan argued.

"What that?" Jak said, coming to a complete stop and reaching out a hand to slow Ryan.

A hissing noise could be heard. Ryan had missed it. The labored rasp of his own breathing mixing with the sound of the leaking pipes overhead had masked the soft sibilant sound. Now that the group had stopped moving, they could feel the warm moisture hovering in the dank air, mixing with the tepid downpour from above.

"Keep moving. Slow until we get around the corner," Ryan ordered.

As the new corner was turned, the group discovered the source of the sound.

Down the passage, a broken steam pipe had fallen inward, blowing what seemed to be an endless wet heat out in a billowing cloudy mass.

"This could be a problem," J.B. stated, his glasses already fogged over with condensation.

"Yeah, I know. Can't shoot a cloud of steam."

"We could wait," Mildred offered. "No supply of hot water is endless. Let it run until the supply is exhausted, then go past."

"No time. I don't want to get caught down here with nowhere to run or hide."

"Jesus!" Mildred suddenly screamed. "I felt something brush against my leg!"

"Everybody, freeze," Ryan said.

"I feel it, Ryan," Mildred said. "Or felt it—whatever it is. The damn thing rubbed up against my leg."

J.B. pulled his Tekna blade. "Think we got a snake. Big one."

Ryan swiftly drew his own panga. "I hate snakes."

"So much for leaving Freedom unmolested," Doc said. "Perhaps this snake is nonpoisonous."

"What, you're a herpetologist now, too?" Mildred said in a voice colored with anxiety as she struggled to keep still.

"No, Dr. Wyeth, but I do know that most water snakes are harmless," Doc replied patiently. "While I am not fond of the slithering set myself, the odds are on our side the one you have discovered is merely as lost as we are."

"You want to take a chance on that, Doc?" Ryan asked.

Tanner shook his head. "Of course not. I am merely pointing out some facts."

"Let this thing slither by one of your skinny ankles, and we'll see who calls what harmless," Mildred suggested, her dark eyes scanning the water.

"Primitive man worshiped the serpent as a creature of great supernatural power, you know. The serpent was sacred to Asclepius, the Greek god of healing. The caduceus, a mighty staff with two entwined snakes, was carried by Hermes of Greek mythology, and is our universal symbol of modern medicine. As a physician yourself, I fail to—"

"Screw the mythology lesson. I got enough of that back with Admiral Poseidon," Ryan retorted. Other than Doc's rather one-sided discussion and the pulling of their various hand-to-hand bladed weapons, none of the group had moved since Mildred's warning.

"Yes, yes, of course. But remember the telling passage from the Book of Genesis, 'And the Lord God said unto the serpent—'"

"Stifle it, Doc!" Mildred warned.

"Think see it," Jak said, his usual calm demeanor tossed away as he bent and peered down at the surface of the murky water.

"What's a snake doing down here?" Dean asked.

"For the rats, I imagine," Ryan answered. "Could feast a long time on the amount of rats slinking around under here."

Jak continued to stare at the water.

"Didn't pull your blade, Jak," Ryan said flatly, noting the albino's hands were empty.

"Don't need it," the teen replied.

Then, faster than anyone's eye could follow, Jak's hand disappeared under the murk up to his elbow...and came back up with a quivering snake held tightly in one hand. Jak had timed his strike well, catching the reptile firmly at the back of the head so that he wouldn't have to fear being struck by the creature's poisonous fangs.

Jak squeezed, and the snake's mouth opened wide, revealing a white lining and throat. Needle-sharp fangs glistened.

"That's a hell of a water moccasin," Ryan said.

The long body of the snake was brown, with wide black cross bands that enclosed lighter tan centers. The belly was yellow and heavily marbled with dark gray. Over and through the reptile's glistening, lidless eyes were dark black stripes that matched the jet-black top of the coiling tail.

"I thought those bastards weren't supposed to get any longer than six feet," Mildred said breathlessly, her adrenaline surge now dissipating in relief. "That thing's at least ten or more."

"They're not," Ryan retorted. "But you're looking at snakes from your time, Mildred. Not ours. A hundred years seems to have stretched him some. And I've faced larger."

"Seen bigger home in bayou," Jak noted as the snake twisted, trying to worm out of his grip. "Hide in swamps. Eat rats, birds, fish, kids. Mean."

"Could've been worse," J.B. said. "Could've been two of them."

"Dear God," Doc whispered, his face whiter than usual. "I think there *are* two of them. I distinctly felt something foul slithering by my leg."

"Probably just a turd. Come on, we've got to hurry up and get the hell out of his cesspool, free steam bath or not."

"Go ahead, Jak. Chill the bastard," Dean urged, watching the serpent continue to coil in the albino's grip.

"No," Jak said, then moved back down the tunnel. Once he was a good distance away, he boldly tossed the snake down the passageway as far as he could.

"What did you do that for?" Dean demanded when the older boy returned.

"Snake's all confused. We'll be gone long time before he gets back over here."

"Let's forget about the damn thing," Ryan stated. "My worry now is seeing how hot it's going to get."

The one-eyed man hunkered down his upper body and braved the billowing steam first. Once on the other side, he was greatly relieved to discover the wet heat had washed over him without causing much discomfort. All of his friends, as well as himself, had endured about as much as any human being could stand in the past four hours.

"Come on through. Go quick. It's not hot enough to burn," he yelled.

One by one, all went through safely.

"Can't be much farther. Seems like we've gone the length of the mall already."

The water had risen to Ryan's stomach by now. Shorter members of the group like Jak and Mildred were having to keep their mouths closed in fear of the foul water splashing up. Only good thing about that was it helped close off the chatter.

Then, as Morgan had said, the tunnel did come to an end, with another flat wall and another rusted yellow ladder going up to the surface. There was no interior wheel to turn this time, merely a heavy lid. Ryan went up the ladder and pushed.

"Stuck."

After a supreme effort that once again made his healing shoulder give off the sensation of being tortured with hot irons, Ryan was able to summon up the strength to shove the manhole cover up and away, where it fell freely over with a clatter to the well-worn pavement above. After Ryan poked his head up to visually recce the area, he gave the all-clear signal and the rest of the group crawled up and out onto the blacktop of one of Freedom's many unused parking lots, this one at the far west end, away from the main entrance and from the secondary front of the stickie attack.

Some fleeing figures could be seen, running along the wall. The pandemonium that had marked the interior of the colossal building still appeared to be going strong, but the tunnel had led Ryan and the others far away from any of the fighting. The group headed back for the tangle of undergrowth that had sprouted up beyond the wide expanse that had been kept cleared for security reasons, and took a wide circle to the start of Hawthorne Road.

Ryan looked back at the burning patches of red and orange in the darkness. "Seem to be making a habit of this," he said.

"What are you talking about, lover?" Krysty asked. The night breeze that had guided the crude gliding devices operated by the stickies onto the roof of the mall was still blowing softly, and felt cool on their wet skin.

"I'm talking about leaving nothing behind us but a damn ruin."

"Not our doing, not this time," Mildred stated. "We were caught in the middle."

"I still can't help but think my being there made crazy mutie-loving Lester decide to attack sooner than he might've. Morgan said they were waiting for more blasters, supplies and men. Might have been able to put up a better fight."

"Ancient history now. I'd say our own kind

brought Freedom down a hell of a lot faster than a gang of stickies,'' Mildred replied.

''What's our next move?'' J.B. asked.

''Don't know. We're close to the underbelly of Virginia. Guess we could stay on foot, try walking for a while and see how far we go. I've been thinking about paying a visit to Nate anyway, see how things are going back home, such as it is.''

Everyone knew Ryan's ambivalent feelings on the stretch of land where he'd grown up. The last time there, he'd left the young Nathan Freeman in charge as the new Lord Cawdor, leader of the clan that shared Ryan's name.

''Still wondering about what Poseidon told you back in Georgia? Trouble brewing up in the Shens?'' Krysty asked.

''Some, yeah,'' Ryan admitted. ''Or mebbe I'm just afraid of what I might find.''

''Long trip to West Virginia,'' Doc said, already feeling his long legs start to ache in anticipation.

''Not if we stick to the highways,'' Mildred replied.

''I haven't made up my mind yet,'' Ryan said simply. ''Be a lot easier to go back to the hospital and take another jump, see where the mat-trans winds take us. Not up to me, though. What do the rest of you want to do?''

There was no response for a moment, and then J.B. spoke for the rest of them.

''Whatever you decide, Ryan, I guess we'll fall in.''

Under Attack!

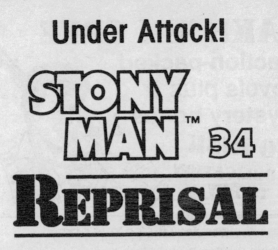

STONY MAN™ 34

REPRISAL

In a brilliant conspiracy to restore the glory days of the CIA, a rogue agent has masterminded a plot to take out Company competition. His stolen clipper chip has effectively shut down the Farm's communications network and made sitting ducks of the field teams. With Phoenix Force ambushed and trapped in the Colombian jungle, and a cartel wet team moving in on Able Team stateside, it's up to Mack Bolan and the Stony experts to bring off the impossible.

Available in April 1998 at your favorite retail outlet.

TAKE 'EM FREE

4 action-packed novels plus a mystery bonus

NO RISK

NO OBLIGATION TO BUY

Where there's smoke...

#111 Prophet of Doom

Created by
WARREN MURPHY
and RICHARD SAPIR

Everyone with a spare million is lining up at the gates of
Ranch Ragnarok, home to Esther Clear Seer's Church of the
Absolute and Incontrovertible Truth. Here an evil yellow
smoke shrouds an ancient oracle that offers glimpses into
the future. But when young virgins start disappearing, CURE
smells something more than a scam—and Remo is slated to
become a sacrificial vessel....

Look for it in April 1998 wherever Gold Eagle books are sold.

Don't miss out on the action in these titles featuring THE EXECUTIONER®, STONY MAN™ and SUPERBOLAN®!

The American Trilogy

#64222	PATRIOT GAMBIT	$3.75 U.S.	☐
		$4.25 CAN.	☐
#64223	HOUR OF CONFLICT	$3.75 U.S.	☐
		$4.25 CAN.	☐
#64224	CALL TO ARMS	$3.75 U.S.	☐
		$4.25 CAN.	☐

Stony Man™

#61910	FLASHBACK	$5.50 U.S.	☐
		$6.50 CAN.	☐
#61911	ASIAN STORM	$5.50 U.S.	☐
		$6.50 CAN.	☐
#61912	BLOOD STAR	$5.50 U.S.	☐
		$6.50 CAN.	☐

SuperBolan®

#61452	DAY OF THE VULTURE	$5.50 U.S.	☐
		$6.50 CAN.	☐
#61453	FLAMES OF WRATH	$5.50 U.S.	☐
		$6.50 CAN.	☐
#61454	HIGH AGGRESSION	$5.50 U.S.	☐
		$6.50 CAN.	☐

(limited quantities available on certain titles)

TOTAL AMOUNT	$
POSTAGE & HANDLING	$
($1.00 for one book, 50¢ for each additional)	
APPLICABLE TAXES*	$ _____
TOTAL PAYABLE	$ _____
(check or money order—please do not send cash)	

To order, complete this form and send it, along with a check or money order for the total above, payable to Gold Eagle Books, to: **In the U.S.:** 3010 Walden Avenue, P.O. Box 9077, Buffalo, NY 14269-9077; **In Canada:** P.O. Box 636, Fort Erie, Ontario, L2A 5X3.

Name: _____

Address: _____ City: _____

State/Prov.: _____ Zip/Postal Code: _____

*New York residents remit applicable sales taxes.
 Canadian residents remit applicable GST and provincial taxes.

GEBACK19

James Axler

OUTLANDERS™

PARALLAX RED

Kane and his colleagues stumble upon an ancient colony on Mars that housed a group of genetically altered humans, retained by the Archons to do their bidding. After making the mat-trans jump to Mars, the group finds itself faced with two challenges: a doomsday device that could destroy Earth, and a race of Transhumans desperate to steal human genetic material to make moving to Earth possible.

In the Outlands, the future is an eternity of hell....

Taking Fiction to Another Dimension!

Deathlands

#62535	BITTER FRUIT	$5.50 U.S. $6.50 CAN.	☐ ☐
#62536	SKYDARK	$5.50 U.S. $6.50 CAN.	☐ ☐
#62537	DEMONS OF EDEN	$5.50 U.S. $6.50 CAN.	☐ ☐

The Destroyer

#63220	SCORCHED EARTH	$5.50 U.S. $6.50 CAN.	☐ ☐
#63221	WHITE WATER	$5.50 U.S. $6.50 CAN.	☐ ☐
#63222	FEAST OR FAMINE	$5.50 U.S. $6.50 CAN.	☐ ☐

Outlanders

| #63814 | EXILE TO HELL | $5.50 U.S.
$6.50 CAN. | ☐
☐ |

(limited quantities available on certain titles)

TOTAL AMOUNT	$
POSTAGE & HANDLING	$
($1.00 for one book, 50¢ for each additional)	
APPLICABLE TAXES*	$ _____
TOTAL PAYABLE	$ _____
(check or money order—please do not send cash)	

To order, complete this form and send it, along with a check or money order for the total above, payable to Gold Eagle Books, to: **In the U.S.:** 3010 Walden Avenue, P.O. Box 9077, Buffalo, NY 14269-9077; **In Canada:** P.O. Box 636, Fort Erie, Ontario, L2A 5X3.

Name: _____

Address: _____ City: _____

State/Prov.: _____ Zip/Postal Code: _____

*New York residents remit applicable sales taxes.
 Canadian residents remit applicable GST and provincial taxes.

GOLD
EAGLE ®

GEBACK20A